NESSUS THE CENTAUR

By
Henry Hollenbaugh

For information contact:
ALONDRA PRESS PUBLISHING COMPANY
Houston, Texas 77043
www.alondrapress.com
lark@alondrapress.com

ISBN 978-0-9814523-3-3

Library Of Congress Control Number 2008944227

Printed in the United States of America

Cover design by Alpha Graphics of Houston, TX
Edited by Penelope Aletras-Leight

Nessus
The Centaur

A Novel by Henry Hollenbaugh

WWW.ALONDRAPRESS.COM

PROLOGUE

I'm moving again. But this time not to another cruddy, crappy little apartment. Oh no, this time I'm going to Greece, to fulfill a dream I've had for the past two years – to retrace the hoof prints of Nessus the Centaur, and the footsteps of other personages, demigods, and heroes of ancient Greece.

As I pack the things I plan to take with me and fling the stuff I'm discarding into large garbage bags, I turn once more to the pile of things I still haven't decided what to do with. I found a place to store my books some time ago, with Sam Gentile. I should have included some of this other stuff, which I simply can't throw away. Like my lucky porcelain owl, which quite possibly is what has made this trip to Greece possible, and my nineteenth century world globe, a rare garage-sale find. And then there's my lucky desiccated spider, preserved in its tiny medicine vial, like Lenin in his glass case, dreaming forever of succulent bugs in spider heaven.

And speaking of dreams, among this pile of things that I simply can't throw away are my manuscripts. One of them is a sort of diary – about two hundred typed pages. Well, not really a diary, but something that I've thought of converting into a book of some sort, like maybe a nonfiction novel, or a historical work of true fiction, or something. I could call it *Nessus The Centaur*.

I pick it up now to heft it in both hands, pondering on the many days and nights of work that went into it. Under that first manuscript are two others, *The Aztec Calendar of Divination,* a tremendous outpouring of research and erudition, and *A Short History of the Centaurs.* The owl and spider, I could take with me. I could make room for them with my socks and shorts – stick the spider inside a sock, and wrap the owl in a couple of shorts. But these manuscripts . . . It would be a lot of extra weight and volume to be lugging around in a strange country. And I can't take them to Sam. He hadn't been too eager to take my books, the slob. Will I have to toss those hundreds of pages into the trash? I've already sent *A Short History of the Centaurs* to more agents and publishers than I can remember. I hesitate, hefting the bundles in my hands, in a crisis of indecision. Keep them? Throw them away? Then I

5

sit cross-legged on the floor and examine the first manuscript as I mull it over. As a novel, it has some difficulties with the tense I could never resolve – couldn't decide whether to use the present or the past. It would take considerable doing to sort it out. Throw it away. The same for *A Short History of the Centaurs.*

On the other hand, maybe they wouldn't be so hard to fix . . . a shame to throw all that work away. Maybe nobody would notice those little problems of past and present tense. Maybe I could combine both manuscripts into a single book, and still find a publisher. It could make me a pile of money. Then I could stay in Greece for as long as I wanted. Maybe I should also change a name or two that I've used in my diary. Daphne, the dumb bitch, might decide to sue me if she ever read it.

My flight is still twelve hours away, and I'm almost finished with my packing. So I stretch out on the floor, my head on one of the pillows I'm throwing away, and begin to reread my diary-manuscript. And the more I read the more convinced I become that it's an excellent work, its little defects notwithstanding. Ditto for *A Short History of the Centaurs.* Those agents and publishers I sent it to were simply lacking the sufficient gray matter to appreciate it. Sons of bitches, dumb cocksuckers . . .

Still toying with the idea of making one manuscript out of the two, I begin to insert pages from one manuscript into the other, scribbling short transitions here and there. The hours slip away unheeded, and I continue at my task, now sitting at the one chair and table I haven't yet thrown into the dumpster. Finally, with only five hours left to catch my flight, I begin to reread it again from start to finish. When I settle down somewhere in Greece I'll polish it up some and then I'll try to think of someone to send it to. It goes something like this:

NESSUS THE CENTAUR
CHAPTER ONE

Last night I went to bed with the same problems, hundreds of them, marching in lockstep through my mind. My law suit against the city; my dwindling inheritance money; the disturbing noises my car was beginning to make; the increasing difficulty I was finding in keeping up my deception of Daphne . . . Okay, I know that's only four problems, not hundreds. But each of these problems, like the abstractions in Greek mythology, seem to beget a hundred offspring.

When I finally went to sleep I dreamed again that I was Nessus the Centaur. This time, however, there was a marked difference in the substance of my dream. This time I actually managed to accomplish a sexual union with Dejanira.

* * * * * *

Strange about last night's dream – how the anatomical differences between Dejanira and I were so effortlessly vanquished. I think what it means is that this particular dream, at once pleasurable and poignant, was really nothing more than an ordinary dream, and not the usual reliving of my past life as Nessus the Centaur. Because that's the way dreams are, of course. Strange things happen in dreams, things much stranger than a centaur having sex with a woman.

I can't tell Daphne about it, because she's already told me she doesn't want to hear me talking about such things. The fact is, I try not to tell Daphne about *any* of my dreams. But sometimes they're so startlingly vivid that I find myself telling her, even when I know I shouldn't.

The memory of the dream produces a vague feeling of discomfort. Reliving a past life in dreams is one thing. But why should I be having a *normal* dream of having sex with Dejanira, in an equine fashion, moreover, and while engaged to be married to Daphne? But then I tell myself that It's Daphne's fault. If she would slip me something now, before we marry, maybe I wouldn't be having such dreams.

I began having these dreams of a past life some months ago, and was immediately struck by their most peculiar quality. They are not really dreams, but that is what I will call them, because I can't think of a better word. In my first experience of this sort I was a grown centaur, but this grown centaur had memories of its centaur childhood, and I brought back those memories with me to this life. So that now I clearly remember galloping gleefully over Magnesian meadows as a little centaur colt behind my mother and a thundering herd of centaurs. Even though I have not actually relived those childhood experiences. I only began reliving my centaur life from the days just before I fell in love with Dejanira.

Daphne only stares at me with a sort of fish-eyed look when I tell her about my belief that I'm a reincarnation of Nessus the Centaur, and she seems to worry that I'll go around telling other people this.

She shouldn't worry about that. I wouldn't have told even her, but one morning after I awoke from the dream I was so overwhelmed by the sudden epiphanic knowledge that I felt I just had to tell someone, or I would burst. I had told her before about the dreams, but it had only been something to laugh about. "Hey," I said to her the first time, "I had the queerest dream. I was a centaur – you know, a half horse-half human. My name was Nessus. The darnedest thing I've ever dreamt. I was looking at a woman named Dejanira, and got a, um, you know, an erection, with my horse's member and everything."

"If you think you're going to get me interested in your disgusting stories of bestiality," she said, with that prudishly affected air she sometimes assumes, "you're very mistaken. I've told you before I don't like that kind of filthy conversation."

At that moment, getting her "interested" in my story had been the furthest thing from my mind. Even though she couldn't sit there and tell me that my talk actually disgusted her. Maybe I'm not so smart, but I know something about women of Daphne's type. Yeah, sure, maybe I shouldn't be talking about her like this, seeing as how I'm actually trying to marry her and all. But the truth is, for all her high-flown airs and classy looks, there's a lot of the common floozy in Daphne.

Not that I don't try to do that – get her aroused, so she'll go to

8

bed with me, I mean. Because the fear that she'll break off the engagement at any moment is always present. And then all that money already spent on her will have been totally wasted. I think she's begun to suspect I don't really have those great amounts of money I talk to her about. Maybe if I could get her in bed I could make her forget about money for a while and make her love me just for what I am. Keeping up the deception is hard work, let me tell you. If a guy could apply the effort and ingenuity that goes into something like this to something honest and productive, then real money could be made.

I was saying, I would never have told Daphne of my belief that I'm a reincarnation of Nessus the Centaur, except that one day the realization struck me with such startling clarity that I told her all about it before I could stop myself.

"I just realized," I told her, "why I've been having this dream."

"Have you been dreaming that centaur thing again?"

"Yes," I said, "but this time it was so realistic that it was – it was.... those dreams have always been vivid and realistic, but not like last night. This time I actually *experienced* it. I felt what it's like to have a horse's body. I could feel every one of my horse's muscles! I clearly remember tiny details, the sound of my hooves clip-clopping over the stones and the grass, my tail switching off gad flies, my withers quivering . . . Everything was clear – not confused, like an ordinary dream is. I could see and feel everything, just like I can right now."

I think something happened to me, something knocked out of whack in my brain or something, that made me begin to dream of my former existence. It began shortly after a couple of bad knocks to the head. The first one was entirely my own fault. One day, fishing off an antique little wooden bridge some miles outside the city, trying to get my mind off my personal problems, a sudden gust of wind blew my cap off. I made a quick lunge for it, trying to catch it before it fell into the water. I missed it, and instead, went crashing through the rotten wooden railing to plunge headfirst into the shallow water below, banging my head on one of the bridge pilings. I was lucky I wasn't killed.

That night at home, and throughout the following day, I felt strange. The world looked and felt different. Daphne came to see me the next day when I told her I'd been hurt, and *she* looked and sounded different. It seemed like when she talked, I would hear her words before she opened her mouth. Time was not flowing normally, but rather seemed to go both forward and backward. Time was out of joint, like I think Hamlet said.

"I might be hurt bad," I said worriedly.

"Why don't you go see a doctor?" she asked me.

"Oh, it's probably nothing serious," I answered, back-pedaling. I didn't want to tell her that I wouldn't go to a doctor mostly for economic considerations.

"It's just like you," she said, "to get hurt away from the job. Why couldn't you have done something like that at work? You could have sued your employer, or at least gotten some workers compensation. Even if you're already rich, more money wouldn't hurt, you know." There was a faint hint of malice or mockery in her tone. Or maybe it wasn't so faint. Maybe the impact of her remark was softened to my ears by my somewhat befuddled state, which made her words sound distant and slowed, like she was talking through a long tube.

I replied, my voice sounding to my own ears as if it were emerging from a deep brass tub, "Next time I get hurt, I promise it'll be while I'm at work."

I felt no resentment at Daphne's apparent unconcern for my injury, no anger that her only thought at such a time was the fact that my accident could produce no profit. I was too bemused by the strange humming and buzzing that filled my head.

Just three days later I received another bad knock to the head. On a muggy night on my way home from work I had stopped at a quick market on Westheimer to buy a loaf of bread. As I walked out I came upon a ruckus on the sidewalk that fronted the store. Two tough-looking, scruffily dressed men were tussling with a pretty young girl. She began to scream for help. I've always been a sucker where women in distress are concerned. I moved in to her rescue, not without some trepidation, I confess. "What's going on here?" I asked the men.

The brutes were trying to wrestle the girl away from a high-line pole she was tenaciously clinging to. One of them, without letting go of the girls arms, snarled at me, "Move along, buddy!"

The poor girl screamed like a banshee in her distress. "Help! Help! Help! Oh, please don't let them do this to me!"

The man's rude and belligerent voice and the girl's pitiful wails produced an equal effect on me, provoking me into action. I grabbed one of her attackers by the arm, the one who had snarled at me, to pull him away from the girl. He spun swiftly around, trying to elbow me in the stomach, as he barked, "I told you to move along!" I slugged him in the face with my loaf of bread, and then, as he lunged towards me, I sidestepped smartly, at the same time sticking my left foot out, causing him to trip and stumble to his knees. The other man had wrestled the girl away from the pole and was twisting her arms behind her back. I grabbed his shoulder with my left hand and launched a haymaker at his jaw with my right. I missed, but I made him lose his grip on the girl. She dashed off across the street through the dangerously rushing traffic, losing her high-heeled shoes as she fled. She also left her purse behind on the sidewalk. Wherever that girl is now, I hope she always remembers me and my heroic action.

Both men then turned their full attention upon me. Their slab-like faces, yellowish under the sickly light of the street lamps, their eyes venomous with rage, were a frightening sight. Centaur blood flows in my veins, I now know, and we were known for our fierce courage. I had lost my only weapon, the loaf of bread, which now lay squashed on the sidewalk, but I put up my fists and challenged them, "Come on, you sons of bitches!"

They didn't wait for a second invitation. One of them kicked me in the groin. The other one stepped swiftly in and clubbed me with a ten-pound fist in the side of the head. My glasses went flying. I hit the sidewalk like the proverbial sack of potatoes, luckily landing on my loaf of bread, which broke my fall somewhat.

Through the ringing in my ears I heard one of them say, "Put the cuffs on him." For it turned out they were plainclothes vice cops, and had been trying to arrest the girl for prostitution. They tossed me into the slammer that night; at the worst of possible times, Friday night. So I spent the entire weekend locked up while the sons of bitches tried to establish a link between me and the girl, trying to book me on a pimping charge. They knew it wasn't true; they knew I had honestly thought the girl was being attacked by muggers or rapists. But they did this to cover up their own fault. They had never identified themselves as cops.

Monday morning I was finally able to contact a lawyer I knew,

11

named Sam Gentile (although I think he's actually Jewish), and he got me out that same day. The story provided material for the local news media for several days. I was sometimes referred to as a Good Samaritan, and commended for my courage in attacking two tough men single-handed in order to rescue the girl. But sometimes, also, there appeared to be a faint suggestion in the news stories that I was a fool. Daphne was of this latter opinion. She told me so without mincing words. "What was that prostitute to you, anyway? You made a fool of yourself." So the whole affair made me feel both proud and embarrassed.

Shortly afterwards I began to dream that I was Nessus The Centaur.

* * * * * *

The first time I had the dream I only had a vague notion of who Nessus The Centaur had been. I told Daphne the little I knew about Nessus and the centaurs. What I knew wasn't very much, but it was a lot more than Daphne knew. Daphne never reads anything beyond an occasional best seller or romance novel. She has no interest whatsoever in history or literature. Every reference I ever make to these subjects – or to any other, for that matter – is always a trampoline for her to leap off of into the talk of money and material possessions. She tries to guide the conversation into disclosures on my part of exactly how much money I have. She wonders, without asking me directly and outright, why I live the way I do, and I know she has never really accepted the explanations I have provided or hinted at.

I remember how shocked she was when she first saw the crummy apartment I lived in. I had taken a chance letting her see how I lived, but it was something unavoidable – she would eventually have had to find out –, and I had a story ready to explain my appearance of poverty, my cheap and shoddy furnishings, which I mostly obtain from trash dumpsters. I acted mysterious, and let her gather, without declaring it outright, that the way I lived was actually a cover, a deceptive façade adopted for certain purposes . . . "Hey," I said to her, "I can handle a bit of hardship. This is nothing compared to some things I went through in South America." And I told her a tale or two of my adventures in the Amazon, some true, some concocted from the adventures I had heard told by other travelers.

12

But Daphne isn't interested in the Amazon. She wants to know why I work at Crompton Markets as a stock clerk when I have such rich parents and other sources of income. I always tell her I work at Crompton Markets because I want to study the business from the bottom up. Besides, the Cromptons once did my father a great financial service, I tell her, and we owe them.

She turns this revelation around in her slow but inexorably logical mind and comes up with the uncomfortable question, How did working for them as a lowly stock clerk repay for that financial favor?

Hey, I say to her, there are many things in life that don't have a simple answer. Some day maybe I'll be free to explain everything. And I add, "Oh, it's probably silly of me, but I have nothing else to do right now, and anyway, receiving the salary from that job doesn't hurt. Money is never superfluous." I don't tell her that I loathe and detest my job, that I work there because it's the only job I could find, and that the money I spend on her so freely, taking her to those fine restaurants, and buying her five-thousand dollar engagement rings, came from a small inheritance - forty-five thousand dollars – that my great-uncle Phillip left me when he died, and that that money is now almost all gone.

I would probably have plenty of real money if I hadn't lost six years of my life in Central and South America, the best years of my youth, searching for chimerical fortunes in the form of Mayan and Inca treasures and medicinal plants. And I would have gone to college and gotten a degree in something – a real degree, not that fake diploma hanging on my wall.

Yes, if there was any fairness in life I would be entitled to a diploma just on the basis of the thousands of books I've indiscriminately read. I've even written one – The Aztec Calendar of Divination, which would have been my graduation thesis, if I had ever truly gone to college.

That book is something else I should never have mentioned to Daphne. "Who was it published by?" she wanted to know. I never claimed to have had it published. It was hard enough to write the sonofabitch. It's a big, thick hefty book. I can hardly pick up all those typewritten pages in both hands. But when I showed all those pages to Daphne once, hefting them before her, trying to impress her with the enormous expenditure of intellectual effort they represented, she looked

13

at them with the same expression as anyone will look at a big stack of good paper that's been ruined.

For the last few months I've also been working on another book, *A Short History of The Centaurs*. Having actually existed as a centaur, no one is better qualified to tell their true and accurate history. I try to talk to Daphne about these literary endeavors, about Greek mythology, the life of Nessus the Centaur, and the jungles of South America. But she is equally bent on talking about money, and about how much of it I have. I doggedly keep trying to impress her with my erudition and the vast knowledge I have acquired from my years in South America and the reading of ten thousand books, a good many of which I inherited from my great-uncle Phillip. Somewhere in the back of my mind, I suppose, I'm hoping that this wealth of the mind will supplant the wealth in the pockets that I don't have as an object for Daphne's admiration and esteem. A forlorn endeavor. Daphne doesn't give a diddly squat about Greek mythology.

I have to admit I didn't know much about Greek mythology myself, until I started to dream. In my dreams everybody called me Nessus, so I began to visit the library to read Diodorus Siculus, and Apollodorus, and Hyginus, and other such old stuff that I didn't have in my own library, looking for confirmation of what I thought I knew – about the way in which Nessus died, and why. Then I began to wish there was some way I could warn myself in that other life, warn Nessus that those hots he had for Dejanira were going to cost him his life.

But there is no way I can do that. Here in this life I am completely conscious of my former existence as Nessus, but Nessus has no knowledge whatever of his existence as me, Jonathan Nestus. It's like there's a connection from there to here, but not from here to there. If there was, then maybe Nessus could inform me of my future. He would probably know what the thirty-two years of my life have been like, and about any bad stuff down the road, and how to avoid it. He could maybe even tell me of some way I could have Daphne.

After I began to dream, I thought I had discovered an additional reason why I pined and yearned for the love of Daphne. Her name, her name alone. Because I now knew who the original Daphne had been. Daphne! that chaste and lovely maiden of flowery meadows! So chaste and virtuous that she even refused to have sex with the god Apollo

14

himself.

This is the story as I heard it told in the centaur caves. Apollo was chasing her across a meadow one day, trying to have sex with her. Daphne was running like it was for her life, with her long filmy robe hitched up to her shapely thighs, to give her legs freedom of movement. Apollo was toying with her, like a cat with a mouse, running easily after her while he taunted her with words such as, "Oh, my goodness! Don't run so fast. You might fall and hurt yourself, and scratch those pretty legs. Run a little slower, and I promise that I'll chase you a little slower too." He was reaching out with his hands to grab her. But poor Daphne, running as swiftly as a ground-skimming swallow, called out in desperation to her father, who was the river god Achelous, "Oh, father, father! If you have the power, save me from this fate!" And instantly she was transformed into a laurel tree. Apollo, reaching out to grab her, slammed into the tree full tilt, and only got an armful of rough bark and tree trunk. He kissed it and rubbed himself against it in his lecherous horniness but only succeeded in bruising himself.

The name Daphne, then, held for me connotations of virtue and chastity. Though base desire has always ruled my life, I nevertheless have noble and lofty inclinations, too.

But, no. Lovely name or not, I would probably have wanted Daphne just as badly if her name had been Gorgophone, or Lamia. From the first time I laid eyes on her as she stepped out the door of Prescott Mobile Home Sales, with the light behind her shining right through the thin dress she was wearing, limning out the voluptuous perfection of her thighs and hips, the lines of her panties faintly visible, an ineffable longing had possessed me. Partly, I suppose, because I instantly perceived Daphne as the epitomized representation of the type of woman I could never have. Ah! if only I was rich, I bet I could have her then! In a curious way, this was the thought that popped into my consciousness from some odd corner of my subconscious, almost before my eyes had fully taken in the sight.

And then, as I stood before Daphne, telling her what I was looking for, a pernicious little voice whispered to me, You *are* rich. You've got forty-five thousand dollars.

I don't have forty-five thousand dollars anymore. That money is mostly gone now. She's going to find out soon – that I'm not really rich

– and then it'll all be over. I've most likely ruined myself for nothing, on account of my unbridled desires – for trying to have a woman that's beyond my class. And in that other life I lived three thousand years ago that same propensity cost me my life.

CHAPTER TWO

In the bathroom I gaze into the mirror at my lower body, and fresh in my mind is the memory of my equine parts, so recently left behind in my dream. I draw my finger wonderingly across my abdomen, to trace an invisible line at the indistinct point where a horse's chest would begin.

Across the teeming city, home with her mother, Daphne is probably getting ready for work too, at her job selling mobile homes. Immediately after receiving my inheritance, flush with all that cash, I had pondered on the wisest way to put it to work. Finally I had decided to buy a mobile home, a great investment, I told myself. In four or five years it would pay for itself in the money I'd save on rent. That was how I met Daphne. I was examining the trailer homes she sold, smugly congratulating myself on my wisdom in having so sagely decided how to put my money to work, when she came smilingly out into the yard to help me.

She was wearing a dress, as I mentioned before – a thin dress, which clung to her body in the light breeze, especially in the vicinity of her genitalia. A tiny whirlwind that swirled up and around the office trailer steps at the precise moment that she stepped onto them lifted it for the briefest of moments above her knees, almost exposing her thighs.

Strange, I have often reflected, how the sight of a woman's legs, no matter how shapely, can leave us coldly indifferent when they are purposely exposed, such as when the owner of those legs is wearing a bathing suit. But let that same woman – or even a woman with totally unattractive legs – accidentally expose some thigh while she is wearing a dress, and we are immediately all agog with lust. Or at least that's the way it is with me. But maybe I'm a pervert, like Daphne tells me.

Anyway, that was the kind of impression Daphne made on me that first time I saw her.

I also felt a sort of hopeless desire, much like the hopeless desire that Nessus feels for Dejanira, immediately recognizing in Daphne a type of female forever beyond my reach. Only a rich person, or a handsome man, or a professional, none of which I was or am, could aspire to something like this.

I asked her about the price of one of her mobile homes. Cash price, I told her. I never bought anything on payments. Nothing but cash on the barrel head for me, I said. I liked to earn interest, not pay it. This somehow led her to believe that I was loaded, which in a way, I was. Somewhere in the back of my mind, I suppose that was what I wanted her to think. Even though a rich person will not normally be buying a trailer home.

But I didn't buy a mobile home that day. I cultivated her acquaintance and invited her to dinner instead. And very soon after that, buying a mobile home became out of the question. So much for my wisdom.

Having unintentionally, more or less, led Daphne to believe that I was rich, how did I manage to perpetuate the impression? At first, it wasn't so hard. First impressions are very important. And, when we really set our mind to do something like that, there are many resorts. The key to carrying it off successfully is to adopt a sort of half-cautious, half-condescending air. But not too condescending, because you'll stir up resentment. You may disclose your fictitious wealth, but only by disclosing some other peripheral matter, so that conclusions can be drawn. You reveal those peripheral matters reluctantly, seemingly compelled to do so by the context of the conversation you are engaged in at the moment.

There are many tiny little tricks and stratagems that serve to reinforce the deception. As I have said, if we really put our mind to it, it can be done. In the matter of revealing information while apparently trying to conceal it, we can learn from the example of Honest Iago and his deception of Othello. And yet, If I may say so, compared to my intelligent application of the principle, Iago was an ass, and the object of his deceit no less so. Another difference between Iago and me is that I am really an honest and decent person at heart. I did what I did forced by the strength of my love for Daphne – to be completely honest, the strength of my desire to get into her pants.

18

But let me give a concrete example or two of my cunning at work. When Daphne would visit at my apartment in those early days, I would take care to leave fake documents lying around where she could see them while I went to the bathroom – such as notations or letters showing I had sent two or three hundred thousand dollars to some bank or other. Returning to the table, I would furtively subtract them from sight, as if belatedly realizing I had left those documents there, and was hoping she hadn't seen them. Later, I even went so far as to have a friend make phone calls, posing as an investment counselor, to talk about my supposed investments. At my end of the conversation I would speak – in a dissembling, roundabout way – of hundreds of thousands of dollars, which I should perhaps withdraw from the stock market.

My friend at his end of the line would be chuckling and saying, "Man, you sure do have some gall. Who are you feeding this bullshit to, anyway?"

"Yes," I would answer, "you're probably right. Maybe we should put a couple hundred thou of those funds into subordinated debentures." Although I wouldn't know what a subordinated debenture was if one bit me on the ass.

And then I would say, "Look, you caught me at a bad moment. Can I call you back?" And I would apologize to Daphne, glassy-eyed from hearing all that talk of hundreds of thousands of dollars. One of these days, I would tell myself, maybe this talk of huge amounts of money will get her so excited that she'll hop right into the sack with me. Yes, I know all this is despicable. I hate trickery of this sort just as much as anybody. But the alternative, to see Daphne lose all interest in me, would be too painful. What ever do I intend to do when the moment of truth comes? But little moments of truth are forever popping up, and I dispose of them as they arise. I find myself forced to continue with the charade because she has set her mind on marriage, and refuses to slip me a small sample in the meantime. I can't understand why this is a problem with her. I don't think she's a virgin. A woman couldn't get such a luscious and curvaceous body like she has just from selling mobile homes. I think others have plowed her fields and reaped a harvest without having to marry her. But I tell myself, even Napoleon had to marry Josephine. The only man who had to marry her in order to enjoy her intimacy, as a personage of those times once remarked. And

19

besides, I'm going to have a stunningly attractive woman for a wife when we get married. Just the first night of holy matrimony with Daphne will repay me for all my trouble. I'll have a story ready to spring on her immediately afterwards, about bankruptcy, and a bank failure or something. I might even just tell her the truth. Maybe by then she will have fallen in love with me just for what I am. At any rate, by then I will have gotten something in return for the money I've spent on her.

* * * * * *

While at work I know I should forget about Nessus the Centaur. Allowing the mind to wander on the job can lead to bad blunders. But today the memory of last night's dream keeps intruding upon my consciousness.

What a peculiar dream. The memory of my organ miraculously penetrating Dejanira's vagina as I had clasped her in my arms and kissed her, something that I know would have to be an impossibility in the real life of Nessus, remained with me almost as a memory of a real event. It was disturbing, in a way, because I had *enjoyed* it. I shouldn't have been enjoying it with a horse's organ instead of my own.

Then, suddenly, I realized what my dream had meant, and the surprise caused me to give an involuntary jerk to the pen in my hand, smudging the numbers on the page on which I had been recording prices and quantities. I had been reliving a *dream* of Nessus the Centaur. Nessus had been asleep, dreaming, when I had relived that tiny portion of his life.

* * * * * *

There have been other occasions when the previous night's dream disturbed my concentration at work. There was the time when I first met Dejanira at a crossing of the Avenus River. I had been hunting nearby that day, far from my cave on Mount Oeta, and had stopped at the river to refresh myself. Dejanira came by with a group of other girls – supposedly maidens – on their way to perform the annual rites at a nearby shrine of Demeter.

The river was quite low that day, but I had offered to carry them across the shallow water on my back. The other nymphs had all gaily agreed, laughing and teasing, clasping me around the waist as they sat on my sleek back. But Dejanira had demurely declined, hitching her

20

robes up to wade across. I had heard of Dejanira before. Her beauty was a common topic of conversation among Greeks and Centaurs alike. Now, finally seeing her in the flesh, I was so struck by that far-famed beauty that I could scarcely tear my eyes away from her. The water was almost thigh-deep, and she had to hold her robe high above her knees to keep it dry. The gleaming smoothness of her legs out-sparkled and out-shone the rippling white water that swirled around her. It was a captivating sight. She saw me staring, and blushingly cast her eyes downward as she carefully walked over the rocky bottom, her seashell eyelids hiding the violet blue of her eyes. I fell in love with her that day.

Later, on other occasions, on other chance meetings, I often thought that she might even be in love with me. On certain occasions I had caught her looking surreptitiously at me, quickly averting her gaze when I would turn towards her. True, once I had also surprised a look of – what was it? revulsion, perverse fascination? – as she stared at my horse's member, which at that moment dangled in a semi-tumescent state.

One meeting in particular remains seared in my memory. Again, it was at the Avenus river. Dejanira was returning from Demeter's shrine at Hypata. I had known she was due to pass the river that day and I was there to catch a glimpse of her, pretending it was only a chance meeting. From the far bank the other girls called merrily out to me. "Nessus, come across and help us over!"

Women of those times liked to tease us centaurs. They knew how much we liked Greek women. Many of them were afraid of us – deeply uneasy about our strange double nature of man and horse, added to our reputation for reckless behavior where sex was concerned. But there were others whose fascination with us overrode their fear. They would try to draw us out and make us talk of the sensations we felt. They would joke with us about the size of our organ, and so forth.

I forded the shallow waters to bring the girls across, two at a time. But, again, Dejanira chose to hitch up her robes and wade across herself. As they were all preparing to leave, picking up their bundles and rearranging their robes, I moved towards Dejanira, trying to think of something to say to her. For one magical instant we stood face to face, only inches apart. If I had lived continuously for these three thousand years since that day, no other experience could erase the memory. She was wearing a snow-white robe of flimsy material, with a chasing of gold thread catching it up just beneath her swelling breasts. She wore no brassiere – we didn't have them back in those days (why modern women have chosen to deform the natural appearance of their breasts with brassieres is a source of never-ending puzzlement to me) –, and her breasts, like pale pink roses, not too large, not too small, not aggressively bursting forth, nor listlessly drooping, were tantalizingly discernible beneath the thin cloth.

There was something about Dejanira . . . Hers was not a raw sex appeal, but something far deeper. Not that a sex appeal wasn't there, but it was mixed with something else – an almost magical magnetic attraction, that perhaps even Aphrodite herself could have envied. As I stood before her that day, our eyes met for the briefest of moments, and something from her soft violet eyes penetrated searingly into the depths of my soul. At the same time, and almost instantaneously, I felt the more tangible effects of that animal urge we centaurs were so susceptible to. That is to say, I got an almost instantaneous erection.

Dejanira was also affected with emotion of some sort. Her eyelids fluttered almost imperceptibly, there was a slight trembling of her lips, and one of her delicate hands went nervously to her throat as my enraptured gaze coursed involuntarily up and down her body.

The nymphs, already moving away, called out to Dejanira, "Come along Dejanira! What do you want with Nessus?" They snickered and giggled when they noticed my erection. "And you, Nessus," one of them called out. "You'd better look out. Dejanira is going to be Hercules' wife. He'd better not hear you've so much as looked at her."

And then Dejanira hurried off after them, leaving me standing there with my tremendous and futile erection.

So, Dejanira was going to be Hercules' wife. It was the first I'd heard of it. I should have known, though. She was the loveliest girl in the country, and Hercules was a single man again. I'd always hated Hercules' guts and at this moment I hated him more than ever. But my hatred was almost equaled by my fear, and I nearly decided then and there that I would never look at Dejanira again.

To explain what must surely sound like a most cowardly reaction, it should be understood that Hercules was the most feared and

22

deadly man of his time. Nobody crossed Hercules or stood in the way of anything he wanted. He would as soon kill a man or a centaur as blink his eyes. As further proof that I'm not a coward, I am among the few who ever dared to meet with Hercules in single combat. I wrestled him once in the Nemean games, a couple of years before our trouble over Dejanira, and he injured me badly.... cracked a couple of my horse's ribs. In that match I wasn't allowed to use my hooves. Otherwise maybe I could have kicked the holy crap out of him.

* * * * * *

I can reconstruct the entire life of Nessus The Centaur from his childhood to the day he died, but not because I have relived every bit of it in dreams. I may dream one day in that life, and ten days later, another day. And in each dream the memories of many intervening days, or even months, are present. That is how I know everything about Nessus from his days as a child onward.

When I first realized I am a reincarnation of Nessus the Centaur I began to take a deeper interest in his problems, and to feel an ever deeper involvement in his love for Dejanira. I began to wish there was some way I could warn him of what was to come, to help him change his destiny in some way, and, since it seemed clear he would never give up his love for Dejanira, to help him win her love.

But this has been impossible, as I have said. I keep trying, though, to establish a two-way line of communication, racking my brain for some way in which it can be done. Among other resorts, I've tried writing little notes to Nessus on the back of my hand just before going to sleep – a simple little note saying, "Nessus, Jonathan Nestus brings you greetings."

Something else has begun to worry me lately: The memories of my other life are beginning to intrude, more and more, into my present existence. Sometimes I forget that I am Jonathan Nestus and when I am asked for my name, or when I fill out an application of any sort, I have to make an effort not to answer, or write, "Nessus the Centaur." The other day – in the presence of Daphne, to boot – I found myself stamping my left foot when I felt an itch in my ankle, just as a horse will stamp its hoof to ward off a buzzing gadfly. But I can't stop reliving the life of Nessus, even if I wanted to. That concussion I suffered – either the fall off the bridge or that cop's blow to my head –

23

is the cause.

Maybe something good will come from it yet. A few days after Sam Gentile got me out of jail that day, he called me at home with a suggestion. Sam was born in New York and he lived in England once, so his accent is a curious mixture of uncouthness and faint traces of a spurious Oxford accent. "I've been studying your case," he said, "and I think you should sue the city. There are several points of law on which we can base a suit. First, they din't identify themselves as cops. Second, they shouldna hit you on the head. There's a police rule against that. And thirdly" (he pronounced it turdly), "they shouldna taken you to jail. I'm sure all this caused you plenty of distress, and trauma, and so forth."

He had his eye on some big bucks, maybe half a million, he said.

Half-a-million dollars! I would be truly rich again. Wait'll I tell Daphne this, I said to myself. 'Bet she'll warm up to me again. For she had been growing increasingly cool and distant over the days.

I called her that evening to tell her, trying to sound casual, as if half-a-million bucks was just chicken feed to me.

But when I told her, she said, "You won't collect a dime. You can't win against the police. You should sue the county instead, for not putting a safe railing on that bridge."

CHAPTER THREE

Daphne believes in reincarnation, but she refuses to believe that I'm a reincarnation of Nessus the Centaur. She says centaurs never existed, that it's only a fantastic myth.

"What do you eat, when you're a centaur?" she asks me, "you can't eat meat like a person does, can you? or grass and hay, like a horse? And besides, a horse grows up a lot quicker than a man does. Your horse half would be full-grown when the rest of you would still be a child."

I tell Daphne that Lucretius had those exact same arguments. In *De Rerum Naturae* Lucretius says, "There are not, nor have there ever been centaurs ... the habits of man and horse are discordant. Their senses are not gratified by the same stimuli." Horace, also, once scoffingly remarked, "Who has ever seen a half man-half horse?" And modern scientists have many ready arguments to show that the interbreeding of man and horse is impossible. They bring up such matters as chromosomes, DNA, chemical incompatibility . . .

I don't know anything about chromosomes and all that. I only know that I have lived as a centaur. I have felt a centaur's sensations in every fiber of my horse's body. I know what wine tasted like to a centaur. I have felt the soreness in a centaur's muscles after a hard gallop. I have urinated and defecated as a centaur. I have had sex with a female centaur.

As to the apparently thorny problem of what we ate, there's plenty of stuff both man and horse can eat. Carrots, corn, cabbage, apples . . . anything green, in fact, and that includes the common grass known as mallow, which the poor of those times used to eat, although it's hard to believe humans could ever have eaten anything so bitter.

And then, there are those little melons some people today call horse melons, which weren't so bad. And we ate meat, of course, whenever we could get it – mutton, beef, venison, and wild pig. Any

25

horse owner today knows that a horse can develop a liking for meat, and this can be seen in the case of Diomedes, who trained four of his mares to kill and eat human beings. I never saw those mares myself in my other life, and I never met Diomedes. I'm not going to lie and say I did. But I knew Hercules, of course, and know that when he stole those mares during his eighth labor they killed and ate his hanger-on Abderus. And in Herodotus we can read that the inhabitants of Lake Prassias fed their horses and pack animals on fish.

Besides, there was something remarkable and unique about centaurs. We were not really hybrids, but actually a *meld* of man and horse. We had two sets of internal organs. We had two pairs of lungs, two stomachs, two hearts, two livers, and two sets of kidneys. But we only had one horse's rectum, of course, and one set of horse's private parts.

We were, in fact, much like that well-known phenomenon of conjoined twins, of which many examples can be seen on earth today, twins who each have a pair of arms, a heart, and lungs, but who share only one lower body, with one pair of legs between them, while each head has its own separate psyche and its own personality. The centaurs were a similar phenomenon except that instead of one body and two heads, we had one head and two bodies, and we could reproduce our own kind.

Today everyone has seen examples of conjoined twins on television talk shows. The possibility that we may some day also see an example of a conjoined man-horse on one of those talk shows cannot be discounted. Or a conjoined example of any other pair of creatures, although the centaur, since it has already existed in past ages and has probably left its genes and DNA in the blood pool of the human or of the equine race, is a much more likely possibility.

Even for the casual observer it's easy to deduce the fact of a double set of organs in the centaur. Of course his human chest and torso could not have been a mere empty shell, enclosing only one huge trachea and esophagus leading to the horse's lungs and stomach. Our trachea, incidentally, was divided in such a way as to continue all the way into our equine parts, as was our esophagus. We had to ingest huge amounts of food to provide adequate nutrition to both man and horse, and we had the capability of controlling which foods or liquids went to our human and which went to our horse's stomachs. Centaurs were mouth breathers, and sometimes we may have appeared to be hyperventilating, because we required great, deep gulps of air to keep both man and horse supplied with oxygen.

Another curious detail about centaur physiology is that we didn't have the same control over our bodily functions as all other creatures have. Our equine half had a certain degree of autonomy, often subtracting itself from the control of its human brain. We never befouled our own caves, but otherwise, we tended to urinate and defecate anywhere, it didn't matter who was present or where we were. A long period of adjustment was necessary before we could learn to control these bodily functions in certain places. We would fart a lot, too, I admit, because of the peculiar diet we followed, which caused a great deal of flatulence.

As to the other objection raised by Daphne – about the uneven growth of man and horse (which is also mentioned by Lucretius) –, I once heard Cheiron explain why the equine half of a centaur could keep apace with the growth of its human parts, so that a five year old child still retained the body of a young colt. It was a certain something in the centaur mother's breast milk, he said – today it would be called an enzyme –, that influenced this evenness of growth. Centaur women knew, by the way, that the centaur mother should never suckle her child at her mare's udders because this would throw the child's development out of kilter. Some centaurs considered this to be only a superstition, but everyone observed it, nevertheless. The observance of the supposed superstition was made easy by the fact that the centaur child did not have easy access to its mother's mare's udders.

In short, Wise Cheiron, most famous of the centaurs, would have had an answer to every one of those scoffing doubts expressed so long ago by Lucretius and Horace and by Daphne today. Cheiron was one of the few centaurs in my time who could read. He had books, in the form of scrolls, written in the ancient alphabet in use at that time, which he kept in a large jar in his cave. He could have explained to Daphne – and to Lucretius and Horace, too – that the accident of nature that was the Centaur race came about because of a strange chemical and atmospheric condition which at one time prevailed over earth in the region of Mount Olympus.

27

This condition caused a suspension in the normal rules and laws of nature, contributing to an abnormal interaction between the seed and ovum of diverse creatures, bringing about a proliferation of freaks and monstrosities on earth. The lecherous half goat-half human satyrs also came into existence at that time, along with the mermaids, those lovely half-fish maidens, whom I have heard singing on moonlit nights in their clear and silvery voices on Magnesian beaches.

It's my belief that the first mermaids were born as a result of the custom amongst the Cyclades Islanders of mating on the seashore, sometimes in the sea itself, giving rise to many instances of spilled seed in the waters. This led, eventually, to the accidental impregnation of passing fish. Although it is not entirely out of the question that there could even have been a man so depraved that he did not draw the line at making love to a cold, slimy fish.

Or, just as likely, a woman swimming at a sandy beach could have come into contact with floating fish sperm. Or a woman could have been unintentionally impregnated by one of those fish which deposit their eggs in any handy crack or crevice. Or even purposely impregnated, against her will, by a large, sexually deprived fish, such as a grouper or rock bass.

Also quite probable, a woman could have had intercourse with a dolphin. Perhaps long ago, a fair maiden, victim of a shipwreck, struggled in the foaming sea. In her desperation, she would shed her robes in an effort to remain afloat as long as possible. Along would come a school of sporting dolphins, which, following the inclination that has been observed in this species, would nudge her gently to the shore and safety. Just before reaching land, one of them, aroused by her lithe naked body with her golden locks flowing around her in the foam-flecked, green sea, would decide to reward itself for its good deed. The maiden would not have resisted, but rather, most likely, have given herself to it with grateful passion.

On second thought, however, this last speculation may be groundless, because dolphins don't have scales, and mermaids did, as I know from personal observation.

Sirens are traditionally depicted as mermaids. To such a degree, in fact, that most people are surprised to learn that these daughters of the Muse Terpsichore had bird's bodies. They were about the size of a

28

small ostrich, but with short legs, almost no neck, and a girl's face. Not that I ever saw them in my other life, but I've seen a picture of them in an ancient engraving. They had been turned into birds by Core because they had been with her when she was kidnapped by Hades, and yet had not told Core's mother. They couldn't fly, of course, being so large and heavy. They took up residence on a tiny island in the Adriatic Sea, and there, moved by a cankering resentment at their fate, they vented their spite upon the world by luring many a mariner to his death with their bewitching song. They sat amidst a pile of bleached bones and rotting corpses, singing sweetly to anyone who passed within earshot.

At least that is the story told about them today, and even during the life of Nessus. But I personally think they were the result of interbreeding between humans and some species or other of large birds, as a result of the atmospheric condition previously mentioned.

Returning to the mermaids, In my other life I've seen them, and I can affirm that they were much as they are traditionally depicted; lithe, smooth-skinned (albeit slightly slimy), and with small, firm breasts. The great deal of time they spent in the water gave them a finely formed, athletic physique. Contrary to their conventional image across the centuries, however, they had no buttocks, and their anus was located on the underside of their bodies, the same as an ordinary fish. Their external sex organ was situated just above the anus and just below the line dividing their girl's body (in the case of the females) from that of the fish. It was covered over with a sort of finely scaled carapace, which would part to facilitate sexual intercourse, whenever they were so inclined. It was quite devoid of pubic hair.

There were of course mermen, too. I've never seen one. I'm not going to lie about it and say I have. But the historian Pausanias has left us an idea of what they looked like. He refers to them as Tritons, and they were evidently rather ugly, according to his description of one which he saw at Tanagra:

> Tritons are certainly a sight. The hair on their heads
> is like that of frogs in stagnant water: not only in its
> frog-like color, but so sleek one hair can hardly be separated
> from the next – they have gills behind the ears
> and a human nose, but a very big mouth and the teeth of

29

a wild beast – from the breast and belly down they have
a dolphin's tail instead of feet. Pausanias; IX 21

This Triton that he speaks of was not alive, but a specimen pickled in brine, and it is also mentioned by the learned Damostratos, who wrote a voluminous book on marine monsters, according to Aelian. But it couldn't have had a dolphin's tail. The mermaid's tail, although it was situated horizontally, the same as that of the dolphin, was scaled and slimy, just as in a fish.

Although they had men of their own species, mermaids often consorted with normal humans, proving that they were quite attractive and desirable (and also, perhaps, proving that the males of their own species were as ugly as Pausanias describes them). When they had sunned themselves for an hour or two on a sandy beach their slightly slimy skin would dry and lose much of its fishy qualities.

The unforgettable spectacle of a group of bare-breasted mermaids sunning themselves on boulders strewn about a sun-splashed, foamy beach, the flashing silver of their tarpon-like scales framed by the sun-worked gold of their thick tresses, their shapely arms plying cockleshell combs retrieved from the ocean's depths through their flowing locks – this spectacle, we may assume, made such an impression on the many people who were fortunate enough to behold it that the memory of it was passed on to succeeding generations and survives strongly to this day as an inherited memory.

Some mermaids were brunettes and others among them had golden scales, much like goldfish. These mermaids, with scales like 'doubly-hammered leaves of finest gold' had platinum hair and green eyes, and a blue, phosphorescent streak running down their flanks to their tail. Nearly all fish have this streak, which is a sensor to detect changes in water pressure, and serves to warn the fish of approaching predators.

Mermaids could dive to depths of three or four hundred feet and remain submerged for up to eighteen minutes. To suckle their young, they would either swim to shore or float languidly on their backs, while the merbaby clung to its mother's breast, its little tail gently fanning the water to help both mother and baby remain afloat.

There was a time when large colonies of merpeople thrived on many beaches on the Cyclades Islands and on all the shores washed by the Aegean Sea. In fact, they were found all over the Mediterranean.

But with each successive wave of advancing civilization, the vast congregations of mermaids which had thronged the beaches of Paros, Naxos and Seriphos, singing merrily as they shucked clams and oysters, grew smaller and smaller. Finally, shortly before or after the Trojan war, the last surviving mermaids failed to return to their favorite beach after an excursion seaward to gather food.

Mermaids loved to sing, a fact noted by Physiologus, as Geoffrey Chaucer reminds us (". . . for Physiologus says that Mermaids do sing most merrily"), and their voices were as clear and pure as the tinkle of silver bells. This is perhaps the reason they are so commonly confused with the sirens.

* * * * * *

The mermaids and the centaurs, then, as well as all the other weird creatures that populate the Greek myths, were the result of interspecies and intergeneric breeding. The inhabitants of the ancient world, unhampered by modern scientific thought, could clearly see that this was indeed the case. To them, seed was seed, and they could see no reason why a woman, mounted by a bull, for example, would not inevitably give birth to a Minotaur. And I happen to know they were right. Of course such instances would not always result in a hybrid. There is that matter of chemical and biological incompatibility. But across millions of years, and across hundreds of thousands of cases, should we not expect that occasionally one of these unions would give rise to an entirely new species?

If the centaurs once lived on earth, why did they then become extinct? The laws of evolution tell us that a new species, to survive, must have an advantage over the old race from which it has evolved and with which it must compete for a livelihood in the same environment. Otherwise, it will inevitably die out over the course of time.

Let us look at the equine half of the centaur, then, to see if they enjoyed any sort of advantage over a mere horse. At first sight it would appear that they did, indeed. Here was a horse that had an intelligent human brain to guide it, and keep it out of trouble. A human half that would take especial care never to mistreat it – never to force it on long rides, and thus bring about an untimely demise from exhaustion. The

31

human half would never forget to allow it access to water or good pasturage; he would be attentive to the horse's every need, and would care for it as lovingly and carefully as if it were himself, which in fact it was.

But who else would be interested in this horse's welfare? This horse already had an owner, the centaur himself. No one else could ride it, or harness it to a chariot. It was useless for breeding purposes. In short, this horse, as far as anyone else was concerned, was totally worthless. No one else, therefore, would have been interested in seeing it thrive and multiply.

Now let us look at the human half of the centaur. Here, again, a superficial look seems to suggest that he was endowed with enormous advantages over mere humans. A centaur was a man who had a horse at his instant disposal, day and night. They were each, so to speak, born in possession of a magnificent saddle horse. When a centaur wished to go on a trip, he did not have to go through the tedious process of catching a horse, gathering saddle, bridle and bit, saddle blankets . . . No. He merely switched himself lightly on the rump with a small stick, and he was off. A centaur never had to worry about earning the money to pay for a horse. This would have enabled them to dedicate all their time to procuring food and shelter, and to procreate. Compare this to modern man's dilemma of having to spend a lifetime of slavery to pay for a car, thereby squandering valuable resources which could otherwise be employed in raising offspring. And then compare this modern man to a hypothetical race whose offspring would emerge from the womb at the wheel of a tiny car, say a little Yugo or Toyota, that would grow apace with the child through the years.

But the advantages that the centaurs enjoyed in their great strength, their fleetness of hoof, and maneuverability in battle, were offset by the numerous problems which beset their daily lives. All of the things which we do so easily were of great difficulty for the centaur. The centaur could not stoop, or bend, or even sit in a chair at a desk or table. If centaurs had survived up to our times, what sort of occupation could they have engaged in to earn a livelihood?

Add to this the fact that sometimes the powerful virile passions of a horse would surge uncontrollably upward into the human half and render the centaur incapable of resisting its beastly urges.

32

It seems likely, then, that this uneasy alliance of man and horse overshadowed the apparent advantages of the centaur. His occasional equine inclination to a headstrong stubbornness and a complete lack of human delicacy and restraint got him into all kinds of trouble with his human neighbors, as we shall see later on, and contributed to his eventual extinction.

* * * * * *

Sometimes I tell Daphne all these things, carefully tailored so as not to give her an excuse to pretend to be offended, but I have not convinced her. She tells me that I read too much when I tell her what Lucretius and Horace said. On one of those increasingly rare occasions in which she has deigned to enter my apartment she looked distastefully at all my books, many of them inherited from my great-uncle Phillip, usually piled in every free corner of my cramped apartment, but on that occasion arranged as neatly as I could manage in several large book cases, and said, "That's what's wrong with you, not those blows on the head. When we get married the first thing I'm going to do is throw all your books in a dumpster."

It was exciting to hear her say, "When we get married . . ." She hadn't uttered that word for a long time. As for throwing my books in a dumpster, I have news for her, which I keep to myself. That's not the first thing she's going to do if we ever get married. The first thing she's going to do is get in bed with me, so I can fornicate her (I know fornicate isn't an active verb, but I prefer to use it that way) until she's cross-eyed. Then she can do what she wants. Much as I prize my books, connected as they are to the memory of my great-uncle Phillip, I would sacrifice them all in exchange for going to bed with Daphne.

I have doubts, however, about her sincerity when she says "When we get married . . ." At times, the uneasy suspicion strikes me that the only victim of my deception now is me, that on Daphne's part the glowing admiration she once held for me as the possessor of huge hoards of cash has long since been supplanted by a gnawing anger and contempt at what she probably perceives as a gross fraud. Because, though Daphne may not be very smart, she's also not so dumb. But I never lied to her. I never actually told her, in so many words, "I'm worth over a million dollars." If she came to that conclusion, it's her own fault. Although, to tell the truth, whenever she would talk about buying a

33

beautiful home in the suburbs once we were married I never mentioned to her that for this to occur, certain financial difficulties would first have to be resolved.

Soon, only the memories of my inheritance money will remain, the memories of those expensive restaurants that I took Daphne to, that trip to Atlantic City and Trump's Casino; my expensive suits, bought for the sole purpose of impressing Daphne, now gathering dust and moths in my closet . . . Then I won't have bugger-all. Not even a decent car. And I wonder what my great-uncle Phillip would say or think if he could see the way I've spent his money. He wanted me to use it to go to college. Poor Uncle Phillip. He didn't realize that forty-five thousand dollars would barely have seen me through two years of a real college.

And, most disturbing of all, someone's been telling me that I still owe the IRS money.

* * * * * *

My only hope these days is my law suit against the city. Five months ago, when the incident happened, Sam Gentile felt we had a good case. He talked about half-a-million dollars. But then he began to talk of an out-of-court settlement . . . maybe a hundred thousand or so. We might ought to go that route, he said. A court settlement can take years.

My first impulse was to say, Let's make an out-of-court settlement; let's grab what we can and run. But as the days went by after that conversation with Sam, I began to reflect: after his legal fees I would be left with maybe sixty thousand. After divvying up with the IRS I would only have forty. Could forty thousand dollars bridge the widening rift between Daphne and me?

And as more days went by, and as my pitiful little inheritance continued to dwindle, with Daphne growing increasingly cool and distant, forty thousand dollars seemed less and less.

So, when Sam called me again the other day I said, "You know, a hundred thousand doesn't seem like very much, after what they did to me."

"I know what you mean," he said, "but that's just about the going rate for a simple slap on the head. If you was suffering from any physical damage – somet'ing besides the humiliation – it would be a diff'ernt story. But you di'nt even go to a doctor."

34

"Well, there's those dreams," I said. And I gave him a short account of my dreams, and how they had started almost immediately after the beating.

Sam was at first doubtful. It didn't sound like something that could be attributed to a blow on the head, he said. But, as we continued to discuss it, he grew more enthusiastic. "Maybe that would work," he finally said. "I know a psychiatrist that would testify as to how a blow to the head can do somet'ing like that – and about the emotional distress it can cause. Come down to my office, and let's go over your story. We'll amend our suit and stick those sonsabitches for five million dollars."

I was elated. I immediately called Daphne and told her, "I'm not going to collect just a measly half-million dollars. It's going to be five million buckamentos!"

But Daphne was more skeptical than ever. "You can't win against the Police Department," she repeated again. "You'll be wasting your time. You should have followed my advice and sued the county over the bridge thing."

I didn't allow her views to dampen my hopes and my enthusiasm. She would sing a different tune when I had that money in the bank. She would look at me differently then. She would begin to really love me, and I would regain the admiration I think she once had for me, when she thought I was rich. I would buy a fine house and a new car for each of us.

My only worry was that I might become a laughing stock when the full story was made public.

CHAPTER FOUR

In my unique condition as a reincarnation of Nessus the Centaur I quickly realized the tremendous advantage I had as a historian of that nebulous era. A few weeks after my first dream, I began to write *A Short History of the Centaurs.* In this literary endeavor I was driven partly by the need I felt of responding to Daphne's statements about the delusive nature of my former existence as a centaur. Any discussion of a remotely intellectual nature I have ever had with Daphne has revolved around this matter, i.e., the historical or mythical basis for the existence of the centaurs. So I gave her a chapter of my new book to read, to refute her arguments, and also, I suppose, hoping to hear an expression of admiration from her for my erudition, knowledge, and writing skills. Here is the first chapter I showed her:

Chapter Two of
A Short History Of The Centaurs

In all of Greek mythology there runs a persistent thread of logic and consistency, wherein all things and persons spring from consequential beginnings. So, it is only natural to find that the primordial progenitor of the centaur race was named Centaurus. However, in the ancient literature, the centaurs are frequently referred to as "children of Ixion." This is because Ixion was the father of Centaurus, and Ixion is a much more prominent personage – he was the king of Elis, for one thing – than was his perverted son. We find the first supporting evidence for our premise that the centaurs actually existed as half-horse, half-human creatures, therefore, in the fact that they do not simply pop into Greek mythology from out of nowhere. They have a well-documented genealogical origin. And the fact that the ancient writers singled out Ixion as their most prominent ancestor, while giving Centaurus only scant mention, lends further solidity to the legend of their origin.

The mother of Centaurus, Nephele, is also a prominent personage in the Greek myths, and her name crops up at various junctures in the ancient histories. In later chapters it will be seen where and how. For the time being, we will only mention that she was a sister-in-law to that famous Sisyphus, who labors eternally with a large boulder in Tartarus. Like Ixion, who is commonly referred to as the father of the centaurs, she is known as their mother, although she was only a grandmother to the first members of that race. Centaurus, on the other hand, is strangely absent from all subsequent events in mythology. There is a reason for this, just as there is a reason for every other aspect of Greek mythology.

The centaurs themselves seem to have thrived over a long period without leaving any distinct lines of descent. A long list of centaur names can be gleaned from Ovid's description of the fight at Peirithous' wedding. Yet, only rarely is any mention made of a centaur's paternity; rather uncharacteristic for Greek mythology, where almost all personages have a father and a mother. This teeming host of fierce centaurs seems to have no other genealogical origin than Centaurus himself. This is perhaps one of the reasons that their existence has been dismissed as fictitious and purely mythical. In later chapters, however, we will advance some reasons to account for this apparent lack of genealogical progression and blood-lines in the centaur race.

But let us proceed with our history: It begins with the story of Ixion, king of Elis, who was frequently the guest of Zeus in the halls of Olympus. There, he actually enjoyed the privilege of sitting down at the Olympian banquet table with gods and goddesses, to shamelessly stuff himself with nectar and ambrosia, oblivious to the stiff demeanor and disdainful glances of Hera and the other gods. They didn't like the idea of a lowly mortal sitting at the same table with them, but they had to put up with it, whether they liked it or not.

And why did Zeus have such a high regard for Ixion? Actually, it appears that he had no regard for him at all. He only invited him into Olympus in order to get him out of the way, so that he himself could then descend to earth and fornicate with Ixion's wife, Dia.

From thus hobnobbing with gods and goddesses, Ixion became infatuated with Hera, and conceived the idea of seducing her, a most despicable and blasphemous notion. True, Zeus was himself fornicating with Ixion's wife, but Ixion, if he knew of it, should only have looked upon this as a great honor. He should have been proud that the supreme god would deign to confer such a distinction upon his wife. For almighty Zeus could pick and choose only the best of females on Earth and in Heaven

From the moment in which Ixion allowed the horrible thought to cross his mind, omniscient Zeus knew of it. He decided to lay a trap for Ixion, to see just how far he would go. Out of a passing cloud he created a woman in the image of Hera, and contrived to leave her alone with Ixion. This false Hera, later named Nephele, allowed Ixion to seduce her.

If things had proceeded to a normal conclusion, Ixion could have been highly pleased with himself. Seducing, and enjoying sex with, the supreme Olympian goddess on snow-capped Mount Olympus was something he could have bragged about to his friends with justifiable pride.

But simultaneously with the consummation of Ixion's passion and his crime, grim-visaged Zeus burst in upon them.

Nowhere in Greek mythology, to my knowledge, is this scene ever described or touched upon at any great length. But what a terrible fright it must have been for Ixion. Consider: He was fornicating with (as far as he knew) the supreme Olympian goddess. Her husband, a being of awesome power, capable of the greatest extremes of harshness and cruelty, had caught him in the very act. An experience of this sort, according to modern psychiatrists, can lead to subsequent problems of impotence. This, of course, would have been the least of Ixion's concerns. He would have known that he had things other than mere impotence to worry about.

And what about Nephele? Did she know this was going to happen? Was she collaborating with Zeus in the entire matter? If she wasn't, then she deserves our most heartfelt sympathy, subjected as she was to the horrible embarrassment of being interrupted in the act of procreation. Either way, the fate of Nephele illustrates the petty, vindictive, and egotistical nature of the ancient gods, thoughtlessly creating intelligent life with all its suffering, shame, humiliation and sorrow, all to satisfy their own perverted sense of justice.

As for Ixion, Zeus first had him savagely whipped by Hermes, until he repeated the words, "Benefactors deserve honor." Then he had him nailed to a wheel, which was set afire and made to spin eternally through the heavens.

Another version of the myth says that he was consigned to Tartarus, likewise nailed to a flaming wheel. Ovid, in his *Metamorphoses*, says that Hera saw him there, in that part of Hades' dominions which is known as the Abode of the Accursed, when she descended there to ask a favor of Tisiphone, who is one of the Three Furies. She looked around her, says Ovid, to take in the sight of various of the tormented inmates, such as Tantalus, reaching futilely for the water he can never drink, and the overhanging fruit, which forever eludes his grasp; Sisyphus, now pushing, now pursuing his 'shameless' stone; the Danaids, carrying water in their perforated pitchers; the giant Tityus, killed by Apollo because he tried to rape his mother Leto, and now pegged down over nine acres of ground while three vultures tear at his liver . . . Ixion was there too, on his flaming wheel. "She glared fiercely at them all," says Ovid, "especially at Ixion." This gives us a clue as to how Hera felt about a lowly mortal presuming to seduce her.

What an additional torment it must have been for Ixion, knowing now how he had been deceived. Knowing now that he had never really enjoyed Hera herself, but only a cheap facsimile fashioned from a cloud.

From this brief union of Ixion and Nephele, a child was born, whom Nephele named Centaurus. It is not clear exactly where this child was born, or why Nephele chose to name him Centaurus. But it's possible that she gave birth while she was still in Olympus, thereby justifying the term, "the cloud born," that Ovid and other poets apply to Centaurus' offspring. But of course the term would apply at any event, because Nephele was shaped from a cloud, and that is what her name means. It is said that, her purpose served, Zeus couldn't decide what to do with her, and she wandered disconsolately around the halls of Olympus for some time. Finally, however, Zeus gave her to Athamas, king of Iolcos, to be his wife.

As for Centaurus, he grew up an outcast, shunned by gods and mortals alike, being the child of such a notorious criminal. Isolated by this ostracism and excluded from a normal social intercourse with his fellow humans, he wandered alone through the years, northward from Iolcos across the River Penaeus into Magnesia.

Imagine, if you will, the following scenario: It is a pleasant spring day on the foothills of Mount Pelion, on a day shortly after the first full moon of the spring equinox. The air is filled with the joy of blooming flowers and freshening grass. In the far distance, snow-capped Mount Olympus, the abode of the gods, lifts its majestic head to survey the primeval panorama at its feet – emerald meadows, splashed with the riotous color of poppies, violets, goldenrods, bluebells, and daffodils. Like necklaces of dark-green jade, forests of venerable oaks, willows and elms ring the bejeweled meadows, and a cool breeze from the east wafts in the sweet odors of the Myrtoan Sea.

It was to one such meadow that Centaurus wandered on just such a day, there to chance upon a herd of brood mares, placidly grazing on the lush grass and clover . . .

We must remember, Centaurus no doubt felt deeply wounded by the treatment he was subjected to for something that was no fault of his. He was probably very lonely. He could not turn to a fellow human being for consolation. In fact, he was probably substantially dehumanized by his long period of exile from the human race. We mention this, not to excuse his actions, but as an explanation, of sorts, for his behavior. As to how he managed to accomplish the mission for which he had been destined by the Fates, who can say? Perhaps he found some pieces of rope in the meadow, with which he haltered and hobbled the mares. But this is immaterial.

Centaurus hung around the meadow for several days, taking his pleasure, until he was chased away by the indignant owner of the mares.

* * * * * *

Thus was the race of centaurs conceived, "A host wondrous to look upon," says Pindar, "resembling both their parents." Nephele always preserved a soft spot in her heart for her son's children. She was said to retain some control over the clouds from which she was conceived and at the fight at Pholoe between Hercules and the centaurs she is said to have sent down a shower of rain to loosen Hercules' bow string and make the ground slippery beneath his feet.

* * * * * *

To the owner of those mares, that nameless and anonymous horse breeder, gazing for the first time at the little creatures his mares had foaled, they must have presented a weird and repulsive sight, not immediately revealing in their aspect what they were. He would have seen only deformed foals, with most of the body of a normal colt, but, instead of a normal neck and head, a growth of hairless flesh, with ugly appendages, disturbingly suggestive of human arms and head. Moreover, from out of a tiny slobbering mouth, set in a blind, wrinkled little face, there would have proceeded nerve-wracking shrieks as the monstrosities stumbled about, unable to find their mothers' udders. We can surmise that he brought neighbors and friends from a nearby village to show them the disquieting sight, hoping someone could tell him what the strange deformities meant. Some of them would have known at once what they were looking at. From other similar cases – not too uncommon in those times – they would have known that they had before their eyes the results of interbreeding between man and horse. With this puzzle settled, the horse breeder would have remembered the incident of the previous year, when he had chased Ixion's outcast son Centaurus from the meadow. And everyone knew what Centaurus had been doing. So, the question of who the father of these little creatures was, would have been immediately answered.

All this we can only surmise. Possibly, the true sequence of these events was known for thousands of years, and the knowledge eventually lost to humanity forever when the chain of oral traditions was broken by wars and shifting populations.

* * * * * *

It seems likely that the foals, instead of being left with the mares, were taken away by their owner and various of his friends and neighbors. This was fortunate, because it is doubtful that they could have survived if the mares had suckled them. Possibly, the mares' milk would have induced a too rapid growth of the equine part of the little creatures, causing an atrophy of the human parts. And this would effectively counter the skepticism of Lucretius, who based his disbelief in centaurs on the disparate growth rates of man and horse.

Over the next few years the villagers were able to observe the curious way in which the infants grew and developed: Probably raised on goat's milk – or possibly, even by a few lactating women who were not squeamish about suckling the little creatures at their breasts – , man and horse kept apace in their growth until, after ten years or so, the equine parts somewhat resembled a cross between a modern thoroughbred and a medium-sized draft horse. In the same time-span the human half melded onto the chest and withers of each horse became a nearly mature individual. In the case of the males (for there were probably an equal number of males and females), they were muscular and broad-shouldered, with heavy chests, thick arms, flatly chiseled facial features and shaggy heads of sandy colored hair and beards. Being somewhat craggy-browed, some of them wore a habitually scowling expression. This typical, scowling countenance was one of the factors which contributed to their later reputation for fierceness, sometimes unjustly applied.

The females, on the other hand, were strikingly beautiful, with a lithe, well-shaped bust and torso, and with facial features somewhat reminiscent of that well-known French painting of Lady Liberty, leading a charge of armed men into battle. Or perhaps comparable to the face on the Statue of Liberty in New York harbor, except that they did not have such large mouths, nor, of course, the same vacant stare. Thus the first centaurs came into existence.

End Of Chapter Two Of
A Short History Of The Centaurs

42

* * * * * *

When Daphne brought the pages back two or three weeks later, I asked her what she thought of the chapter.

She gave a sort of faint shrug of the shoulders. "Who's going to publish that?"

"Oh, I don't know," I answered her, "I haven't decided. But more than one university press has expressed an interest in it. Of course I haven't told them why I am so uniquely qualified to write about the centaurs. And also, in my history I can't say everything I would like to. I have to pretend that all my knowledge of the subject has been gleaned from published material. A shame, really. There are so many things I know, from having actually lived those times."

Her expression conveyed the faint suggestion of a skeptical sniff. "But all that – that . . . bestiality. I've told you I don't like to hear those things."

"Daphne, this is history. I don't necessarily like that stuff either."

She changed the subject. She was having car trouble again. It was going to cost her four hundred dollars to have it repaired. She didn't know where she was going to get the money, with the house payment due, and everything, and she hadn't sold a trailer for three weeks.

This was where I was supposed to say, "Why don't you let me lend you the money?" But I didn't say it. I was worried about my old car myself, and I was beginning to suspect by now that giving money to Daphne was throwing money down a bottomless well – a dry well, to no purpose. She was never going to give me anything in return. Also, I was miffed at her lack of enthusiasm for my writing talent.

* * * * * *

Money, house, car . . . the IRS. Nessus the Centaur never had problems like this. These problems were three thousand years away for him. We lived in caves, excavated on mountain sides. Transportation was something we were born with. I have pleasant memories of my childhood as a centaur. Riding on horseback is an unrealizable dream for most modern human children. I recall, as a little boy on my uncle Phillip's farm in Ohio, pretending to ride on horseback everywhere I

43

went, straddling an old broomstick and urging on an imaginary mount with a little stick, striking myself on the butt with it, sometimes until I was black and blue. All for the pleasure of imagining myself on horseback. As a centaur child I didn't have to do this. I had a fleet and powerful colt always at my beck and call, to carry me galloping swiftly through life.

Then, as a grown man, I was handsome and muscular. I didn't wear glasses back then. I had cool hair and a thick, sandy beard. I didn't have to worry about not being loved for what I was. I never had to pretend to have money in order to enjoy the companionship of females of my own kind. Of course, where *human* females were concerned, there was this drawback of being half horse, a grave defect, from those human females' point of view. But, since this was something I couldn't change, I had learned to live with it.

All in all, I must say that Nature had both blessed and cursed the centaurs in many subtle ways. Blessed with a horse's strength and power, and the speed of a horse's thundering hooves, which often evoked admiring glances from Greek women who would watch us racing with the wind across the fields, we were also, by these same attributes, barred from ever having a meaningful relationship with the daughters of ordinary man, to whom we were always greatly attracted. And additionally, we carried the heavy burden of having to control a horse's passions with only a normal human brain.

People today may wonder: If there were centaur females, why were so many centaurs always chasing after human females? Life as a centaur was already complicated enough. Why did we insist on further complicating it by chasing after women, spurning a normal relationship with one of our own kind? Why couldn't we accept the fact that a woman's shapely long legs and undulating hips were something forever beyond our domain, and that a mare's hard bony rump and clip-clopping hooves was our assigned portion in life?

Centaur women were certainly not unattractive. The least attractive of them could still be described as handsome. Their eyes were large – usually chestnut or brown – with arching eyebrows and long, thick lashes. They wore their hair unbound, streaming over their shoulders, sometimes serving to cover their breasts whenever Greek men were around, staring goggle-eyed at their sun-highlighted splendor,

44

since centaurs, males and females alike, never wore clothes.

The breasts of centaur women were always firm and youthful-looking, even when they were lactating, and nursing infants. This was perhaps due to the equine heritage of centaur women. If you have ever had occasion to examine a mare's udders, you will have noticed their small size, as compared to a cow's huge, flopping ones. The trim primness of a mare's udders was thus transposed into the demure and genteel size of the centaur female's human breasts, a far cry from the ungainly, baggy mammaries – perhaps the word is mammae – one might expect, given the fact that they served to suckle a fifty-pound, or one-hundred pound foal.

Centaur children, by the way, were weaned at a late stage. I clearly remember, when I must have been four or five years old, sucking at my mother's breasts and I remember that they were turgid and firm, not floppy and sagging like an ordinary woman's breasts would be after suckling a child for five years.

And yet, despite this natural beauty of the centaur woman, centaur males still persisted in chasing after Greek women, sometimes trying to rape them. Other Centaurs, besides myself came to a tragic end because of this unbridled lust for human females. Like Eurytion, who even tried to marry one once, a girl named Mnesimache. And the marriage would have gone through, too. Her father had already agreed to it. But Hercules showed up just before the wedding and shot Eurytion through with an arrow, because he wanted Mnesimache for himself, and he claimed that Eurytion had frightened her father into consenting. Hinting, thereby, that no man would willingly give his daughter in marriage to a centaur, and that no woman in her right mind would want to marry one.

And yet most centaurs always thought of Hercules as a friend, strangely blind to the bigotry that this one act showed. It was a general attitude that all people held towards Hercules, a view which is hard to understand today. No one was revulsed or shocked at his homicidal excesses, seeming to view his many murders as heroic deeds. Some of his more well-known victims included his best friend, Iphitus, whom he threw off a tower because Iphitus had mistakenly thought that Hercules had taken some of his cattle. He killed a poor farmer, Theiodamas, who refused to give him the ox he was plowing with so Hercules could eat it;

45

he killed his music teacher Linus, who was a cousin of Orpheus, breaking his lyre over his head because Linus had rapped his knuckles when he plucked the wrong strings; he mutilated the Minyan heralds, cutting off their ears, an act which would normally have been considered the most heinous and unpardonable of crimes in anyone else. He killed his wife Megara and his own children . . . His many other murders would fill an entire volume.

But his worst crime of all, as far as I am concerned, is that he killed my best friend, Homadus the Centaur.

He claimed to have done it because Homadus was trying to rape Alcyone. But Alcyone was actually the sister of Hercules' worst enemy, King Eurystheus. Why would Hercules have been so concerned over the safety of his enemy's sister? He was no great champion of womanhood. He once shot a priestess of Hera through both breasts with an arrow, after a religious argument of some sort. This was the principal reason that the goddess Hera hated his guts. Aside from the fact that he was a bastard child of her own husband, of course, if there was any truth in the tale that Hercules himself had no small part in spreading.

To me, his murder of Homadus shows that Hercules, despite his professed friendship with the centaurs, really hated all centaurs and used every pretext he could think of to kill one.

And yet, his many murders only evoked universal admiration, instead of condemnation. The Greeks had a penchant for making the most despicable of murderers into demigods and heroes. The reason for this is that the human mind was different back in those days. The human brain has evolved far more than most people realize today in just that relatively short period of three thousand years. I know this because I have felt the difference. I think differently in that other life, even though my own mentality was of a more advanced frame than that of the common Greek or centaur. I can almost feel like a sort of 'click' in my brain upon awaking from one of those dreams, as if a different set of mental gears were enmeshing when my thought-mode switches from then to now. This is the reason, as I say, that the ancient Greeks seem so strangely tolerant towards the criminal defects of their heroes . . . Achilles, a homicidal maniac; his father Peleus a fratricide, who with his brother Telamon murdered their brother Phocus; Odysseus, who talked Agamemnon into sacrificing Polyxena to the ghost of Achilles,

46

and who threw the infant Astyanax from the walls of Troy; Jason, who treacherously murdered his brother-in-law Apsyrtus, and abandoned his wife Medea; Perseus, who tried to kill his blind father-in-law . . .

In the case of Hercules, this tolerance – tending towards sheer adulation – was partly due to the fear and terror he inspired. After I killed him – because, yes, I can say that it was I who rid the world of this mad-dog killer – that adulation culminated into worship. They claimed that he had become a god, that he had become a gatekeeper in Olympus, and he had shrines and temples where many people prayed to him, just as they did to the real gods. It was as if people refused to believe that a mere human could have committed such a varied catalogue of crimes – that only a god could be capable of such enormities.

I was already dead myself by then. But if I had still been alive I would have spit and pissed on his shrines, and told any Greek that their greatest hero and popular god, Hercules, had been nothing more than a surly, sullen, murderous, vicious, and no-good son of a bitch.

CHAPTER FIVE

As a reincarnation of Nessus the Centaur I know exactly how the Ancient Mariner must have felt, with his overpowering urge to tell someone the strange experience he had lived through. As for me, the only person I had to whom I could reveal my former existence as Nessus The Centaur was Daphne. And Daphne had nothing but skepticism to offer, and advice about how I could "cure" myself of my "delusion."

If only there had been someone else to whom I could have talked about the things that perpetually entertained my longings, my interests and my imagination, and if I could have maintained before Daphne an entirely different façade, as a sober person, a cold-blooded manipulator of assets, a man of substance and of means, with no room in his head for nonsense and literary preoccupations, in short, a guy with plenty of money. That way, I could have kept alive my hopes of eventually winning her unconditional respect and admiration – my hopes of eventually getting into her pants, to put it crudely.

But there was no one else. All I had was that tenuous relationship with Daphne, for whatever it was worth. And so, despite my uneasy, unclearly formed knowledge that by doing so I would inevitably destroy those tenuous ties, I began to use my *Short History of the Centaurs* as a way of convincing her that the Centaurs had truly existed, that they had been real, and that my other life as Nessus the Centaur was not a delusion. So, even after her curt dismissal of Chapter Two of my new book, I gave her another chapter to read:

Chapter Three of
A Short History Of The Centaurs

When the first centaurs were born, the fortunate people who then inhabited the earth had many other engrossing events to entertain their fancies and provide them with endless subjects of conversation. Flying horses, hydras, chimeras, griffons and multiple-headed dogs competed for attention. Minor

49

gods, goddesses, wood nymphs and dryads populated every river, lake, pool, and woodland. The Olympian gods themselves frequently walked on earth and mingled with mortal man. The darker and more distant corners of earth were ruled by Titans, giants and serpent-tailed monsters. The foaming, roiling seas that girdled fair earth teemed with mermaids, sea nymphs, nereids and tritons.

Still, despite this plethora of wonders, when the first centaurs appeared on earth the entire Mediterranean world buzzed with gossip and commentary. The reason for such a keen interest in the matter stemmed partly from the fact that the culprit involved – Centaurus – was such a prominent personage, with connections to the Olympian gods themselves, as we have seen. All the attention that the incident received probably caused him a great deal of shame and embarrassment; for he disappeared shortly afterwards as if the earth had swallowed him, never to be heard from again. At any rate, all references to him in Greek mythology end at the point where he is identified as the father of the Centaur race, with never a hint afterwards as to his ultimate fate. However, it appears he earned his status as an outcast principally because of the criminal and blasphemous manner of his conception, rather than because of his bestial acts.

It would be extremely interesting to some day discover, perhaps in some lost manuscript which survived the destruction by fire of the Alexandrian Library, some further reference to this cryptic and tragic personage. But, in the absence of such an unlikely event, we must content ourselves with the occasional references to centaurs we can extract from those works that we do have, and from the writings and commentaries of modern scholars, who have the patience and dedication to scrutinize many obscure and deadly-boring texts, and fragments of texts, in Greek and Latin. It is by analyzing these ancient works and the writings of these modern scholars, that we can sometimes find an occasional reference to centaurs.

In *Physiologus*, for example, we can see that at one time there were not only the common horse-centaurs we are most familiar with, but also ass-centaurs, apparently native to the Middle East. Because Physiologus, citing the book of *Isaiah*, says that sirens, hedgehogs, and ass-centaurs will one day dance in Babylon. This would be invaluable evidence to prove my contention that the centaurs truly existed; for, who would dare to say that the Bible lies? I must confess, however, that I searched in *Isaiah* for the reference cited by Physiologus and could find no mention of centaurs, ass or otherwise. But this does not prove or disprove anything.

In the notes to a chapter in *The Greek Myths* the late Robert Graves, speaking of the centaurs, says: "Members of this neolithic race survived in the Arcadian mountains, and on Mount Pindus until Classical times and vestiges of their pre-Hellenic language are to be found in modern Albania." This is an astounding bit of information to toss off so casually. Surely, the knowledge that there are people on earth today who speak the language of the fabled centaurs, however vestigial, should appear to us as the most incredible and wonderful of revelations. But Robert Graves, of course, perversely contended that the centaurs were ordinary tribes people, who were depicted as equine only because they had the horse as their totem animal.

And anyway, very few people care today. The pressures of modern life have eroded our interest in those things which for so many centuries preoccupied mankind, so that the centaur, who with the dinosaurs should be an object of deep and almost reverential awe, has been summarily dismissed as a complete figment, and is no longer a topic of drawing room conversations.

What is the reason for this? Surely, anyone who has a realistic view of mankind and his innate perversity should have no problem accepting the fact that five thousand or so years ago a man named Centaurus could have mated with a herd of mares. If we can accept that fact, why should it be so difficult to believe that progeny could have resulted from such a union? Even today, man routinely indulges vicariously in the procreation of hybrid creatures, crossbreeding animals such as the horse and the ass, for example, to produce the mule. The cow and the buffalo and a multitude of other creatures and plants have also been successfully cross bred. Modern genetic science has demonstrated that the most grotesque of creations is possible.

Admittedly, the examples of interbreeding we are familiar with all result in hybrid creatures unable to reproduce themselves. This, perhaps, is the principal consideration that makes the centaur so hard to believe in. It would appear, at first glance, that no other case could be brought to mind as a parallel. But there could be many examples all around us, which have simply never been looked at in this light. The giraffe, a most extraordinary creature when we pause to consider it, must surely be the result of interbreeding between some ordinary ruminant and an extinct, long-necked reptilian. The giant anteater of South America, the manatee, the tapir, the armadillo – all these could be the issue of two completely disparate species, some of them extinct, some still living. The world's only flying mammal, the bat, is most likely descended from a brief affair between a sparrow-like bird and a rat, or mouse. The larger species of bat,

51

such as the flying fox, could be a cross between a hawk or buzzard, and a possum or fox. The platypus of Australia and Tasmania is another obvious example of interspecies breeding. It is of course nothing more nor less than a cross between a duck and a beaver, which probably occurred during Eocene or Paleocene times.

Then, too, the product of interspecific breeding does not always take the spectacular turn such as in the case of the centaurs and the other possible examples mentioned above. Sometimes the result can be, instead of a distinct double-creature, simply a subtle blend of one animal's body and another's temperament. I believe crossbreedings of this sort are quite common and often pass unnoticed. These types of hybrid are so ordinary and unremarkable that they are unrecognizable as anything other than a mild variation of a species. The dog-faced baboon could be one such creature. It could be a cross of either dog and ape, man and ape, or man and dog.

Sir Walter Raleigh, in his *History of the World*, says that the hyena is a cross between dog and cat. He came to this conclusion because of the hyena's canine head and feet and because it urinates backwards like a cat. But the hyena's barrel-shaped body, its grotesque hunchbacked stance, its insane giggle, seem to suggest other, more intriguing, possibilities. Could not these features indicate a canine with human bloodlines in its ancestral background? Its human-like giggle could be the result of prenatal influence, stamped upon the ovum or homunculus before impregnation by this remote ancestor, who perhaps giggled uncontrollably as it committed its act of bestiality.

Even with such a repellant creature as the snake, there is always the possibility of interspecific breeding, whether accidental or intentional. Although it could with justice be asked, "Who, or what, would want to mate with a snake, except another snake?", yet we can see in some species of lizard the possibility that they are descended from the union of snakes with various types of small rodents or frogs. In some American deserts, for example, there is a species of lizard that has only rudimentary forelimbs. The back legs are entirely absent. And there are other lizards and salamanders which at first glance are indistinguishable from a snake. The elongated body of the weasel also suggests that there could be a snake somewhere in its family tree. Perhaps, on various occasions in remote epochs, as a constricting snake crushed the life out of a small rodent or frog, it was aroused to reptilian, erotic passion, and instead of devouring its prey, proceeded to fornicate with it instead.

Fantastic as it may seem, even the interbreeding between Man and snake is not something entirely improbable. (Everyone has heard the expression, applied to certain promiscuous persons, "He/she would fornicate a snake if someone would hold its head.") While in Bolivia, I once heard a curious story told by an old man who claimed to have had dealings with an Indian tribe known as the Toromonas. This tribe has since vanished from its former territory — possibly to some unknown location in the Peruvian Amazon — after a brush with the Bolivian army and air force which destroyed their villages after they had attacked a small town to kidnap several of the women there. The story this old man told was that once a woman of that tribe had been attacked by a monstrous anaconda, possibly twenty-eight feet long. (Zoologists today tell us that only the female grows to that size, but I believe there are exceptions.)

The Toromonas habitually went completely naked, men and women alike, so that the huge anaconda, as it wrapped its slimy coils tightly around the naked woman, apparently became sexually aroused as it tried to squeeze her life out. As the Toromona woman gasped for breath, her eyes popping out of her head, she suddenly felt the monstrous reptile's organ penetrate her vagina. At that moment, several men of the tribe came running up with shouts, and the snake rapidly released the woman and slithered away. She subsequently gave birth to a weird abomination, which was quickly put to death by her husband. Whether the snake purposely fornicated with the woman or whether it was simply accidental is hard to say.

The Pelasgian (pre-Hellenic) creation myth, by the way, says that Eurynome, the great Mother Goddess, had sex with her pet snake Ophion, and that from this union the universe and everything in it came into existence. Strange, that the Pelasgians should choose the snake as the procreator of the universe when there were so many other less objectionable creatures they could have chosen from. The choice seems to make a statement upon the innate perversity of human nature.

The myth goes on to say that Eurynome afterwards felt ashamed of what she had done, and killed the snake with a stick. This could possibly be the true origin of the enmity that exists between man and snake, the book of Genesis notwithstanding.

As further proof that animals of differing species will sometimes transgress Nature's bounds there is the recent widely reported instance of a moose in Maine persistently trying to mate with a cow in a farmer's pasture. Many other similar cases go unremarked and unreported. It can be assumed that sometimes these confused animals succeed, that sometimes hybrid births result, and that in rare cases those offspring are amphimictic.

From time to time the world continues to hear of strange instances of hybrid births of the strangest sort: a half-fox, half-rabbit; a half-cat, half-rabbit; a sow dropping a litter of piglets, with one of them a mixture of pig and monkey (in this last case, a monkey had been observed molesting the sow), and many other cases, too numerous to mention. Incidentally, most of these reports come from tropical America, which would seem to indicate that climatic and atmospheric peculiarities contribute to the phenomenon. If dumb beasts can successfully accomplish interbreeding, what then shall we say of man, who across the ages has applied his cunning and his ingenuity to satisfy occasional urges of the same sort?

Perversions aside, it can be seen that when men of science are furnished with the proper incentives they are quite capable of producing a hybrid creature of any sort, biological incompatibilities notwithstanding. So, if science and technology can create the conditions necessary to breed such creatures, then it is also possible those same conditions once existed naturally on earth, accidentally created by climatic and atmospheric abnormalities. The advent of the centaurs, in other words, would be entwined with the laws of chance and probability.

Incidentally, the hypothesis proposed here – of the interbreeding of disparate species, such as can be seen in the evidence of interbreeding between man and horse – would account for the abrupt appearance of many species on earth without any apparent progression from one species to another. This hypothesis would not entirely supplant the theory of evolution, but could be a valuable adjunct to it. It would explain why naturalists are often unable to produce intermediate species from the fossil records. Darwin, who sneered at Lamarck's theory of the inheritance of acquired characteristics, was just as wrong as Lamarck. They both failed to recognize that interspecies breeding has contributed just as much as mutation, and just as much as the inheritance of acquired characteristics, to the origin of species and the diversity of life forms on earth.

If fossilized remains of centaurs were available to display in museums, then there would be little reason to doubt they had once existed. But unlike dinosaurs, which roamed the earth for millions of years, the centaurs lived for only a few centuries – the briefest flicker of time, the time it takes to blink, compared to the eternity of one hundred million years. No doubt many thousands of other species have come into being on earth, to struggle briefly for existence against a harsh environment, the hostility of competing species and the whims of nature, only to die out, leaving no trace of their passing because they did not survive long enough to leave evidence in the fossil records.

While on the subject of fossils, we might also remark that the fact that no fossilized remains of a centaur have ever been found does not mean that some will not be unearthed some day. The centaurs lived in caves around Mount Pelion and the rugged environs of Arcadia. While the chemical composition of the soil in these areas and the climatic conditions extant from their time to the present day are unfavorable to the preservation of fossils, still there is some chance that at one time, while they still lived, a cave collapsed on a family of centaurs, preserving them under tons of limestone rock, frozen in the activities they were engaged in four or five thousand years ago. I predict that the discovery of such a cave with its fossilized occupants will someday be made.

As for the armadillo, which I have already mentioned, once we have learned to look at odd creatures with the possibility of interspecies breeding in mind, it immediately becomes evident that it is a cross between a turtle – or tortoise – and a mammal, perhaps a small prehistoric pig. The armadillo's pig-like habit of grubbing for food with its snout, its little pig eyes and ears, and its indistinct diurnal and nocturnal habits all attest to its porcine ancestry, while its hard shell, its ability to partially retract its head and feet into it, its voicelessness, and its ability to walk beneath the water on the bottom of a pool or stream, reveal its reptilian antecedents. Perhaps, millions of years ago, a female tortoise was sunbathing on a rock or a log, when a lonely pig came snuffling around. With nothing better to do at the moment it would have commenced to idly molest the tortoise. Assuming that the pig's attentions were unwelcome, the tortoise could not have run away. She could only have retreated into her shell. And there, she would have discovered, she was still vulnerable, because of a pig's peculiar genital configuration (ask any pig farmer of your acquaintance). There is no need to go into the question of incompatibility between pig and tortoise. We need only remember that the laws of chance and probability dictate that such an event was bound to occur, given a time frame of millions of years and a pig's idle and promiscuous nature.

So, the end result of this chance encounter between pig and tortoise is the armadillo, a curious and entertaining little creature.

Here, let us pause to reflect over the deep mysteries of life and fate. How many of the species which share our earth today, to delight us with their strangeness and variety, originated through the idleness and aberrant lust of their progenitors? The answer, probably, is that there are a great many, and we can further ponder over the fact that something worthwhile can be born of vice, idleness and lust. Many of the world's richest treasures in art and literature also exist today because of certain aberrant passions in the artists who created them. Like Percy Bysshe Shelley, to cite one example, whose infatuation with a common, hash-slinging waitress inspired him to compose some of the most deathless and poignant poetry in the English language. It is unfortunate that such tortured and twisted passions were necessary in order for us to inherit such treasures, but how fortunate for us that these treasures do exist.

By the same token, we can be thankful that various birds and beasts in ages past transcended the bounds of natural behavior to mate with individuals of a family and genus other than their own. For, how poor the earth would be without the myriad life forms which populate it. And especially, how poor the earth would be without the legend of the glorious, cloud-born centaurs, brought into being through the idleness and bestial lust of their progenitor, Centaurus.

The end of Chapter Three of
A Short History Of The Centaurs

CHAPTER SIX

The more I wrote the more was I filled with enthusiasm and admiration for my own work. I felt that my work would convince the world of the reality of the centaurs. I couldn't furnish concrete proof; not even if I was to publicly announce that I knew for a fact that the centaurs had existed, because I was a reincarnation of Nessus the Centaur. The scientific community would shrug me off as a nut case. But my well-thought-out reasons might convince the general public.

I talked to Daphne again several days later on the telephone, and we agreed to meet at Kingstown Skating Rink so she could catch a skating exhibition she wanted to see. I asked her to bring the pages I had given her, if she was through with them. I was hoping to hear some expressions of admiration for my work, and that we would discuss my theories as we watched the performance. But when we met she handed me the pages without comment, other than her usual complaints about the weather and her trailer homes. As we watched the skaters, I dropped several leading hints to give her a chance to comment on chapter three. Two or three times she began to say something about it, but each time she interrupted herself with things like, "Oooh! what a fantastic leap," and "Oooh! that was a perfect camel!", so I gave up.

Maybe Daphne's lack of interest in my writing was a good thing. I no longer worried about offending her with my opinions and the direction in which my theories inevitably took me in my treatment of the history of the centaur race. Sometimes I would ask myself, Why do you give her your stuff to read, anyway? What does Daphne's opinion matter. Did Shakespeare, Melville, Dickens, or any other literary giant need some cheap floozy to encourage them by praising their work? (For, yes, in my private thoughts I sometimes refer to Daphne as a cheap floozy, even though I'm trying to marry her.) But then I would tell myself, Well, never mind what other writers may not have needed, that was them, but I'm me. I'm no literary giant. Me, personally, I need encouragement and feedback of some sort. I don't have it in me to struggle away with my writings, like a blind mole burrowing from root to root, without some immediate evidence that there will be an audience out there to derive some pleasure from my work.

So, some time later I gave her Chapter Four to read, which goes like this:

A Short History Of The Centaurs
Chapter Four

In further support of our thesis that man, in his unbridled love of horses fathered a new race, let us consider the special relationship that has always existed between man and horse. Throughout the ages man has lavished care and affection on his equine companions. Even in prehistoric times, cavemen scratched crude representations of their favorite animal, the horse, on cavern walls. In the ancient Greek world this love of horses was even more accentuated. Horses figure prominently in many of the Greek myths, be it dragging Hippolytus to his death behind his chariot, or as a prefix in the names of many heroes and personages. Several of the gods and minor deities assumed the shape of a horse on various occasions. One of the names by which the great Mother Goddess was known was, "The Mare Headed Goddess," and she was represented as such in carvings and icons.

Today the same fascination with horses continues. There are modern artists whose sole subject is the horse. They paint or sculpt horses in an endless variety of poses and attitudes – galloping, trotting, rearing . . . And there are people – both men and women – whose entire lives are centered on their love of horses. Which is curious, when we stop to consider that horses are rather undemonstrative creatures, apparently incapable of returning even a small part of this love.

All this is by way of saying that, since this love does exist – one-sided though it may be on man's part –, no one should marvel that at one time in history it was manifested by the appearance on earth of its strange fruits.

In support of the above, there is a book, *The New Evolutionary Timetable*, by Professor Steven Stanley, which presents an interesting new view on evolution, not entirely refuting the conventional theory, but in certain aspects modifying the long-held views of the Darwinists. Professor Stanley affirms that new species evolve when small groups of individuals break away from the main group, to develop in isolated communities. He calls his theory "punctuationalism" as opposed to Darwin's "gradualism." It so happens that Steven Stanley's theories agree completely with my own. He stops short, however, of the most important detail of all – the evolution of new life forms through interspecific and intergeneric breeding.

Incorporating Professor Stanley's respected hypothesis, we can come up with the following alternative scenario to explain the emergence of the Centaur race: Let us say a group, or clan, of outcast, misogynic tribesmen retire into the wilds of Arcadia, away from the main body of their tribe. Perhaps they are a clan of horsemen and horse traders, or horse breeders, and the group is occasionally replenished by recruitment or desertions from the main tribe. Developing in their isolated community, they are subjected to what evolutionists call severe selection pressure. This pressure, combined with the special atmospheric conditions of the time and place, as we have already suggested, and further aggravated by the complete absence of women, would finally result in the birth of the first centaurs.

The first offspring of these grotesque unions were probably misshapen creatures, crippled and twisted; sometimes a humanoid horse and at other times an equine human. Imagine a horse with normal hindquarters, but with hairless, rudimentary forelegs, with thick, gnarled fingers and a massive human head and face on a horse's neck. Or an even more nightmarish variation, such as an erect-walking creature with horse's hooves, a hairy, humanoid body with a long, equine head and face on a human neck, and enormous human genitalia. Or a nakedly hairless horse with human hands and feet on the ends of its horse's legs, a horse's ears, and rubbery horse's lips on a human face.

Eventually, fate and destiny had their way and the amphimictic, dichotomous centaur as we know him came into existence. It seems likely that this group of people were known as Centaurs even before they evolved into *Equus centauri*, named after their first king or chieftain, Centaurus. This would explain many an ancient narrative in which they appear as normal human beings, and it could be that the ancient authors were confused on this score.

* * * * * *

If the preceding opinions on the interbreeding of man and beast seem too preposterous, there is an even more startling possibility to consider: the interbreeding of flora and fauna. Onan was not the first man – nor the last – to spill his seed upon the ground, nor has man been the only culprit. All manner of birds and beasts have been guilty.

Certain animals (especially monkeys) have been observed rubbing themselves on large fruits, vegetables, and other inanimate objects. I have personally watched a pet capuchin monkey making determined efforts to fornicate with a hen in a vegetable patch. And when the hen escaped from its clutches and ran away, squawking indignantly, the monkey continued its endeavors with a sort of large zucchini squash, humping it industriously.

So, when we pause to scrutinize the possible consequences of these animal acts, and recognize that there is a strong chance that many of the plants, fruits, and vegetables, which we are so familiar with are actually hybrids of plant and beast, or man and plant, then the seemingly preposterous premise of a half-man, half-horse, becomes a quite tame proposition.

Mandrake, or mandragora, is a striking example of a plant that was probably engendered by spilled seed, possibly the seed of Onan himself. The species that exists today is not the same one that existed in ancient times, when its root had the exact shape and form of a tiny little man, as we are told in the ancient Bestiaries.

In the Greek myths, there are many stories having to do with the birth of strange beings from spilled blood or seed. So prevalent is the theme and with so many variations, that it seems there must have been many instances in which the phenomenon was observed.

We are told, for example, that aconite – *Aconitum napellus* – was engendered by the foam from the slavering jaws of the hound Cerberus, when Hercules dragged it out of hades into the light of day. And then there is the story of how the drops of blood from the severed head of the Gorgon Medusa, which fell upon the burning sands of the Libyan desert as Perseus flew high overhead on his way home, bred a swarm of vipers, which still abound in northern Libya to this day.

A more pertinent case, having to do specifically with spilled seed, is the legend of how Erichthonius was born, a king who instituted the worship of Athene in Athens, and whom we can see today in the heavens as the constellation of Auriga. They say that Athene, was visiting Hephaestus' smithy one day, having ordered a set of armor from him so that she could take part in the Trojan war. But Hephaestus was the victim of a practical joke by Poseidon, who had made him believe that what she really wanted was some sex, and that the armor was only a pretext for visiting his shop.

So, while Athene was standing there, innocently admiring his handiwork, he suddenly whipped out his organ with one hand, grabbed her around the waist with the other, and attempted to insinuate his attentions on her. Athene angrily wrenched herself away, but not before Hephaestus had spilled his seed all over her thighs. She wiped it off with a handful of wool and threw it off in disgust. Down it went fluttering to earth and fell near Athens, where it accidentally impregnated Mother Earth, who nine months later gave

60

birth to Erichthonius, a weird child with a snake's body from the waist down.

Mother Earth frequently became pregnant from accidents of this sort. The castration of Uranus was another such instance. Uranus was castrated by his own son Cronus, at his mother's behest, using an adamantine sickle she had given him for the purpose. "Eagerly he harvested his father's genitals," says Hesiod in his *Theogony*, "and threw them off behind." They went plunging down to earth, and from the bloody drops that spattered over her, Mother Earth gave birth to the titans and the ash tree nymphs. She also gave birth to the furies – the relentless fiends who hound those guilty of parricide and matricide. Cronus himself was apparently immune to their sting. It is never mentioned anywhere that he was troubled by remorse, as if depriving his parent of his genitals was not the most horrendous of deeds.

The aforementioned genitals – organs of a colossal size – floated on the sea for many months, much like the vast whale carcasses described by Melville, which, marked by dashing foam and screaming sea birds, would sometimes be recorded in ships' logs as uncharted reefs.

Eventually, from out of this foam, the goddess Aphrodite also was born. She came floating into the shore at Cyprus on a large sea shell, completely naked, covering her breasts and her pudenda with her richly flowing locks. Little winged cherubim hovered above her, showering her with rose petals and blowing on conch shells to herald her arrival, according to a painting I have seen somewhere. Hesiod says in his *Theogony* that one of the names by which she is known is "Philommedes, from the genitals by which she was conceived." Philommedes means, literally, genital loving, and Dorothea Wender in her translation of the *Theogony* says that, "This may be a corruption of Philomeides, 'laughter-loving', a more usual (and daintier) epithet of the goddess." It is well known, however, that Aphrodite, as befits the goddess of love, loved nothing better than the male organ of procreation. But we won't argue with Ms. Wender about this matter.

As for the divine genitals themselves – so as not to leave them just hanging there – we may presume that they finally rotted away and succumbed to the corruption and ravages of time, nibbled away at by little fishes and ravenous sea monsters. The indestructible atoms of which they were composed are still around, of course, spread over all the globe, and present in minute quantities in the sea, and in the very air we breathe.

I feel obliged to repeat these apparently irrelevant stories to illustrate that in those times there were things much stranger than the appearance on earth of the centaurs. The reason these occurrences appear so improbable and weird to our eyes, could be because, as I have said, different rules of time and causality prevailed in those days. Perhaps time in its passage drags reality behind it, like an interminably long, partitioned screen on which are depicted set after set of inconsequent realities, which pass before the eyes of humanity, watching, from the isolated bleachers of its own independent time, the varying events thus presented to its view. Sometimes these realities – like a painting which gradually blends one color into another – overlap, with their elements surviving into succeeding realities. Others are intended and suited for one particular time only: the painter has washed his brushes and begun anew. These last pass by us without leaving any other trace except a few confused memories and myths, when the period of that reality gives way to the next. The centaurs, I believe, were in the first category, and therefore it's possible, as I have already mentioned, that their bones or other concrete evidence of their existence, will someday be found.

Returning to the subject of interbreeding between flora and fauna – today the earth still teems with forms of life so weird and twisted that reason is sometimes stretched beyond credulity when science tries to explain its origins. The slimy slug; the stick insect, almost indistinguishable from a dead twig; the katydid, which resembles a fresh green leaf; carnivorous, insect-devouring plants; maggots, worms, dung beetles; innumerable species of spiders and parasites – many of these life forms could have sprung into being in prehistoric times from plants and flowers accidentally pollinated by man and beast. Or even purposely impregnated. In Pliny's Natural History he mentions one Passenus Crispus, father-in-law to Nero and consul of Rome, who fell in love with a tree, a beech tree, growing in a sacred grove in Tusculum. Not only would he spend hours lying in its shade, but he " . . . would sprinkle it plentifully with wine, clip and trim it, and embrace and kiss it otherwhiles," according to the Philemon Holland translation.

"Wonderfullest things are ever the unmentionable," said Herman Melville, and however obscure the meaning of the words in the context in which they were uttered, they seem made to order for all that we have mentioned above.

End Of Chapter Four Of
A Short History Of The Centaurs

CHAPTER SEVEN

I wish I had never told Daphne about my other life. But then, what the hell good is a real girl friend if you can't tell her anything? And yet.... A man doesn't tell even his wife everything. Some things should be kept quiet. Maybe I should have kept this centaur business to myself. Daphne has lost her respect for me as a result of my openness, and she's beginning to treat me like dirt. Her words to me are often tinged with sarcasm and she's even gone so far as to express her wonderment at how someone so dumb could have as much money as I supposedly have.

* * * * * *

Yes, candor, frankness, and honesty may all be great virtues, but they can be harmful, too. In the evening, after my supper of beans and chili, I had more proof of this as I watched a news program on TV that contained a reference to the time, some years ago, when the president had fired one of his cabinet officials for publicly advocating that masturbation should be taught in the schools, as a way to combat the spread of AIDS. Whatever possessed that obfuscated woman to express such an opinion? Moreover, what youngster has ever needed to be *taught* about masturbation? Even an idiot child will learn it on his own.

This was something else, by the way, which we centaurs could not too easily do. Along with the natural human proclivity to scratch the behind. Because of the distance of those parts from our hands, you see.

Though, to tell the truth, we could often find gratification of that sort at the hands – or perhaps I should say, *in* the hands – of a Greek woman. This has to do with the fact that the love man has always held for horses is much more marked in women. A woman can fall instantly in love with a man if she sees him on horseback. But take that same man off his horse, and the woman may quickly lose all interest. Yet her attention may still linger on the horse itself. Psychologists know the underlying reason for all this, and they could furnish us, if they wanted to, with a stripped-bare exposition of the repressed urges women feel when they admire a fine horse. Repressed and sublimated, to a certain

63

extent, because of the grave danger they would run of getting kicked in the head.

Back in those times, women could safely indulge those repressed desires. In the centaur they had a creature that was both man and horse, and only too willing to allow them to give their perverse desires free rein. Hippodameia, who married the Lapith Peirithous, was one of those women. Everybody knew it back then, except for dumb Peirithous. In fact her name, Hippodameia, which means Horse Tamer, wasn't her real name. It was only a nickname, given to her by wagging tongues because of her love for centaurs – centaur males –, a penchant which in later centuries, and in slightly different form, was shared by Catherine The Great, according to some stuff I have been reading recently. So widely used was Hippodameia's nickname that I don't even recall her real name.

So, Peirithous wasn't very smart, despite what Homer quotes almighty Zeus as saying about him in the Iliad: "Never have I been so in love," he says to Hera, "Not even when I loved Deia, who bore me the wise Peirithous." Maybe either Homer or Zeus were being sarcastic.

As further proof that he wasn't all that wise – that he was actually rather foolhardy –, he and Theseus later shared an incredible adventure, with tragic consequences for both of them, but especially for Peirithous. Peirithous had helped Theseus abduct Helen, later to be known as Helen of Troy, because even at the age of twelve she was already famous for her beauty and Theseus wanted her for his wife, even though he himself was already fifty years old. He recruited the aid of Peirithous with the understanding that Theseus would then help him abduct a wife of his own, which he had yet to choose. So, although Castor and Pollux later rescued their sister from his clutches, he still had the obligation to assist Peirithous. And to his dismay, Peirithous decided that he wanted none other than Persephone, wife of Hades, for his own.

Other Greek heroes successfully harrowed the depths of Hell. But they had other things going for them besides sheer audacity and courage. Orpheus had his magical lyre and his incomparable singing voice. Odysseus had his animal cunning and the aid of the witch Circe. Hercules, who supposedly descended into Tartarus more than once, had the aid and blessing of Zeus in all his undertakings. But Theseus and

64

Peirithous got a little out of their depth when they went down to Hell, and things didn't go too well for them. They descended by a back entrance, and Peirithous, with the hilt of his sword, knocked on the massive bronze doors leading into Tartarus. While the sound was echoing and reverberating through the subterranean chambers, Theseus nervously tugged at Peirithous' sleeve saying, "Well, it looks like nobody's home. We'll come back another day."

But almost immediately, Hades in person was at the door, smiling politely, and asking what he could do for them. When they made their outrageous intentions known, he asked them to step inside. Theseus, who had much more sense than Peirithous, was probably wishing that he was a thousand miles away, but he was too courageous a man to back out now. He felt he had to honor his promise to help Peirithous, so he followed him into Hades' chambers. Hades asked them to have a seat on a nearby stone settee while he considered their demands. But as soon as they sat down they froze fast to the seat.

For four long years they sat there, while the furies lashed them mercilessly with their whips; snakes and serpents hissed and coiled around their necks, and the dog Cerberus snapped and snarled and chewed on them with all three of its heads.

Finally Hercules came along in his quest for the dog Cerberus, his ninth or tenth labor. As he sat chatting amiably with Hades and trying to make arrangements for the loan of the dog (Hades told him that if he could catch and subdue it he was welcome to take it) he noticed Theseus and Peirithous sitting nearby, stretching their arms to him in mute entreaty. He had a quite close friendship with Theseus, so he asked Hades if he could please let his friends go. Hades told him that he could take them if he could free them from the stone settee. So Hercules grasped Theseus by the shoulders and gave a mighty heave. There was a nasty, ripping sound and Theseus came free.

Hercules next prepared to try the same procedure on Peirithous but the earth trembled ominously and he therefore desisted. This was only fitting, since Peirithous had been the leading instigator of the foolhardy endeavor.

I must tell the truth here. I don't know of all this at first hand, I've read about it in some mythology or other. And I don't know what Peirithous had done with the wife he already had, Hippodameia. If all this really happened it must have been some time after my death, the death of Nessus, that is.

When Theseus was pulled free of the settee, by the way, he left behind a good part of his buttocks. Aristophanes claimed, according to an ancient commentator on one of his lost works, that this was the reason Theseus' Athenian descendants had such a small behind. I myself have wondered if the episode could have given rise to the colloquial expression, "he lost his ass," applied to persons who embark on ill-advised enterprises and lose everything. I'm not going to lie and say I've heard the expression used in my life as Nessus the Centaur. Because, as I have said, all this must have happened some time after my death. If it ever happened at all. There are some chronological problems involved.

* * * * * *

I don't have any first-hand knowledge of Hippodameia and her centaur-loving tastes. I never sought her out as other centaurs did. My mind was too filled with thoughts of Dejanira. From the first day I laid eyes on Dejanira, her image constantly floated in and out of my mind. She was always dressed in a snow-white robe of flimsy linen. She braided her ash-blonde hair in rich and luxuriant tresses, which she coiled around her head to frame her smooth white face and forehead. Her eyes were like the stuff unattainable dreams are made of . . . clear and limpid, half somnolent under the Nordic folds of her eyelids and thick over-arching brows.

Even as a maiden, Dejanira's body was of a buxom type, resembling, in its generous proportions, the human parts of a mature centaur woman, and I wouldn't have been greatly surprised if we had actually been able to consummate a union together. From the day of that first meeting on the River Avenus, all my fantasies revolved around Dejanira. In my fantasies she loved me just as passionately as I loved her. She would curry and brush my flanks, and comb the burrs out of my silvery tail. We would walk together, side by side, across cool meadows. I would encircle her buxom waist with one arm, then draw her to me and hold her tightly to my body as I kissed her radiantly fair face. Then I would thrust my monstrous organ into her vagina. In this part of my fantasy conveniently blocking out of my consciousness the fact of our incompatible anatomies.

From these fantasies it was natural that I finally progressed to the notion that perhaps I could ask her father for her hand in marriage, following the example of Eurytion with Mnesimache. Such a marriage would certainly raise eyebrows, and possibly make us the laughing stock of the entire Greek world, but I wouldn't care. And if Dejanira loved me, she wouldn't care either.

There was a lot of prejudice against centaurs in those days, something that people don't realize today. Reading between the lines of the ancient myths and histories the discerning eye can detect this subtle undercurrent of prejudice against the centaurs. Bullfinch says, somewhere in his *Mythology*, that the Greeks were too fond of horses to consider the centaurs monsters, and that they "magnanimously" accepted them as friends and companions. Bullfinch was right, to a certain extent. Any acceptance that the centaurs won in human society was not because we were half human, but rather because we were half horse. The ancient Greeks were ready to embrace the horse and overlook the fact that it was half human, but they were not willing to embrace the human half and tolerantly accept the fact that it was half horse.

Throughout Greek mythology, it can be seen that the centaurs are constantly referred to in less than eulogistic terms. Even Homer, from whom we would expect a less jaundiced view, refers to them as "shaggy monsters," or "monsters of the mountains." If we had been less human I think we would have won wider acceptance and aroused less feelings of hostility. To understand what I mean, imagine what it would be like if all dogs could talk, just as we do. Would people love dogs more than they presently do? No, the opposite would be the case. Many people who are presently dog lovers would loathe and despise them, while dog haters would hate them even more, regarding them as vicious, savage brutes with the capacity of speech; sworn enemies of mailmen, meter readers and all defenseless little creatures; with a predilection for sniffing at each other's rectums; driven to fight savagely amongst themselves; with a habit of fornicating openly, without the least regard to who might be watching, whether human or their fellow canines. Their power of speech – and the ability to reason that such a faculty would presumably confer on them – would divest them of all excuse for such behavior.

67

It was the same with us. No one despises a horse because of its tendency to fart, urinate, and defecate whenever the notion seizes it, or to unconcernedly flaunt its organ in an erect condition. A horse can do all these things, and men and women will love them all the more.

But the same faults were not acceptable in a centaur, a creature that was half human.

Incidentally, the worst insult that could be offered to a centaur was to call him a hipporrhus – horse's ass. In fact, I happen to know that the modern epithet has its roots and origins in those times, when it was applied disparagingly to the centaurs.

To better understand the prejudice against centaurs, try to imagine yourself living back in those times. Imagine yourself meeting a centaur – a female centaur, let us say – for the first time, and engaging her in polite conversation. At first, no doubt, your gaze would linger for long moments on her buxom, naked torso, her smooth, well-turned arms and turgid, swelling breasts, with a mass of tawny hair spilling over soft shoulders. Maybe, if she was coquettish, she might casually toss her hair back, away from her breasts, to fully reveal them in all their bursting splendor. If you kept your gaze riveted on this enthralling spectacle of lovely face and breasts you could preserve the illusion that you were talking to nothing more remarkable than a beautiful naked woman. But then, your eyes would be drawn inexorably down to where her smooth abdomen gave way to a mare's bay hide and hard equine chest. And as she spoke to you, in well-modulated tones, she would perhaps stamp her hooves restively and fretfully switch her tail to swat away at buzzing gadflies. And, to your embarrassment, she might suddenly spraddle her hind legs, arch her tail, and proceed to urinate vigorously, while she tried to distract your attention by pointing to something off in the distance.

Imagine all this and you will have a fuller idea of what strange beings we were, even in those times so full of marvels, and more readily agree that the prejudice of which I speak must surely have existed.

While on the subject of prejudice, an interesting question may have occurred to the reader: How did centaurs get along with horses? Other people can only speculate, but I know the answer: We had a strong aversion to them. This conclusion could be reached by modern scholars, moreover, by considering one significant fact: The names of

68

many individual centaurs have come down to us through the ages, from famed Cheiron to obscure Antymachus, and Pyrachmus, and Monychus, and none of the names begins with the prefix 'hippo.' In contrast, other ancient Greek names range from Hippolochus (born of a mare) through Hippalcus (horse strength) and Hippeus (horse-like) to Hippocoon (horse stable), to say nothing of Hippasus, Hippomedon, Hipponous, Hippolytus, and many others. Even many Greek women, such as Hipponoe, Hippothoe, Hippolyte, Hippodameia, Melanippe (black filly), and others, had names which showed the love and admiration the ancient Greeks had for horses.

But the centaurs wanted nothing whatever to do with anything that would remind them of their singular deformity. The centaurs looked upon horses much as a modern race today will regard any historical evidence of the uncivilized behavior of their remote forebears, such as cannibalism or institutionalized infanticide. To the centaurs, the horse was an uncomfortable reminder of their own less than noble and lofty descent. The horse represented all that was base and lowly in the centaur race; the horse was a stupid beast; the horse was incapable of speech or reason; the horse was barely a notch above a dog or a cow; the horse was a horse was a horse, as Gertrude Stein might have phrased it.

So the centaurs were not entirely free of snobbery, any more than were the Greeks, and we steered wide of horses, going to great lengths to avoid them.

The centaur woman, especially, felt decidedly uncomfortable in the vicinity of a stallion. Of course the centaur woman was quite capable of looking after herself. She would have been in no danger of being mounted, against her wishes, by a horse. The centaurs never had to worry about the safety of their females, in this regard. Their women were so chaste and virtuous that the men were thereby relieved of that curse of canine jealousy, which so often is the real concern of *Homo sapiens* when he pretends to hold such solicitous regard for the well-being of his mate.

Stallions aside, there was little danger of a centaur woman being raped by a human. A centauress could outrun any man then living, with the possible exception of the twins Calais and Zeetes, who it was said were children of the North Wind. And besides, what man would have

69

been so foolish as to even try? He would have been kicked silly. On top of that, few men would have had the desire in the first place. True, the sight of a luscious, naked centauress could easily bestir a man's admiration. Their rich, silken locks flowed in a glorious cascade to their withers. Their skin was smooth and unblemished, and their full breasts were firm and always youthful-looking. Their features could best be described as handsome, though some were decidedly beautiful, with a straight nose, arching eyebrows over large chestnut eyes, a delicately turned mouth and finely chiseled chin. But then, after drinking all this in, a hypothetical admirer would have inevitably noticed that the object of his admiration was half mare.

And, should an occasional admirer have decided that this was only a minor consideration, he would have come up against the centauress' cool and aloof nature, which would have quickly discouraged him from attempting any familiarities.

Because of the Greek prejudice against centaurs I know it was wrong of me to fall in love with a human female. There were many fine and noble centaur women I could have married. There was Ocyrhöe, for example, daughter of Cheiron. She was a seer and diviner, quite good at the science, and she revealed to me many secrets of the future, including the fact that my passion for Dejanira was going to cause me serious trouble. I didn't listen to her because I was too hopelessly in love. Nothing could have led me away from that fatal obsession. Also, I thought that Ocyrhöe's warnings were only prompted by jealousy, because she wanted me for herself.

Ocyrhöe was a pretty centauress. She had coppery red-gold hair that flowed down to her withers, a smooth, unblemished complexion and eyes of an obsidian black. She had had a crush on me since we were children, galloping across fields and meadows behind our mothers. But then I left Mount Pelion to live in the Pindus mountains with my friend Homadus, and I saw Ocyrhöe only infrequently. She had stayed at Mount Pelion with her father after her mother died, and he taught her the art of divination. Many centaur women liked me, by the way, though it may seem vain and immodest of me to say so. I had a reputation for fierce courage, partly because of that encounter with Hercules at the Nemean Games, and more than one centauress had coquettishly told me I was handsome.

70

One day when Ocyrhöe was visiting the Pindus range with some other centaur women I told her about my love for Dejanira, hoping she would see something good in the future for me. It was at this time that she told me something bad was going to happen to me if I didn't forget it, and she said that the love I thought I felt was only an infatuation. Later, maybe out of the goodness of her heart, in the hope that she could make me forget Dejanira, she let me make love to her several times. But even in the act itself, I am sorry to admit, I entertained fantasies of Dejanira.

Afterwards I would feel somewhat guilty and ashamed. I knew it was despicable of me to even be thinking of Dejanira at the very moment of making love, in an equine fashion, to a mostly equine female. It wasn't fair to Ocyrhöe, either.

Ocyrhöe was a red and white paint, by the way, a rare coloration amongst centaurs. Most of us were bays and sorrels, but I myself was black – a shimmering jet-black – and I had a silvery tail, the same as Homadus and Eurytion. It almost seems as if the Fates were somehow driven to choose a similar fate for individuals of this coloration, as the result of subliminal suggestion.

Cheiron, on the other hand, was a gray-roan, as were Crotus and Pylenor. It seems, in fact, that this particular coloration was shared by the wisest among us.

CHAPTER EIGHT

I had never liked Hercules, but this passive aversion towards him turned to active hatred and loathing when he killed my friend Homadus. Thereafter, every mention of Hercules would bring Homadus and the memory of his cruel murder to mind.

Homadus, the same as almost all centaurs, was greatly attracted to Greek women. He became infatuated with Alcyone, she of whom it was later said that she was transformed into a kingfisher when she was grieving for the death of her husband Ceyx. I don't know what Homadus ever saw in Alcyone. She wasn't attractive at all. Her eyes were beady and close-set, and she had a rather long nose. She did have a somewhat regal bearing, since she was the sister of King Eurystheus and married to another king. Maybe that is what attracted Homadus. He went simply nuts over her, and finally one day he tried to touch her or something. Alcyone claimed that he had tried to rape her. Women were always accusing centaurs of rape. But of course a centaur could never really rape a woman. It was next to physically impossible.

What great times Homadus and I used to have. Many a mile had we ranged together over the length and breadth of Aetolia and Thessalia, and even as far north as the River Haliacmon in a centaur's ceaseless quest for food and wine. Homadus was a great archer, excelled among us only by Crotus when he had been young. Among the Greeks, only Hercules and Phalerus were the better bowmen. Many a deer had Homadus and I hunted together, chasing them over hill and meadow on our fleet hooves, to finally bring them down with a well-placed arrow. After these hunts, back in the cave that we shared in the Pindus mountains, we would invite Agrius, a friend and neighbor who had his cave nearby, to the feast. And as the meat bubbled in a cauldron or as it roasted over the coals on hardwood spits, we would contentedly swig our wine, if we were lucky enough to have any, and tell stories as we waited for the meat to cook. Stories of Libya, land of wild beasts and strange tribes; stories of the western ends of the earth, where it was said the Titan Atlas lived with his daughters the Hesperides; stories from the eastern confines of the world, where the sun god rested each night with his silvery horses in their golden stables. Stories from the far north, land of the Hyperboreans and the one-eyed Arimaspians, where the griffins guarded a fabulous hoard of gold.

East, south, west, and north – the world surrounding us was a vast repository of riches, a treasure house of unconfirmed rumors and reports of monster-populated seas, perpetually fog-shrouded lands, weird serpents, giants, spirits, multiple-headed creatures, and other unsounded mysteries.

Even quite nearby, there were astounding things that many of us could have seen, if we had ever had the time and the inclination to travel for a few days to verify them. If we had traveled for just a few days north along the Adriatic Coast, for example, we could have seen the sirens – or at least the island that they lived on, which was visible from the shore. Homadus had once tried to talk me into going with him to see them. I convinced him that it would be a dangerous and foolhardy thing to do.

After his death, every mention of the Sirens always brought back the image of Homadus. Homadus and I trotting cheerfully over mountains and meadows as we traveled to some distant destination, our bows and quivers slung over our shoulders; Homadus, roasting a haunch of mutton over the fire at our cave; Homadus and I savoring a jug of wine he had stolen somewhere, as he presided over our fire . . . Homadus dying, with a foot of arrow protruding from his chest. And then my hatred of Hercules would smolder. Hercules had not yet begun to poison his arrows when he killed Homadus, so at least he died a clean death.

I grieved deeply over the death of Homadus. But most other centaurs to whom I spoke of the matter, suggesting that we should avenge his death, only shrugged their shoulders. They thought it was Homadus's own fault, for failing to notice that Hercules had been near by. As for the Greeks, they all universally acclaimed Hercules for this cold-blooded murder. It showed great nobility, his sycophants said, to thus avenge an insult to a sister of his worst enemy.

Homadus and I, with some other centaurs, had lived on the mountains of Othys and Pindus, about a hundred miles from Pelion. But when he met his tragic death most of us moved to Mount Oeta where old Crotus had his cave.

* * * * * *

Crotus enjoyed a certain prestige among the Greeks, who thought his knowledge and wisdom rivaled that of Cheiron himself. Part of the reason for their opinion of him was perhaps because of his gray color, which the Greeks had come to recognize as a hall mark of the wise centaur. Though, to be fair, I should say that Crotus really did possess a sly sort of wisdom, combined with a fair knowledge of medicine, augury, and other sciences. Also, Crotus never got stinking drunk, like most centaurs. No one loved wine more than Crotus, but he had developed the ability to shunt the alcoholic fumes into his equine parts, so that it never got the best of him.

We did not require a great deal of wine to get drunk, by the way, as some might suppose, given our great size. A centaur would normally retain wine in his human body; we had the ability to control our circulation in such a way that alcohol would confine itself mostly to the blood circulating in our human half, so that none of it was wasted on our equine parts. This was one of the reasons a centaur could easily go berserk when he was drunk. Because his equine half, no longer under the wise guidance and restraint of his human brain, could then freely indulge its equine urges and passions, just as a common horse will sometimes take the bit in its teeth and completely ignore its rider. Some centaurs had even been known to attempt sexual intercourse with common mares when in this state, and for a centaur this was even more disgraceful than those far more common instances of attempted rape upon Greek women.

This inordinate love of wine in centaurs was one of the reasons Hercules seemed to have so many centaur friends. Wherever groups of centaurs gathered, wine would be present, and wherever there was wine, Hercules would not be far. Because Hercules was absolutely a pig where wine was concerned. He would drink it to the point of madness. He murdered his wife and children, in fact, while in a crazed state brought about by a prolonged drunken orgy. My own liking for wine did not reach the pernicious extreme that it did in other centaurs I knew – Phocus, Agrius, Pylenor. These, and many others, all died on account of wine, at the wedding of Peirithous, and in that fight with Hercules at

75

Pholoe. And when Homadus allegedly tried to rape Alcyone I think he'd had more than a few.

Cheiron often lamented this centaur propensity to guzzle wine to excess. I can see him today, his snowy white hair and beard shining faintly in the dim light within his cave in the winter, as he spoke gravely on the evil which the unbridled love of wine had always caused the centaur race. He would often congratulate me on my restraint, which he mistook for wisdom. The fact is, too much wine just didn't agree with me.

I think Cheiron had cast his eye on me as a likely husband for his daughter Ocyrhöe. He didn't know that I had ever had sex with her. And, although he was famed as a seer and diviner, he didn't know that Ocyrhöe was also being fornicated by a Greek named Aeolus. Ocyrhöe turned to him, I think, when she realized that my infatuation with Dejanira was too deep to ever be set aside.

Strange, that I, half equine myself, should find Ocyrhöe's equine half turning me off, to go chasing after an unattainable human female, while Aeolus, who was not a bad-looking human, could conceive such a passion for Ocyrhöe's human half that he was willing to overlook the fact that she was half mare.

There were other cases of centaur females consorting with Greek men, and afterwards giving birth to fully human babies. The birth of a human child to a centauress, however, was not necessarily an instance of interbreeding between man and centauress. We didn't have the science back in those times, but we knew that these things could happen.

* * * * * *

After the death of Homadus I would often travel to Cheiron's cave on Mount Pelion with Crotus and Agrius. Crotus liked to visit Cheiron in order to maintain his own claim to wisdom and knowledge. For Cheiron enjoyed a great prestige among the Greeks, despite their deep-rooted prejudice against centaurs. As a way around their own prejudice, many of these bigots claimed that Cheiron was not really a centaur, that he had been fathered by Cronus on the nymph Philyra on an island in the Black Sea. Cronus had been surprised in the very act by his wife Rhea, and Cronus, in his panic, had turned himself into a horse and galloped away. He didn't even withdraw completely from Philyra's embrace before turning himself into a horse, that's how terrified he was of his wife. And this was the reason, they said, that Cheiron was born half horse.

After he died, strange to say, they even began to claim that he had actually been immortal, and that he had only relinquished his immortality because he was weary of life. The Greeks did not find the story too preposterous because when Cheiron died he was very old for a centaur – about eighty or so. Our normal life span was usually about forty-eight, which is the sum of a horse's life span and a human's life span divided by two. And Cheiron had such a vast store of knowledge of all the sciences – medicine, astronomy, history, augury, zoology – that the Greeks felt he must surely have something other than a common centaur parentage.

Crotus, for reasons of his own, had no small part in the propagation of this belief. Crotus, bullshitter and liar though he might have been in some respects, was a fairly accurate seer himself, specializing in looking into the future through the study of sheep entrails. He was also a good physician, and he sold love potions, and cast spells for a moderate fee. Many Greek men and women came to see him for these reasons.

In his capacity as physician he liked to examine Greek women, making them strip completely naked in his cave while he felt them all over, with a grave and professional expression on his face. Crotus, though approaching middle age, was still somewhat of a lecher, a fact that he slyly managed to conceal from his Greek clientele.

Once he passed me off as a medical colleague, and I stood by as he examined a young woman named Helice, as she lay on his stone examination table. He smeared something he called oil of Asclepius (though I happened to know it was nothing but adulterated olive oil) all over her naked body, passing his hands lingeringly over her thighs and breasts – looking for lumps, he told her. He called me to his side and said, "Feel this side of her pudenda Dr. Nessus. Do you detect anything abnormal there?" And I squeezed lightly on the woman's private parts, assuming the same grave expression as Crotus, to finally say, "Why, no. It feels quite normal to me."

He gave Helice some herbs to make into a tea, and was paid for the consultation with a small jug of wine, which we later drank together.

* * * * * *

I kept my love of Dejanira hidden. Nobody knew about it for a long time except for Ocyrhöe, and I had sworn her to secrecy. But one day I told Crotus about it too. We had been talking about marriage and related subjects, and he had said, "Why don't you marry Ocyrhöe? Everybody knows she likes you, you know, and Cheiron would be pleased to have you as a son-in-law."

"Look, Crotus," I said, "I can't marry Ocyrhöe." And I told him one of the reasons. "The other day, while I was hunting around Mount Parnassus, as I was resting beside some large boulders at the foot of the mountain, I saw Ocyrhöe come trotting up through the boulders, with a man on her back. It was that guy, Aeolus, the Thessalian. When they came to a low ledge, he dismounted and they started hugging and kissing. Then he got behind her, stood up on a rock, and they had intercourse."

"No! you don't say!" exclaimed Crotus. "Who would have thought Ocyrhöe would do something like that? She looks so demure and chaste. She'd better be careful. She could wind up pregnant, and her father would be very annoyed. You know how he opposes those interspecies relationships. It degrades the centaur culture, he says. Centaur couples don't live together like the Greeks do. Our females support themselves, and live apart. We only have to help them excavate their caves, and take them an occasional haunch of mutton, and so forth. Hylonome and Cylarrus are the only centaur couple I know who actually live together, just like they were Greeks."

Crotus's observations made me slightly uncomfortable. But I needed someone to confide in; the constrained pressure of my obsession with Dejanira was something too powerful to keep bottled up within me. And besides, Crotus could help me. So I told him the other reason I was not interested in Ocyrhöe. I was in love with Dejanira. "But this is just between you and me," I added.

Crotus was highly amused when I told him. "I thought you had more sense than that," he said, laughing. "Greek women aren't something to fall in love with. You're only supposed to play with them, get them to fondle you, and so forth. But not fall in love with them." And then, turning a bit more serious, he continued, "And besides,

78

Hercules has already cast his eye on Dejanira. Everybody knows that he's going to ask her father for her hand in marriage. You don't ever want to cross Hercules. You want to stay out of that maniac's way. And anyway," he summed up, "Dejanira could never marry you. How could you ever have a normal relationship?"

"I know my love sounds absurd," I said, "but I think she could love me back. She looks at me in a certain way . . . I think she likes me, at least. Could you fix me up with a love spell that might help? Or could you do me a favor and look through some entrails to see what the future might hold for me in regard to Dejanira?"

The amused look on Crotus's face gave way to a fully serious expression. "I can see that nothing I say will make you come to your senses. Let's you and me go see if we can pick up a sheep, so I can look into your future. I know of a place where we might find a lost sheep not too far away."

We centaurs did this occasionally, I mean appropriate stray sheep that were sometimes left behind when the flock moved on. True, we would often cause them to be left behind by cutting them off from the flock. Strictly speaking, this wasn't stealing, though. We considered it more as a sort of grazing fee, because it was centaur land those sheep were grazing on. The Greeks were inclined to dismiss any centaur pretension to land ownership, saying that centaurs had no more right to own land than would a common horse. So they unconcernedly grazed their flocks on our hereditary fields and meadows, encouraged in this trespass by the indolence of the centaurs, who failed to press their legitimate claims to those lands. Crotus and I trotted off to a field where a large flock of sheep grazed. We found a fat young ram that had separated from the flock and interposed ourselves between it and its companions. We kept a watch on the shepherd and his flock, some distance away now, as we adeptly drove the ram farther away. This isn't an easy thing to do, by the way. A sheep is absolutely obsessive in its determination to rejoin its flock. When he considered that it was sufficiently far away from the flock to justify our taking of it as simply taking an ownerless sheep, Crotus brought it down with a mercifully well-placed arrow. The slight pangs of conscience I felt at our actions were tempered by the anticipation of the delicious feast we would have.

Back in Crotus's cave we quickly dressed the ram, and built up

79

the fire in drooling expectation. We had a jug of wine and a large loaf of bread, and some vegetables to cook with the meat. We used long-handled spits whenever we roasted meat, because we couldn't crouch or stoop around a fire. It wasn't true, as some Greeks claimed, that we ate our meat raw. This was a malicious slander, intended to show that the centaur was more beast than human.

But first, Crotus had to examine the entrails. He extracted them from the carcass and spread them out on a waist-high slab of rock. As he pondered over the message they told him, I offered up the bones and fat to the gods, as Prometheus taught us we should do, and then began to prepare the meat, looking over towards Crotus occasionally to watch his progress.

"Come here," he said to me after a while, having studied the internal organs and entrails with glazed eyes for long moments, occasionally poking at them with a stick. "Look at the loops these entrails have formed. I see both good and bad things for you there. I see you holding Dejanira in your arms. That little dark spot on that part of the intestine there, means she is resisting. Even though this little blob of fat here could mean that she is melting in your embrace. And over here, this nodule could represent the repressed and pent-up love she holds for you. But over here – this is what I don't like. That is Hercules, in a terrible rage. This entire intestine here represents his bow – not good, not good at all. However, over here, in the liver, I see what could possibly be Hercules writhing and groaning in agony. I'm not sure what that means. Maybe that you've killed him. And in these lines and striations in the heart and kidneys, I see . . . I see . . ."

But Crotus could see nothing further. We finally disposed of the entrails and other evidence and proceeded to cook the meat. We roasted the quarters and boiled a potful of mushrooms and other vegetables. I continued to pester Crotus for more details of his prophecy as we cooked the mutton and drank the wine. How would I kill Hercules, I wanted to know. That sonofabitch led a charmed life. He was protected by Zeus himself. No arrow could touch him. And it would be madness to try to overcome him with just brute strength.

I knew this from personal experience. I had wrestled him at the Nemean Games shortly after the death of Homadus. No one else had had the courage to step forward when Hercules had paraded his seven-foot, four-hundred-pound mass of sinew and muscle before the ring, challenging anyone to wrestle with him. So finally I had stepped up. I had been hiding my rage towards Hercules for the death of Homadus, and continued to disguise it now. But a smoldering anger consumed me. When the match began I had flown at Hercules in a quiet fury, determined to break his neck. I had almost gotten the best of him. For a long moment I had him in a headlock and then I tried, with a fierce wrench of my entire body, to fling him to the ground. But he broke my hold at the last moment, and turned the tables on me. He twisted one arm behind my back, and then, with a powerful heave threw me to the ground with such force that he fractured two of my horse's ribs.

He was furious at having been almost bested, and he would have killed me right then and there if my friends had not saved me.

Such awe did Hercules' superhuman strength and his unerring marksmanship with the bow inspire that it was even said he was a son of Zeus himself. The story told by those wandering minstrels among the Greeks, known as Aoidoi, went that when he was born his mother Alcmene had been so terrified of what Hera would do to her when she found out she had been in the sack with Zeus, that she had abandoned him in a field. But Zeus, in confabulation with Athene, contrived to have Hera stumble upon him while strolling by one day. Athene tricked her into picking him up and nursing him at her breasts, which, in her capacity as mother goddess of the universe were always swollen with milk. So, having sucked at her divine and gloriously swelling tits, the story went, he had thereby become immortal, and nothing could kill him.

Some fawning Aoidoi or other, who had nothing but admiration for Hercules, had added the further embellishment that Hercules had sucked so hard that he hurt Hera's breast, so that she flung him down on the ground. But Hercules was gagging from having sucked so greedily, and he spewed out a stream of milk into the sky, which thereupon became the thousands of stars in the Milky Way.

I could believe this part of the story – I mean about Hercules gagging and barfing up the milk – because he was such a gluttonous slob. He had probably been no less of a slob even as an infant.

These days Hercules was engaged in some supposedly impossible tasks imposed upon him by King Eurystheus. A long drunken orgy had driven him over the edge, causing him to murder his own children and his wife, and the Delphic Oracle had told him he could only be freed from their ghosts if he performed a certain number of tasks for King Eurystheus. So Hercules trekked back and forth across the known world, even to the straits which became known as the pillars of Hercules, engaged in these labors.

But he didn't stop guzzling wine, and committing many other murders and atrocities between his labors. Many people admired him for this, and many others pretended to, because they were terrified of him. Me, I never pretended to admire the sonofabitch. I hated his guts. He had an idea of my feelings towards him, knowing that I had been a close friend of Homadus, and whenever our paths crossed he would scowl at me in a menacing way. I could tell he was looking for an excuse to pick a fight with me.

Besides wanting to know how I could ever get Hercules out of the way, I wanted to know what I could do to win Dejanira.

But Crotus had nothing further to enlighten me with. "After we eat," he told me, "I'll see about casting a spell that will help you. I won't charge you, of course. But maybe you can get us another jug of wine some day . . ."

Wine was hard to come by for a centaur. Equally as strong as our love for wine was our aversion to the hard work that was necessary to earn it. I must admit this because it's the truth. This was another of the reasons for the prejudice against centaurs. That, and our tendency to take stray sheep.

I began to ponder upon ways in which I could get hold of some wine for Crotus.

CHAPTER NINE

"How do you talk to those people?" Daphne asked me once, after I had related one of my dreams. "Do you know Greek?"

No, I didn't know Greek, I explained to her. I didn't know Pelasgian, either, which was the language the centaurs spoke. Most centaurs were bilingual, speaking both languages. In my waking life, my memories of those times do not include a remembrance of the exact words I used when I conversed, or of the words that other people spoke to me. To reconstruct those memories I have had to translate the words into modern English.

Or, to be more exact, I do not actually *translate*. In my dreams I carry on long conversations, which I understand completely. I know what I am saying, and I know what is being said to me, but when I awake, the words we used are only an incomprehensible gibberish. But from the knowledge imprinted upon me at the moment the words were said, I can reconstruct the entire conversation, without retaining any knowledge of the Pelasgian or Greek languages. The impression the words make on me at the time I hear them is what persists.

Occasionally, however, I have retained a complete phrase in my waking memory. Like when I found Homadus dying and he said to me, *"Nessos, elide putade Heracles meamatadus, teneyades phanastos!"* I know he was saying, in the Pelasgian language, "Nessus, I have been most unjustly slain by Hercules."

Or like when Hercules called me a *"hipporrhus,"* horse's ass. This is probably because the word caused me such fury. I think that in time, if I continue to dream, I will eventually become fluent in classical Greek, and in Pelasgian, too. This would be something of incalculable value to scholars and historians. I could write a complete dictionary of the vanished Pelasgian language, the language spoken by the centaurs, something that could be marveled at no less than did Alexander Von Humboldt when he found an aged and loquacious parrot that could speak the language of the Ature Indians. The tribe had long since become extinct, and this long-lived bird, which had been the pet of a tribal member, was therefore the last living creature to still speak their language.

But nobody cares these days. Everyone except me shares Daphne's opinion that the centaurs never existed in fact.

Daphne's questions are symptomatic of our deteriorating relationship. It's becoming harder every day to keep up my deception. In fact, there are times when I no longer even try. There are times when I become convinced that she knows the truth, and is just marking time until the moment when she finally drops me like an old shoe. One thing that holds her back, I believe, is that engagement ring – $5,285.86, it cost me – which, if she has an ounce of decency in her, she would have to return. I would gladly tell her, though, Keep the ring! Just go to bed with me one time, and keep the ring! She could easily get a couple thousand bucks for it, a good price for just one lay.

* * * * * *

As Nessus the centaur I have problems too. I know I said that in my centaur life I never had to worry about such things. But I meant in the times before I met Dejanira. When the idea of asking her father for her hand in marriage first crossed my mind, I also began to ponder that I would have to have an occupation of some sort, just as other people did. Men had flocks of sheep, or vineyards, or they were blacksmiths, potters, traders, merchants, horse breeders . . .

Me, I was nothing. I led a hand to mouth existence, like other centaurs, living each day as it came; conniving with other centaurs to obtain wine or a sheep; spending our time hunting for deer and wild boar; gathering nuts, mushrooms, and edible greens in meadows and forests. Not exactly fleeing and avoiding work, but never actively seeking for it, either. In our unique condition we had some measure of excuse for our attitude towards work. Still, however, there were many tasks for which we were better suited than most people. Any one of us would have made the fleetest messenger in all of Greece. All else failing, we could easily have hired ourselves out to pull carts and wagons. But our pride kept us from doing any of these things. This excessive and sometimes unreasonable pride, some people later said, caused our eventual downfall. Theognis says, in his *Elegies* "I fear, oh Kurnos, that pride will destroy the city, as it did the centaurs, eaters of raw flesh,"

84

In my constant and obsessive mooning over Dejanira I began to muse upon all these things. How could I ever support Dejanira, if she should consent to be my wife? Would she come to live with me in my dark and musty cave? How could I buy her robes and sandals, and trinkets and bracelets, and all the things that Greek women think they need? I couldn't too easily live in a house with her, either, or sleep in the same bed with her, like a husband and wife are supposed to do, to say nothing of the normal conjugal act between husband and wife.

All these thoughts should have made me realize that my love was totally grotesque. But they didn't. I was as incapable of reining in my insane desire as would an ordinary horse be capable of restraining itself in its desire to mount a mare in heat.

One day an idea occurred to me. Actually, Crotus gave me the idea. I had been talking to him about our general condition, about this inability of centaurs to work and live as human beings do, and he observed, "Me, Poseidon forbid that I should ever stoop so low as to take a job. But if you feel that way, why don't you try something? Like a ferryman, for example. There's that guy Phoroneus, who ferries people across the Spercheius for a living. Why don't you look for some place where you could do something like that? You wouldn't need a boat, like Phoroneus has. You could carry people across on your back. You could pick up some good change that way." He grinned knowingly. "You could even support Dejanira in style, and live in a nice house by the river bank."

Crotus wasn't dumb. He wasn't making his suggestion in complete seriousness, but he knew what was on my mind, and why I was thinking about work and a job.

But in my lovelorn longing, I clutched at the idea. I could do that! There was the Avenus river, where I had first met Dejanira and carried those nymphs across on my back as a favor. There was a fair amount of traffic at that river crossing. There were always travelers who hated to get their feet wet, and many of them would pay to avoid that annoyance. I could set myself up in business there, put up a sign, so that everyone would know they had to pay to get carried across. (Oh, maybe I would carry a pretty girl across for free, once in a while.) Then, once established, and in a position to build a good house, a house that would accommodate both Dejanira and my special equine condition, I would

85

go to her father, and ask for her hand. He would probably say no, at first, but persistence and perseverance would maybe convince him. Maybe I could even resort to threats, as Hercules claimed that Eurytion had done in the case of Mnesimache. As for Hercules and his own designs on Dejanira, I would worry about that later. It would be a demeaning occupation, true. But I was willing to make that sacrifice for the love of Dejanira. She would understand, I thought, and far from holding me in contempt for it, she would love me all the more.

I didn't immediately tell Crotus what I had decided. He was always poking fun at me for my pretension of marrying a Greek woman, and this would just make him laugh at me even more. Instead, I now tried to pretend that my love for Dejanira had only been a passing fancy, that I wasn't interested in that anymore.

But it wasn't easy to fool old Crotus. Despite this tendency of his to poke fun at me whenever I confided my innermost secrets to him, Crotus was a pretty good guy. He said, "Hey, let's forget all those unpleasant thoughts of yours for now, about going to work and all that. No female, Greek or otherwise, is worth such sacrifice. I can't help you at all in that regard. And anyway, you got bigger problems than not having a job if you want to have Dejanira. You gotta think about how you could consummate your marriage, for example, something that's very important for a woman."

That problem had been occupying my mind a lot. I said to Crotus, "Yeah, you're probably right. But you know, I've heard a lot of stories that make me think there would be a way around that problem, assuming I was really serious about wanting to marry Dejanira, which I'm not. For example, everybody has heard about Pasiphae . . ."

"You got a point there," Crotus said. "If Pasiphae found a solution, so can you."

"But how did she manage it, exactly? "I've never heard the full story."

"Let's have some wine, and I'll tell you all about it," Crotus said. He went to a dark corner of his cave where a jug of wine rested on a stony ledge I had given it to him a few days before. I had made a deal with a couple of centaur women who were lactating. Wealthy Greek women were willing to pay a good price for mare's milk to bathe with, in the belief that it was good for the complexion. Centaur milk was just

86

as good, coming as it did from the centaur woman's mare's-udders. Milk, moreover, for which a centaur female had no use whatsoever, since a centaur mother nursed her infant at her human breasts. These centaur women had traded their milk to some Greek women for some wine, which they then exchanged with me for some mutton. I couldn't milk them myself, of course, because a centaur can't very well sit at a stool down there, with a milk bucket between his knees. So the Greek women themselves had done this, although centaur women dislike having a stranger fondling their udders. This way the centaur women had gotten twice as much mutton than if they had traded their milk for it directly. And I got the mutton quite cheaply, too . . . for free, actually, so everybody got a good deal.

We set the jug on a flat boulder just at the cave's entrance and filled our cups. In our singular condition of equineness, the many boulders and ledges to be found in the mountains was the reason we liked to live there. Since reaching the ground with our hands wasn't easy for us, we liked to be in areas where there were many such natural projections, which served the same purpose for us as tables and benches.

We poured a few drops on the ground as a libation to the gods Poseidon and Dionysus first. Then Crotus, lifting his cup, took a short swig. "By Sabazius and Poseidon!" he exclaimed, "this is really excellent wine."

I tasted it myself. He was right. This was a full-bodied, sparkling and flavorful wine, very dry and with a rich bouquet. The Greek women who had traded it for centaur milk had assured the centaur women that it was from the vineyards of Great Ancaeus, the Argonaut, who had died tragically before he had had a chance to savor any of it himself, just as a seer had prophesied to him some years before when he had just finished planting the vines.

I tossed off another swig, and prompted Crotus to begin the story of Pasiphae. The entire Mediterranean world had been abuzz with the sordid gossip about Minos, Daedalus, the Cretan labyrinth, Pasiphae, the bull, and the Minotaur for several years now. I knew most of the story. Poseidon had caused Pasiphae to fall in love with the bull to punish Minos. But one aspect of all this still puzzled me.

87

"Why did Poseidon do this to poor dumb Pasiphae?" I asked Crotus. "Why didn't he directly punish Minos himself?"

Here Crotus manifested some of that wisdom he had a reputation for. Minos was generally believed to be a son of Zeus, Crotus pointed out, and it was only natural that Poseidon would hesitate to meddle directly with a son of Zeus. But he could do whatever he wished with the persons around him. Powerful persons – that is, persons under the protection of powerful gods – are never directly touched by misfortune. It always comes to them indirectly, through their weak spots, represented by their relatives and loved ones who are not included in the aforesaid protection.

That answered my question. But the principal aspect I was interested in was: How, exactly did Daedalus solve Pasiphae's problem, enabling her to accomplish the physical act? How did she manage to get the bull interested in her at all? Maybe a magic potion was involved, I suggested to Crotus (and I secretly hoped that maybe Crotus could supply me with some of it to use on Dejanira).

No, there was no magic involved, Crotus said. He took another swig of wine, wiped his mouth with the back of his hand, and began to tell me the full story. He told it all, from beginning to end, with all its plotting and conniving, twists and ramifications, ending with the epic flight of Daedalus and his son Icarus across the Cretan Sea, and the tragic death of Icarus.

"A lot of people don't believe this, though," Crotus observed, referring to the flight of Daedalus and Icarus. "They can't see how a man could flap a huge pair of wings fast enough to get off the ground. But the truth is, he didn't flap those wings. And they weren't actually made with feathers and wax, either. They were stiff, and they weren't glued to his arms. I think the way they worked is he climbed up on a height, and then just sort of dropped off. The warm air currents lifted him up, and carried him right over the sea. You've seen how eagles and buzzards can float high in the sky for hours, without flapping their wings. Oh, Daedalus was a clever fellow, all right.

"And what happened to Icarus is he tried to go higher when there was no warm air current to lift him upward. I guess you could say he sort of – sort of went into a stall, you might say, and then he couldn't recover his stability, and went spinning down into the sea. Too bad,

88

because Daedalus destroyed the remaining pair of wings afterwards in his sorrow, and never meddled with flight again.

"So actually, compared to Pasiphae and her bull, there's really not such a great problem about a centaur and a Greek woman living together. The gods, especially, can't have anything against it. They're always assuming all kinds of weird shapes whenever they fornicate with mortals and demigods on earth. Take Zeus and Nemesis, for example."

He poured himself another cupful of wine. Crotus knew all the stories pertaining to gods and their sexual adventures on earth.

"You know how he got the hots for Nemesis, and chased her all over the world, trying to screw her. She turned herself into all sorts of creatures, trying to escape, but he kept right after her. It was a mistake, changing herself into different animals, thinking to get away from him that way. This only excited him all the more, because he likes to change himself into an animal too, when he has sex. In fact, he can't fornicate with a mortal woman in his true shape. He has to turn himself into something else first, or it's fatal to the woman. His true form is so dazzling that a mortal woman can't withstand it. Semele, you know, found this out to her sorrow. Hera tricked her into insisting that Zeus come to her in his true form, and when he did so, she was burned to a crisp."

As for Nemesis, Crotus said, the last shape she turned herself into was a duck. But Zeus just changed himself into a goose, and fornicated her that way, while she quacked away indignantly. Some country folk passing by witnessed the act, but did not recognize its significance. They only saw what their eyes told them, a gander fornicating a duck, and they shrugged their shoulders in dismissal of the odd occurrence.

Crotus continued with his examples. "He also had sex with Europe while in the shape of a bull, you know, and he's even gone so far as to change himself into an ant, so he could screw Aegina, daughter of Asopus. Don't ask me how, or what kind of pleasure he could have gotten from this; I don't know. And this girl Io . . . you probably know her uncle's grandchildren, who live over in . . . but, anyway, he changed her into a heifer. My point is that sex between two different types of creatures is not impossible. If Zeus can do it, you can do it too."

"Yeah," I said. "Maybe you're right. Though of course I'm not Zeus . . . But tell me about Io. I've never heard the whole story."

Crotus refilled our cups. "The way it happened was he changed her into a cow, so that Hera wouldn't see it was a girl he was with. But Hera wasn't fooled, and she took the cow and gave it to Argus Panoptes to keep watch over it, so Zeus couldn't change it back into a girl again. Zeus had Hermes kill Argus so he could turn the cow loose. Argus had one hundred eyes, you know, big, round blue eyes, all over his body. Some were on his back, and on top of his head, and in back of his head, and on his ass, and even on the soles of his feet. Hermes had to tell him stories, and play on his flute for a long time before he could put them all to sleep. Then he cut off his head and dropped a big boulder on him for good measure. Hera had those eyes placed in the tail of the Peacock when Argus died. She ordered the peacock to spread its tail every now and then, to commemorate his death. That's why peacock feathers are bad luck."

"I've never seen a peacock," I said.

"Well, I have," Crotus said, "and you can see Argus's eyes in its tail, just as plain as day."

Then the talk turned again to Nemesis.

"Could it really be true," I wondered aloud, "that Helen was hatched out of an egg that this here Nemesis laid? They say that Leda found the egg on the edge of a marsh and took it home . . . And the word going around is that Paris has stolen Helen away from King Menelaus in Sparta. Cassandra has prophesied that there will be a long and bloody war on account of Helen. Of course nobody ever believes Cassandra."

"Yeah, that's true," Crotus said. "Like you say, nobody ever believes her, even though a lot of her prophecies have come true. But this time I'm sure she's mistaken. Though, to tell the truth, Helen is something worth fighting a war over. She is absolutely beautiful. Having been incubated in an egg, she has the most perfect and flawless complexion you could ever see."

I tried to find out from Crotus when he had had the opportunity to actually see Helen in the flesh, but he evaded the question.

"As far as I'm concerned," I finally said, in a maudlin mood now from the wine, and throwing all my attempts to deceive Crotus into the

90

wind, "Helen is just a cheap floozy. I'd trade ten years of a hundred Helen's for one moment of Dejanira."

"Oh, no, you're wrong," Crotus said. "Helen's got a face and an ass that could launch a thousand ships."

We talked on and drank wine until sundown. But Crotus did not come up with anything useful to me in the matter of my wish to marry Dejanira, as I had hoped he would. He would shrug off my discreet questions and promptings, wandering tangentially off into tales of other strange deeds and occurrences of those days. Finally, he passed me the nearly empty jug. "Here, drain the rest of this wine, and then let's start thinking about how we're going to get another jug. This was really excellent wine."

* * * * * *

I awoke with the taste of the three-thousand-year old wine still on my palate, the wine from the vineyard of Great Ancaeus, who died before he had had a chance to savor it. He was in the process of raising the cup to taste his first swig of it, laughing at the prophecy of the seer who had told him he would never live to enjoy it, when someone came running in to tell him that a wild boar was ravaging his vines. He set down the untasted cup, grabbed his spear, and rushed out to protect his property. But as he was pursuing the beast it suddenly wheeled around and attacked him, slashing him in the groin with its tusks and killing him. Which gave origin to the phrase, "There is many a slip 'twixt the cup and the lip."

I was deeply intrigued at the information I had gathered from this latest dream. Daedalus had invented the hang glider! The story of the origins of the Minotaur was historical fact!

It was a Saturday. Daphne, the bitch, has never gone out with me or come to visit me on a Saturday, so I sat down at my desk and began to crank out Chapter Seven of my *Short History of the Centaurs*, while the memories of my dream were still fresh in my mind. It goes like this:

Chapter Seven
A Short History Of The Centaurs

Having mentioned Pasiphae and the bull, I must digress from the

91

history of the centaurs for just a moment to tell the entire story here. There appears to be an abundance of evidence attesting to a historical basis for the myth, and since it is another instance of interbreeding between man and beast – of woman and beast, to be more exact – we should not leave the story untold.

The legend of Pasiphae and the bull has always been one of the most fascinating and puzzling tales from Greek mythology. A gloomy aura of secretiveness – of mystery and intrigue – continues to enshroud the whole affair, an aura that has filtered down through the ages to our time, hinting to the acute observer that there are some things about the matter that have never been told.

Like multitudinous tentacles, ramifications of the legend reach out to touch upon many an aspect of Greek mythology. One of those ramifications has to do with the Cretan labyrinth, which in its turn is the story of a proud man's determination to shield his family from scandal. Some versions of the myth say that the labyrinth was carved out of rock and that its center was at the heart of a mountain. But others say that it was constructed of high hedges, forming tunnels of greenery that spread over such a vast acreage that a person wandering into it ran the risk of never finding his way out again.

At the center of this somber labyrinth, King Minos entombed the Minotaur, the fruit of his wife's strange and deviate passion. It thrived on raw human flesh and King Minos treated it annually to a feast of fourteen Athenian youths and maidens which the city of Athens was obliged to pay as tribute to the Cretan king.

Whatever possessed Pasiphae, highborn Queen of Crete, to have a love affair with the beastliest of beasts, a slobbering, drooling bull? This would be a question to sorely perplex humanity forever. But fortunately the answer to it is known. It was the doing of the gods, of the god Poseidon, to be exact, and he did it to punish Minos. We can frequently see other instances of this sort in the Greek myths: The gods of those days believed in teaching Peter a lesson by punishing Paul.

Actually, in this particular instance, there is perhaps some justification for this way of proceeding. Minos was a son of Zeus, and it is understandable that Poseidon, his brother, would be hesitant to meddle directly with Minos himself. If we scrutinize human affairs closely, we can see that this same principle always seems to hold forth. People born rich and powerful, i.e., under the protection of powerful gods, remain immune to the disasters and misfortunes which devastate the lives of the weak and the poor. These powerful people are affected only coincidentally, seemingly by peripheral entities who are understandably reluctant to interfere in the lives of people who are loved and protected by a higher power. There are exceptions, of course, but we can account for these exceptions by presuming that the particular power that has protected these people has abandoned them. When this abandonment occurs, we can then see the relish with which those peripheral powers descend upon the unfortunate abandonee, inflicting upon him or her the cruelest of misfortunes.

But getting back to Pasiphae and the reason she committed her abominable act, it came about as follows: Minos, as a son of Zeus, was highly favored by all the gods. Sometimes it would go to his head and he would boast to his friends that the gods would grant him anything he asked for. One day, while strolling on the beach, certain of his friends, perhaps irritated from hearing this constant boast, asked him to demonstrate that it was true. Minos thereupon built a makeshift altar from the stones that abounded on the beach. Then he raised his arms seaward and asked the gods to send him a sacrificial victim from the sea. And immediately, a beautiful, snow-white bull came swimming in to shore.

It was the most beautiful specimen of bull ever seen, roundly sleek and fat, with a dark streak running the length of its snowy back, its soft brown eyes framed by huge floppy ears and a tiny pair of polished horns. Such a beautiful animal, in fact, that Minos didn't have the heart to sacrifice it. He ordered his servants to take it away to join his herd and had them bring back one of his own scrawny specimens to take its place. "Poseidon won't mind," he thought. "He won't even notice the difference."

But Poseidon did notice, and he minded very much. He determined to make Minos pay for this display of greed and irreverence. However, reluctant to visit his displeasure directly upon Minos, for the reasons we have explained, he came up with the grotesque idea of making poor Pasiphae fall in love with the bull. According to the mythographers, he secured the cooperation of Aphrodite, who in turn enlisted the aid of her son Eros (more commonly known as Cupid).

So one day, while Pasiphae was leaning out of her bedroom window, innocently admiring the bull which her husband had so miraculously acquired, Eros shot one of his golden-tipped arrows into her breast. Almost instantly, she conceived an insane passion for the bull, deciding that she just had to have sex with it, no matter what.

Poseidon's intention was that Pasiphae should suffer from unrequited love. But Eros didn't have to bother shooting a leaden-tipped arrow into the target of her love, the bull, which was the way an affair of that sort was usually arranged back in those days. It wasn't necessary because a bull, of course, will not normally be attracted to a human female, no matter how lovely and enticing she may be. A bull will normally be interested only in a cow, a member of its own species. But Pasiphae, out of her mind with desire, chose to ignore this irrevocable law of nature, and continued to pursue the affair to its final sordid conclusion.

One can only speculate that Poseidon was so astonished to see the lengths to which human beings will go to satisfy their beastly urges that he just stood there watching, shaking his head in wonderment. For Pasiphae, faced with the sublime indifference of the bull and determined to satisfy her raging lust, went to Daedalus, who was then living in Crete, told him about her craving, and asked for his advice.

She couldn't have gone to a better source for help. Daedalus, the cleverest man in the world at that time, loved problems of this sort, since he appears to have applied his cleverness and ingenuity mostly towards idle and frivolous pursuits. He quickly came up with an idea to solve Pasiphae's problem. He fashioned a wooden cow, probably consisting of two hinged halves, with a real cow's hide stretched tightly over it and tacked into place with tiny wooden pegs or bronze nails. It was probably adorned with limpid brown eyes and curling lashes, applied with a paint brush; and as a crowning touch of genius, a real cow's tail, which Pasiphae could twitch by means of a concealed string held in her hand.

He pushed this wooden cow into the pasture where Poseidon's bull grazed amongst Minos' contented cows (Diodorus Siculus says that he had built wheels into it, concealed in the hooves). He helped Pasiphae climb into it and showed her how to place her arms and legs inside the cow's hollow limbs. Then he discreetly retired, though he probably felt tempted to stay and watch. His ingenuity was quickly rewarded, for the bull soon came shambling along. It made a cursory examination of the wooden cow and after a brief courtship, mounted it. Then Daedalus returned and helped Pasiphae climb back out.

With her insane desire satisfied, Pasiphae now felt only an intense shame and embarrassment. She couldn't bear to look Daedalus in the eye, as he solicitously inquired of her if everything had gone all right. "How was it? was it okay?", he asked, carefully concealing any suggestion of a leer. She also averted her face from the sight of the bull, which was still standing nearby, trying to make sense of what it was seeing, a woman emerging from the interior of the cow it had so recently mounted.

Later, came the consequences of her unladylike act. There is always a price to pay when we fail to control our base urges even if, like Pasiphae, we can blame it on the gods: She gave birth to a monster, the Minotaur, which of course, it is redundant to say, was half-bull, half-human.

Apropos of nothing, by the way, this notorious creature, generally known to most people simply as The Minotaur, had a name: It was Asterius, which incidentally, had also been the name of Minos' stepfather. His mother Europe had married the said Asterius after Zeus had finally tired of fornicating her, and Asterius had adopted Minos and his two brothers, Rhadamanthys and Sarpedon as his own.

What is the source for this rather disagreeable story of the Minotaur? Why would anyone go to the trouble of inventing it? It is not really an imaginative tale, but rather one which appears to have been necessary to explain certain otherwise unexplainable facts. Those facts would be that there was a real creature, fathered upon a woman by a bull; or at least, a creature that appeared to be half-bull, half-human, was born to a woman. Pausanias, who Robert Graves refers to as 'a level-headed and truthful writer', says of this creature in I:24,2 of his *Guide To Greece*,

". . . Even in our time women have given birth to much more amazing monsters than this one." One can only wonder what he was hinting at.

* * * * * *

The episode of Pasiphae and the bull took place several centuries after the first centaurs had appeared on earth, and it seems likely that centaurs were a relatively common sight in Greece at that time. The mermaids and the satyrs also thrived in that same epoch, and besides this there was also the chimaera, and many other strange creatures, such as three-headed Geryon and his two-headed hound, Orthrus, monstrous Echidne, the sirens, the Cyclopes, Scylla, snake-bodied Erichthonius, and a long list of other weird monsters. So the birth of a half-bull, half-human creature should really not be such a difficult thing to believe.

Another consideration which makes us believe that the story of Pasiphae and the bull has some solid historical basis, is the fact that the story does not end there, with the birth of the Minotaur. As we have already stated, the story continues, with many ramifications involving Daedalus and Icarus, the struggle of Athens against Cretan domination, the life of Theseus, who finally

95

killed the Minotaur with the aid of Ariadne . . . And by the way, a curious little detail, not often remembered, is that Ariadne was, of course, the Minotaur's own sister, as Dante reminds us in Canto XII of the Inferno, where he has Virgil saying to the Minotaur,

> "Partiti bestia, que questi non vene
> ammaestrato de la tua sorella,"
> (Be off you beast, for this one comes not
> instructed by your sister,)

which is a reference to Theseus' trip into the labyrinth to kill the monster, using the thread Ariadne had given him so he could find his way out again. So Ariadne was helping him to kill her own brother, and Theseus killed the creature which would have become his brother-in-law. As for the way in which the lives of Daedalus and his son Icarus are intertwined with that of the Minotaur, their epic flight across the sea was a direct consequence of Daedalus' machinations in the affair between Pasiphae and the bull. It came about as follows:

Minos seems to have experienced a nasty shock when he beheld the monstrosity his wife had brought into the world. This gave way to shame and embarrassment when he realized what she had done. For one whose name has come down to us as that of a wise and powerful ruler, famed for his strength of character and equanimity, his reaction seems rather more extreme than the circumstances warranted.

The whole incident serves to illustrate the truth of the maxim which tells us that embarrassing situations, in themselves, are usually unimportant. What really endures through the years is the attitude we assume before them. Because Minos' elaborate efforts to cover up the whole sordid affair only succeeded in focusing world attention on it, so that even today, thousands of years later, people who hear about it for the first time can still murmur and shake their heads in wonderment. Instead of going to all that trouble of building the labyrinth, Minos could have laughed the whole thing off as a harmless joke played on him and his wife by the gods, and it would have soon been forgotten.

But he apparently decided that the shame and embarrassment were more than he could face. Having consulted an oracle, he was advised to build the labyrinth. Once it was built, he secreted Pasiphae and her child in the heart of the inextricable maze, and retired into its depths himself. According to Apollodorus, Minos never emerged into the open world again. However, it is elsewhere claimed that he made an ill-fated voyage to Sicily, where he died, so it seems Apollodorus was mistaken.

And who was it that designed and built this famous labyrinth as the solution to Minos' problem? Why, none other than that inventive artisan and problem solver, Daedalus, the man who was responsible for the problem in the first place.

Such an interesting event could not be kept secret for very long. Gossiping tongues soon leaked the story out to the world at large. Then, to aggravate matters even further, Minos learned the part that Daedalus had played in Pasiphae's disgusting love affair and had him imprisoned, together with his son Icarus, in the labyrinth. But Pasiphae, perhaps feeling a certain degree of guilt, knowing that it was all her fault, had them both secretly freed from their dungeon.

However, Daedalus was still faced with the problem of escaping from the island itself, no easy matter when Minos kept a tight control over every ship in the harbor. His solution was to build two pairs of wings for himself and his son, with which to fly across the sea to mainland Greece and safety.

The familiar story tells us that he built these wings out of eagles' quill feathers and fastened them together with wax. Before setting out on the epic flight he instructed his son carefully. He cautioned him against flying too close to the sun, the legend says, because the heat of the sun would melt the wax holding the wings together. But halfway across the sea the heedless boy, driven to recklessness by the exhilarating sensation of free flight, ignored his father's warnings. He soared too close to the blazing sun, which quickly melted the wax. He found himself foolishly flapping his bare arms, Ovid tells us, in a desperate effort to remain aloft. He then went plunging down into the sea which to this day bears his name, in a shower of feathers and melted wax.

Today, with interest in the Greek myths in a sad decline, no one to my knowledge has advanced the hypothesis that the flight of Daedalus and Icarus may have been a historical reality. Perhaps the wings fashioned by Daedalus were actually the first hang-gliders, possibly built in a manner resembling feathers, partly for aesthetic, partly for practical, purposes. There are strong convection currents on the Island of Crete, and many convenient cliffs from where he and Icarus could have initiated their flight. Daedalus' instructions to his son would have centered mostly on the dangers of going into a stall, of trying to soar upwards when there was no corresponding air current to sustain him aloft. With the tragic outcome of the venture, perhaps Daedalus came to abhor his invention and destroyed the remaining wing, refusing ever to meddle with flight again. Succeeding generations, in their ignorance, having no idea how the wings were constructed, have assumed that Daedalus and Icarus flew by flapping their arms.

Daedalus himself eventually reached Sicily where he was granted asylum by king Cocalus, and he repaid the king's hospitality by making dolls with jointed limbs and other delightful toys for his daughters.

His cleverness and his affinity for solving puzzles and problems almost proved his undoing for a second time, however. Minos was combing the Mediterranean with a fleet of ships, determined to find Daedalus and take him back to Crete for punishment. He carried with him a spiral sea shell and a linen thread, and at every harbor he entered he offered a reward to whoever could pass the thread through the shell, knowing that only Daedalus could solve the problem. When he arrived in Camicus, in Sicily, King Cocalus offered to have it done and eagerly carried the shell and thread to Daedalus. The problem was mere child's play for Daedalus. First he bored a hole in the small end of the shell; then he tied a spider web to an ant's leg, and induced it to climb through the shell by smearing honey on its edges. Then he tied the other end of the spider web to the linen thread and thus pulled it through.

Minos paid Cocalus the reward and then demanded to have Daedalus turned over to him. But Cocalus' daughters hated to lose him because of the many pretty toys he made for them. So, together with Daedalus, they hatched a cruel plot. Cocalus had invited Minos ashore and into his palace while he pondered the demand to surrender Daedalus, and while Minos was enjoying a warm bath they poured boiling water over him through a pipe, which Daedalus had passed through the roof of the bathroom.

Thus the life of great and far-famed Minos came to an end, sacrificed to some young girls' desire for pretty playthings. Cocalus turned the body over to the Cretans, saying that he had tripped and fallen into a cauldron of boiling water.

* * * * * *

And what does all of this have to do with the centaurs? Nothing, really, except that by following the pathways of these stories backward through time, we find that they have their profound roots and origins in the legend of Pasiphae and her affair with the bull. The fact that many other historical events spring from that same source is another little bit of proof that the episode itself is factual, and not merely distorted myth. And finally, it is another little bit of evidence showing that interbreeding between man and beast was not unknown in ancient times.

Even today, if I am not mistaken, we can still observe, in carnivals and sideshows around the world, the results of interbreeding between man and nearly every known variety of creature. When I was a little boy I remember seeing, in a carnival freak show, Larry the Lizard Man (who was covered with lizard-like scales from head to toe); Jerry the Giraffe Man (who had a neck at least a foot long); Jocko the Dog Boy . . . Other people tend to dismiss these interesting sideshows as mere instances of defective births and shameless huckstering. But I know better.

The sight of these unfortunate beings – beasts with a human face and a human intellect, visible in the look of stoic suffering with which they stared back at my child's eyes of wonder and awe – woke in me a deep, scientific curiosity in the phenomenon of interspecies breeding; a curiosity that has continued unabated to the present time.

In the late nineteenth century, there was the case of the Elephant Man, David Merrick, recently brought to our renewed attention by anthropologist Ashley Montagu. David Merrick was supposedly a victim of a progressive and degenerative disease of the bones, neurofibromatosis, which had gradually reduced him to his pitiable state. Oddly, no one seems to have ever considered the possibility that the elephant man was exactly what his appellation implied – the offspring of a man and a cow elephant, or possibly, of a bull elephant and a woman. When he was first discovered by Sir Frederick Treves he was associated with a circus and it can be assumed that his father was too. The elder Merrick would have had access to an elephant, since most circuses usually have at least one, and as a circus man, Merrick senior would have been an acrobat, or otherwise endowed with special talents, making it easy for him to accomplish a union with a pachyderm.

If these suppositions are correct, then we would have an explanation for David Merrick's gentle and philosophical character in the face of his misfortune. The part of him that was of an elephantine nature would have been quite at ease with his appearance, since it would have been only natural, as far as an elephant was concerned. Also, a reflective, philosophical, and patient nature is characteristic of the elephant.

Going back to our statement that David Merrick could even have been the child of a *woman* and an elephant, some people may ask, "How on earth could a woman possibly be impregnated by an elephant?" It would appear to be a dangerous undertaking for a woman, to say nothing of the difficulty of securing the cooperation of the creature itself. But there are many ways in which a woman could conceive a child from elephant sperm without actually engaging in intimacies with the beast. She could have come into contact with elephant semen in a swimming pool, for example. Or she could even have gotten it off a toilet seat, or other like manner.

Not without its relevance to the foregoing, Pliny tells us in his *Natural History* that in Egypt an elephant fell in love with a girl who sold nosegays and flowers on the street. But she wasn't just any old street peddler. Aristophanes the grammarian was also in love with her, says Pliny, and this shows, presumably, that elephants have a quite refined taste in women. If I am not mistaken, this was the same elephant that Melville refers to as "Darmonedes' elephant, . . . that so frequented the flower market, and with low salutations presented nosegays to damsels, and then caressed their zones." In plain language, in case any reader has not grasped the genteel and reticent Victorian language used by Melville, it presented bouquets of flowers to young girls and then felt them up with its trunk. This is surely evidence of a certain sexual compatibility between humans and elephants. Although I must admit that it could only be that Darmonedes himself trained his elephant to behave in that manner, and that he derived a vicarious pleasure from watching it do this.

In Livy's history of the Second Punic War, by the way, he mentions that during the seventh year of the war, a baby was born with an elephant's head. It was during this war, of course, that Hannibal crossed the alps with his elephants, so that elephants became a common sight on the Italian peninsula in those years. This constitutes too much of a coincidence to attribute the birth of an elephant-headed baby to a mere genetic defect. At about the same time, at Tarquinni, a pig was born with a human face. All this according to Livy, of whom Dante says in Canto xxviii of his *Inferno*, "–come Livio scrive, che non erra."

End of Chapter Seven
Of A *Short History of The Centaurs*

CHAPTER TEN

Lately Daphne has begun to praise my writing, and she shows a keen interest in my *Short History of the Centaurs*. This pleases me greatly. Even though It does sort of seem to me that every time she expresses admiration for my writing skills and for the enormous amount of research that goes into my work she asks me to loan her some money immediately afterwards. But I tell myself that I'm being uncharitable when I allow this thought to cross my mind.

Anyway, Daphne liked Chapter Seven so much that I felt I had to give her the 300 dollars she wanted to borrow, and then I gave her Chapter Eight to take home and read. She brought the pages back some weeks later. I had expected some objections from her, because of the sexual content of the material, but she only had words of praise. This has given rise to an uncomfortable thought: Is she reading those pages at all?

The disturbing suspicion was reinforced when she began to tell me of her mother's illness. Her mother had a most worrisome pain in her side. She had to go see a doctor; she didn't know how they were going to manage, what with all their unpaid bills, and their insurance premiums, and the light bill, and telephone, and . . .

I found myself saying, grateful for her praise for my writing, even though I was almost sure it wasn't sincere, "Why don't you let me help you? I can loan you a couple hundred . . ."

And before she left I slipped her a check for two hundred dollars, no longer from my inheritance money, but out of my pitiful checking account. She gratefully allowed me to kiss her good night when she left, and to briefly embrace her warm and voluptuous body, which almost made it worth it.

* * * * * *

Sam has advised me to get ready for my deposition. We had a long telephone conversation, and he gave me a general idea of what the questions would be like. He told me not to lie in my deposition, which

101

surprised me. Of course I didn't have the slightest intention of lying; I never lie. But I had thought his advice would rather incline in the other direction. Actually, although he told me not to lie, I think his intention was to subtly encourage me in that direction by asking me several mock questions which he thought the city lawyers might ask, and slyly prompting the appropriate response from me.

He seemed to be greatly pleased at my answers. "So, this here Passy Faye, then," he said, "you say you think she really did have a minnow tar? If you get the chance, you might bring up that subject at your deposition."

It won't be hard. These days my concentration isn't very good. My mind is filled with my dreams and with my new book, *A Short History of the Centaurs,* a topic that frequently crops up in my conversations, whenever I feel it's safe to indulge the inclination. Not when I'm at my job, though. I have to be careful there. It might be hard to find another job.

I've been thinking about Pasiphae and all such related subjects a lot, lately. Of course I know for a fact that there is some solid substance in the story. I've lived in those times and I know. So I spend all my free time doing research, gathering information from Greek mythology and from many ancient texts that might validate my theory – that at one time in the history of the world, the interbreeding of species was the rule rather than the exception. As Nessus the Centaur I never gave those things much thought. In those times it was a fact that was generally accepted.

It was with this knowledge in mind that I wrote Chapter Eight of *A Short History of the Centaurs,* on which I had expected to hear some criticism by Daphne, as follows:

A Short History of the Centaurs
Chapter Eight

Besides the case of Pasiphae and the bull, numerous other instances of strange unions and even stranger births can be found in Greek mythology.

Such stories, though they may not in themselves constitute proof of the historicity of the centaurs, are nevertheless food for speculative thought. They indicate that unknown atmospheric or climatically induced chemical conditions existed four or five thousand years ago that were conducive to a heightened interaction between the seed and ova of otherwise incompatible creatures, accompanied by a high rate of defective births. In some parts of the world it seems these conditions persisted up until relatively recent times, because Pliny, writing in the first century of our era says, "Duris maketh report that certain Indians engender with beasts and produce monstrous mongrels, half beast, half man."

Herodotus, too, makes mention of various strange creatures and tribes of people who still inhabited distant parts of the world in his time. Most of these, however, do not appear to have been the result of interbreeding, but rather instances of grotesque mutations. They proliferated especially in Libya (Herodotus referred to all of Africa as Libya). In this land, Herodotus says, were found the dog-headed men, and headless men, with their eyes in their breast; and wild men and wild women. Here too, were found the Lotophagi, whose cattle walked backwards as they grazed, because their downward-curving horns were so long that they snagged in the ground if they walked forward, and the Ethiopian hole-people, who squeaked like bats when they talked. In India there were ants as large as foxes, and in Egypt there were flying snakes. Also found in Libya were the Aramantes, the Atarantes and the Psylli (from whose name I think the English word "silly" is derived), three tribes with striking psychological peculiarities. The last-named were already extinct in Herodotus' time, because they had marched out one day en masse, to make war against the South Wind and in this silly manner succeeded in exterminating themselves, because they were buried in a sand storm.

These examples might suggest to the observer that the conditions conducive to a high incidence of defective births originated in the hot, dry climate of the southern Sahara, irradiating outward to reach Greece, and other far-away places, such as India, to produce the mongrel creatures mentioned by Duris, and even to the cold regions of the land beyond Scythia, to produce other oddities, such as the one-eyed Arimaspians, who stole the gold guarded by griffins.

Conversely, it's possible that the conditions originated in Greece – perhaps on Mount Olympus itself – and spread outward, to constitute an area somewhat like the Sotadic Zone postulated by Sir Richard Burton. The fact that the conditions still persisted in Libya and other far-away places after they had waned in Greece could be explained by the analogy of a pebble dropped into the water. At the point of impact itself, the water will become calm while concentric rings of wavelets are still spreading outward. In support of this latter view we can point out that, from whichever geographical point we may begin our investigations (independent of time), the pernicious effects of this mysterious effluvia seem to become more pronounced the closer we draw to Mount Olympus.

An intriguing question comes up when we examine and compare the civilizations of Greece and Egypt. Why do monsters and all sorts of misshapen humans and half-humans proliferate so much more in Greece than they do in Egypt? A clue to the answer can be furnished by considering the difference in the two peoples. The Egyptians were exceedingly religious and devout. They dedicated enormous amounts of time and energy to the worship of their gods. Very few examples of blasphemy and godless behavior are known to us from Ancient Egypt.

In ancient Greece, on the other hand, once we scrape away the superficial appearance of religious devotion, we can see that the times were riddled with heresy, apostasy and gross disrespect towards the gods. We have but to remember the incident of Ixion, forefather of the Centaur race, trying to fornicate with the Supreme Olympian goddess herself. The Greek gods themselves were responsible for this loss of respect. They hobnobbed too freely with lowly mortals, and thus lost much of the high regard in which they had once been held, because of the truth in the age-old saying, that familiarity breeds contempt.

Now, here is my point, if the reader has not yet lost his patience with my expositions: Egyptian and Greek gods were closely related; they were really much alike, with the same origins. The greatest difference was that one family of gods – the Greek – were much more inclined to lechery and to lascivious behavior. They were much like certain lordly, regal individuals who take a liking to servant girls (or, in the case of females, to their chauffeurs and gardeners).

But in Egypt, men and gods maintained a respectful and discreet distance from each other. In part because the Egyptian gods were more sober-minded than their Greek counterparts, and also because of the extreme religiosity of the Egyptian people. Thus, there was little or no intermingling between gods and humans. Therefore, in Greece, from the indiscriminate intermixing of human and godly seed – from the unbridled lechery of gods spilling their seed on earth, or impregnating mortal women (and even animals and plants), and moreover, doing this while in the shape of some beast or other

– we have a great variety of monsters, serpents, and deformed humans, while in Egypt we have almost none.

This leads us to conclude that the aforementioned conditions had extraterrestrial origins, that a certain something descended from Olympus upon earth, contaminating it from the unprotected sex that the Olympians indulged in with man and other earthly beings.

Some people might sustain that it was the other way around: that the gods became infected from something they picked up on earth, and that this infection, having gone through certain mutations, was subsequently retransmitted to earth in a more virulent form. For, in Olympus we have several cases of deformities, such as the case of Priapus, love child of Aphrodite and Dionysus, who was born with grotesquely enlarged private parts. Aphrodite also had another deformed child, Hermaphroditus, who had both male and female organs. It could be that Aphrodite, who is known to have consorted with various mortals, picked up some sort of infection on earth, which she transmitted into Olympus.

Whenever the Olympian gods consorted with nymphs, nereids, dryads and other semi-immortal females, chances were strong that their offspring would not be entirely normal. On the Gorgon Medusa, for example, Poseidon fathered the winged horse Pegasus, and also the warrior Chrysaor, who was born with a golden sword in his hand. Both of them sprang, fully grown, from Medusa's blood when Perseus cut off her head. On the ocean Nymph Callirhoe, Chrysaor fathered the monster Geryon, a freak which any side-show or circus in the world today would dearly love to possess. He had three heads – one of them a serpent's, another, that of an indeterminate beast, and the third one, a normal, human head and face, of such a remarkably honest appearance that anyone, on the basis of that face alone, could have sworn that Geryon was the most honest and decent person in the world. But he was really a cruel and treacherous monster. For this reason his name and figure were familiar, up until the middle ages, as the symbol of fraud.

One is tempted to include the Gorgon Medusa, so hideously ugly that her glare could turn any living thing into stone, in the list of weird freaks and monsters born in those days; but she wasn't born that way. In fact, she had once been a beautiful girl – beautiful enough to attract the attention of great Poseidon, who wooed her, and made love to her in one of Athene's temples. This was a very disrespectful thing to do. Especially since Athene herself is so chaste. She was furious at Poseidon and Medusa for defiling her temple, but she vented all her rage on poor Medusa, changing her into the ugly creature we all know – another instance of the ancient gods' warped sense of justice.

Medusa, they say, had snakes for hair, bulging, blood-shot eyes and a bloated, purplish tongue, protruding from between jagged yellow teeth and raw-liver lips. The most charitable-minded of persons would have had to admit that she wasn't pretty. Even in death, her severed head retained its evil power. When Perseus laid it down on some kelp while he freed Andromeda from her chains, the kelp and sea weed turned into the stone which we know today as coral, and long after her death, her sightless eyes continued to turn men into stone.

The god Pan, however, is a clear instance of a freakish birth. Half goat, half human, he was supposedly a child of Hermes. It seems likely, however, that far from being a god, Pan was only the first satyr, the forerunner of his race, and that he was elevated to the status of god by the ignorant people of the times.

Evidence seems to indicate that Pan was only the first of a great many of these half-goat, half-human, beings, which existed contemporaneously with the centaurs. They were apparently highly sexed little creatures, even more so than the centaurs, and today, in many languages, their name – satyr – denotes a lecherous and lascivious person. They could possibly have existed even up to the second century of our era, for Pausanias, in his *Guide to Greece* repeats a curious story, related to him by a sailor named Euphemos. This sailor and his ship were blown off course onto an island inhabited by a great many of these satyrs. As soon as they noticed the ship, says Pausanias, ". . . they ran down to it and without saying a word began to grab the women. The sailors were so frightened that they threw down one of the barbarian women they had with them and she was raped by the satyrs not only in the usual place but all over her body." - Pausanias, I:23,7.

The satyrs evidently inherited every bit of a goat's lecherous and lascivious tendencies. Unlike the centaurs who lapsed only occasionally into unbridled frenzy, the satyrs were perpetually in a state of sexual arousal. They could not so much as look at a woman without experiencing an instantaneous erection. Even more than the centaurs they would pursue their natural inclinations without the least regard to circumstances or time and place. For this reason satyrs were never accepted into society and the family of humankind. To invite satyrs to a wedding or other social gathering where females would be present was unthinkable. Therefore, they lived mostly on the

106

fringes of civilization, in the woods and mountains.

Since they were a rather small race, unintelligent and disorganized, their frequent attacks on women rarely met with success. Still, women hated and feared them, although most men looked upon them with amusement and contempt. They were not a handsome race, being hairy all over, hook-nosed and beady-eyed. The satyr women were also rather unprepossessing, with rubbery, pendulous breasts and round shoulders, their homely faces enframed within a tangled mass of stringy hair that resembled dirty strands of thick yarn.

Some of the myths say that Pan was fathered by Hermes on Amaltheia. Amaltheia! Such a tender and caressing name, evoking the image of a golden-haired damsel; a smooth-limbed nymph of flowery meadows. But actually, Amaltheia was a nanny goat. This is one of the considerations that casts doubt on Pan's godly nature.

Because, why would the god Hermes, who could take his pick of the loveliest maids fair earth had to offer want to make love to a nanny goat? The most likely answer is that it was not Hermes but merely a priest of Hermes, who had assumed the name of the god he served, as was the custom in those times. Such as in the example of the Roman emperor Heliogabalus, who had once been a priest of the god Helius in Syria, and thereafter assumed his name. Or as in the case of the Priest Topiltzin, of ancient Mexico, who assumed the name of his god, Quetzalcoatl, thereby originating great confusion, not only among modern scholars but even among the ancient Mexicans themselves.

Perhaps the goat Amaltheia was named thus by this lecherous priest of Hermes, who was in love with some lovely maiden of that name in a nearby village, and who would murmur the name passionately as he caressed the smelly goat.

On this matter of the true nature of Amaltheia, however, the ancient myths seem a little ambiguous and confusing, since she is also described as a goat-nymph, and as foster mother to Zeus. His mother, Rhea, had entrusted him to Amaltheia's care because his father, Cronus, had developed the distressing habit of swallowing his children whole as soon as they were born. Such vile behavior should not surprise anyone. Cronus, we may recall, had castrated his own father, and these children he was swallowing he was fathering on his own sister. Some sort of incestuous curse seems to have been Rhea's lot, because when her son Zeus grew into manhood he repaid her maternal affection by violating her. She turned herself into a snake, trying to escape him, but he turned himself into a snake too, and raped her that way. His own mother. The

107

evilness of these ancient gods sometimes boggles the mind.

But Zeus also had certain commendable qualities. In gratitude to Amaltheia for nursing him as a child, he later placed her image among the stars as the constellation of Capricorn, the goat. He also made one of her horns into the cornucopia, or horn of plenty. These two details should dispel all doubt as to Amaltheia's true nature: She was nothing more nor less than a common nanny goat.

More evidence that Pan was not really a god can be seen in the fact that there were so many different versions as to his paternity and his birth. Some said that he was a child of Hermes and Dryope; or of Hermes and the nymph Oeneis. When the emperor Tiberius made inquiries as to Pan's origins, scholars at his court informed him that he was a son of Hermes and Penelope, according to Plutarch in his *Why Oracles Are Silent*. Still another version said that he was fathered on Penelope by the swarm of suitors that nearly ate her out of house and home in the years before Odysseus finally returned from his wanderings.

The fact that this last version of the myth exists, by the way (if the reader will allow me to digress still further), indicates that Penelope was not the chaste, virtuous wife she is traditionally depicted to have been, waiting with stoic faith and patience for her husband to return. Indeed, if the suitors had been as unwelcome as she pretended they were, she could have simply ordered them out of her home. But did she? No. Instead, she wove a tapestry during the day, putting out the word that when it was finished she would choose one of the suitors to be her husband. At night, however, she would undo what she had wove during the day – not, as Homer tries to make us believe, because she had no other way of rejecting the suitors, but because she wanted all of them to hang around and entertain her. She was having a great time, and wanted it to last as long as possible.

To further buttress our theory upon the true nature of Pan, there is the intriguing section found in Plutarch's aforementioned essay, *Why Oracles Are Silent*, in which he reports the death of that god. Isn't it strange that of all the Greek gods, only Pan was ever reported to have died, and that many people apparently accepted the report as true? I say that this is only because he was never a god in the first place. In short, all of the foregoing can serve as further proof that Pan was simply another product of interbreeding between man and beast, and that the race of satyrs were Pan's descendants.

And finally, before we conclude with this subject of the origin of the satyrs, which some readers might find disagreeable and in poor taste, here is another curious little detail from Herodotus, a detail with some possible relevance to my entire speculative hypothesis of interspecies breeding, and specifically, to the hypothesis of interbreeding between humans and goats: In his description of the Egyptian province of Mendes Herodotus says, "In this province recently, a goat tupped a woman in full view of everybody – a most surprising incident."

End of Chapter Eight of
A Short History of the Centaurs

CHAPTER ELEVEN

Once Crotus put the idea of becoming a ferryman in my head, my mind was made up. That's the way a centaur was. We were impulsive and, as a general rule, not inclined to reflective prudence. I began to secretly plan my move to the Avenus River. Even though the prospect made me somewhat uneasy. It would be cold there in the winter. The surrounding countryside at the Avenus River was flat, with no caves or other type of shelter. To leave my cave and my mountains would be much like a deer leaving its wooded glens and dells to graze in broad daylight on open meadows, or not unlike a triton forsaking the sea to live on dry land.

I would have to build a house, of course; this was necessarily an integral part of my plan. But that would take some time, and in the meantime I would be like a turtle without its shell. Especially since, as I have already mentioned, centaurs didn't wear clothes, and I would be totally exposed to every inclemency of weather.

In this regard, Daphne often asks me pointed questions about my existence as a centaur. "If you always went naked," she asked me the other day, "didn't it get cold for you in the winter?"

But I pointed out to her the example of certain cold lands, such as Patagonia, where the Indians go about almost naked. People can become inured to the inclemencies of weather. We centaurs did occasionally don a sheepskin cloak in the coldest days of winter. But we felt silly going around dressed only from the waist up. Our nakedness was, I suppose, a concession we made to our equine half. A horse has a natural impatience towards clothing of any kind, be it a saddle blanket or whatever, and so, by keeping our human half free of all covering we also kept peace between our two natures. Although the Centaur Phaeocomes often wore a sort of caparison, which covered him from his human neck to his horse's hocks, a fact Ovid knew and recorded over a thousand years later.

I should mention at this point that in later references I or Nessus the Centaur might make to a shirt, we are really speaking of what nowadays is called a tunic. Everybody wore one back in those days, even an occasional centaur such as Phaeocomes. It was a simple garment with short sleeves, worn belted around the waist, and that reached to just above the knees. Even Hercules wore one, although he always wore a lion skin over it. This lion skin was from some scrawny creature he had killed in Nemea, one of the last surviving lions from the last ice age, I think.

Our nakedness was one of the reasons the Greeks held us in such contempt. It was evidence of our primitive nature, they said, and our savageness. A good part of their attitude was based on envy. The Greek women envied the buxom loveliness of our women, who proudly and nonchalantly flaunted their naked breasts before Greek men. And the Greek men envied the marble - sculptured perfection of the centaur's muscular body, resenting the fact that in our double nature of man and horse we could freely wander around naked, sometimes with our organ fully tumescent, safe from the imputation of indecent exposure which such behavior would surely carry if we had been fully human.

Sometimes it would make the Greeks angry when our organ would involuntarily become erect in the presence of their women. Here, again, envy had a lot to do with this attitude. Our penile configuration and sheer size was so superior to theirs. But the Greeks were obliged to concede that it would be impractical for us to wear any kind of garment that would conceal our private parts.

More than once, by the way, I experienced an erection in Dejanira's presence. There was that first time I met her, as I have already mentioned, and another time that was particularly embarrassing. I had continued to look at her, trying, by holding her eyes with mine, to keep her from noticing it. But a deep blush had colored her cheeks. And after I had momentarily glanced away from her, I caught her staring at it, with an expression I can't define – whether revulsion or fascinated admiration, it's hard to say.

On one occasion on the trail to Hypata, when I and Agrius encountered Dejanira with a group of girls on their way to the shrine of Demeter, I had bantered and joked with the girls, and indulged the equine half of my nature by dancing and prancing around them, high-stepping fancily about, rearing and flashing my forelegs in the air; all the while observing Dejanira out of the corner of my eye. All the other girls had laughed and clapped their hands in approval, their admiration perhaps equally divided between the sculptured perfection of my muscular upper body and the magnificence of the sleek and powerful horse it was melded to. But Dejanira had only stood unsmilingly by with her usual look of gravity and decorum.

Was not her appearance of gravity somewhat forced? I later asked myself. Was she finding it hard to hide the admiration she felt for me – or at least for my equine half?

Maybe that little fit of exhibitionism – that equestrian display – was a grave error on my part, if winning the admiration of Dejanira had been its purpose. Perhaps it only called her attention more fixedly upon the enormous differences between us. But no, it had not been an error. It had only been a manifestation of the equine half of my nature, which I was powerless to suppress. And my passion for Dejanira, on the other hand, was a manifestation of my human half, which I was also powerless to vanquish.

Yes, it was a heavy burden I took upon my shoulders the day I fell in love with Dejanira.

Just as the centaurs were always attracted to Greek women, the centauress also felt drawn to Greek men. I should explain a little more fully on the reasons for this. The centaur, his existence ruled by his human psyche, always felt somewhat removed from his equine half. We were basically human beings – human beings with a deformity, if you will. And, just as a deformed person will not feel drawn to other persons with the same deformity, so it was with the centaur. Dwelling in the back of the centaur mind – of both males and females – there was always the same aesthetic longing. Moreover, where lovemaking between male and female centaur was concerned, a disquieting knowledge was ever present: We were human beings, and yet the performance of the act involved the interaction of a mare's vagina and a horse's organ. This consideration always hovered over all instances of lovemaking between centaur and centauress and tainted with its uncomfortable aura our marital relationships. This, by the way, was one of the reasons for the low birth rate of centaurs and an important contributing factor to their eventual extinction. The centaur's attraction towards humans of the opposite sex was therefore not something unnatural.

113

* * * * * *

Returning to this matter of nudity . . . the ancient Greeks were just as prudish about the naked human body as is modern civilized man. You don't have to take my word for it. There's plenty of evidence in ancient writings showing that, far from considering the naked human body as something quite natural and nothing to get excited about (as one might be drawn to surmise from the abundance of naked sculptures from those times), the ancient Greek would go positively agog with lust and excitement at the sight of a naked body of the opposite sex. And women were no less averse to allowing strangers a view of their naked bodies than are women today.

In Herodotus, for example, there is that story of how the wife of Candaules, last Heraclid king of Lydia, had him murdered because Candaules had arranged to have his friend Gyges view her stark naked as she prepared for bed. She had caught sight of him as he scurried away from behind the door where he had been hiding, and immediately guessed at the truth. She had him brought to her by her most trusted guards and told the frightened man he had two choices: to kill Candaules and take her as his wife or to be struck dead on the spot. "One of you must die," she said. "Either the king, the author of this wicked plot, or you, who have outraged all propriety by seeing me naked."

After some agonizing deliberation Gyges chose to live. The queen hid him behind the same door he had used before when he had seen her in her birthday suit and that night while Candaules slept, his life came to an untimely end. That was the thanks he got from his ungrateful wife for being so struck with her beauty he felt he just had to display her to his friends. Perhaps he was so smitten with her loveliness that sometimes he couldn't believe his good fortune and sought outside confirmation of what his senses told him.

This little episode from Herodotus' *Histories* gives us an idea of the attitude towards nudity in ancient times. In the Greek myths there are other stories which carry this same theme - the harsh punishment meted out to some unfortunate personage or other, who had sought to innocently regale his eyeballs with the spectacle of a naked female shape.

Many of these stories were told around the centaur camp fires at

114

night, sometimes by an occasional Greek who would happen to be passing through our mountains. I remember one time when Nestor was visiting Cheiron, and several of us had congregated there to listen to the gossip he brought from the surrounding Greek world. Nestor was still a relatively young man at the time, but already as garrulous as he was in his old age.

He brought news of what had happened to Leucippus, a young man many of us had known. This boy had fallen in love with Daphne; a futile and fruitless passion, because Daphne, as I mentioned earlier, would not even have sex with Apollo himself.

Since he couldn't get near her, because she would run away, Leucippus had latched onto the idea of disguising himself as a girl, so he could tag along with Daphne and all the mountain nymphs when they held their moonlight revels. And then, having gone this far, he also joined them one day when they went swimming naked in a mountain stream. He pretended he couldn't bathe that day – because he wasn't feeling well, or it was his period or something – and he just stood around with his clothes on, his eyes bugging out of their sockets as he looked at their naked bodies. He took to doing this every day, although the nymphs were probably puzzled as to why he would never actually join them in the water.

But Apollo (Nestor said) became furiously jealous. One day he suggested to the nymphs that whenever they bathed they should insist that all of them disrobe, to make sure that everyone present was a woman. This made them prick up their ears. What on earth could Apollo be hinting at, they asked themselves. Their suspicions fully aroused, they followed his advice. The next time they were bathing, they all took off their clothing, as usual. And as usual, Leucippus kept his on while he stood by, devouring them all with his eyes, especially the luscious and virginal Daphne.

But now, having been forewarned, the nymphs could immediately see that something wasn't quite right about this supposed maiden. For one thing, beneath the feminine robes there was a tent-pole-like projection between the legs . . . They surrounded him and asked him to take off his clothes. He tried to make an excuse. They grabbed him by the arms and legs and began to rip off his feminine robes, immediately revealing him for what he was. They continued to

115

rip until they had torn Leucippus himself limb from limb and scattered his pieces over the mountainside. That's how mad they were at having been seen naked by a man.

We all sorrowed to hear of the tragic fate of Leucippus. He had been a good kid, a friend of the centaurs. We commented about it in bemused wonder for a while, condemning the mountain nymphs for their cruelty. What harm had been done them, just because he had seen them all naked?

And then Nestor reminded us of the equally tragic end of Actaeon, and of Erymanthus. These two had gone even further than Leucippus, because they had intruded upon the sacred privacy of goddesses, Actaeon with Artemis, and Erymanthus with Aphrodite.

Actaeon had been hunting on the mountainside with his pack of dogs, when he heard the sounds of Artemis with a group of nymphs as they bathed. Actaeon, guided by their laughter and the pleasant sound of splashing water, crept up on them. What a spectacle met his eyes when he peered through the undergrowth ringing the pool! There was the radiant goddess of the hunt herself, in all her gloriously lovely nakedness, and surrounded by a bevy of equally naked nymphs.

He thrust his head and face through the underbrush to better take in the view. So enthralled was he at the sight that he never thought to conceal himself. In fact, he even whooped out in glee, going "Woo, woo! look at them titties!"

His eyes were popping out of their sockets, and a lecherous grin distended his slack, drooling jaws. The nymphs let out a concerted shriek of alarm and tried to cover the goddess with their own bodies. But Artemis took it calmly. Scooping up some water in her cupped hands she walked slowly towards Actaeon. She made not the slightest effort to conceal any part of her body. Rather, she afforded him a full frontal view, swaying her hips slightly as she walked towards him. Actaeon's eyes were still bugging out of their sockets and he continued to grin as he made coarse and ribald remarks. The goddess stopped a scant two feet away and stood there for a long moment, her cool eyes surveying him with a distant expression.

A vague feeling of unease swept over Actaeon; he continued to grin, but in a mechanical way, and something now made him blink rapidly in nervousness. Then Artemis splashed the water over his head

116

and said, "Now go and tell whoever you may wish that you saw me naked."

The next thing Actaeon knew, he had been transformed into a stag. Filled with sudden panic he wheeled about and fled down the mountain, with his pack of hounds in hot pursuit. It would almost be funny, except that the knowledge of what happened when his hounds caught him stifles the initial impulse towards laughter.

Erymanthus was blinded by Aphrodite under similar circumstances. He had accidentally stumbled upon her as she bathed stark naked in a pool on Mount Erymanthus, named thus in his memory in later years. And the famous seer Teiresias met the same Fate at the hands of Athene. He, too, had seen her naked by accident. One would think that the experience of Artemis and Aphrodite would have taught her to be more careful. When Teiresias' mother begged Athene not to do that to her son, the goddess told her that there was an unalterable law that no human must ever see a goddess naked without suffering the consequences. But she gave Teiresias inward sight – the gift of prophecy – as compensation.

We all agreed that Actaeon got what he had coming. It was the height of blasphemy to look at a god's nakedness. We didn't dare speak up and say what was secretly in our hearts – that those goddesses, the same as the nymphs who had torn Leucippus limb from limb, had been guilty of unwarranted cruelty. And besides, in the case of Aphrodite, plenty of mortal men had seen her naked before, and she had never made such a big deal of it. A guy named Anchises had fornicated her to the point of satiety, for example. But it wasn't safe in those days to say anything disrespectful about the gods.

Anchises had learned this the hard way. A friend said to him once, "Wouldn't you rather make love to the daughter of So-and-so than to Aphrodite herself?"

And Anchises had nonchalantly answered , "Oh, I don't know; I've fucked 'em both, so I find that a hard question to answer."

Zeus overheard the blasphemous words and blasted him with a thunderbolt, making a cripple of him for the rest of his life. Which was the reason his son Aeneas, whose mother was Aphrodite herself, had to pack him out of burning Troy on his back a generation later.

* * * * * *

The circumstances surrounding the death of Actaeon and the blinding of Erymanthus are well known, which is the reason I have skimmed over them so briefly. But an interesting and little known detail connected to the death of Actaeon, besides the fact that he was reared and educated by the Wise Centaur Cheiron, is that the names of many of the hounds that massacred him have survived in history and are known today because they were recorded in written accounts by the ancient authors. According to Ovid they had names such as Melampus, Ichnobates, Pamphagus, Dorceus, Oribassus, Nebrophonus, Theron, Laelaps.... He names thirty-two and says there were others it would take too long to name. A veritable swarm of hell-hounds, and they must have made short work of Actaeon in stag form when they caught him. Poetic justice, perhaps, because no doubt he had gleefully followed this same savage pack many times, to preside over the slaughter of many an innocent beast of mountains and forest.

It's curious that the names of common curs should be thus immortalized, when many a deserving human, who would sell his soul to the devil for a like honor, goes down to his death in total obscurity. Hyginus says that after they had torn Actaeon to shreds they went howling to Cheiron's cave, missing their master sorely. The wise centaur cleverly hit on the idea of making a wooden image of Actaeon, Hyginus says, with which he consoled them. But I know that Hyginus is mistaken or has invented the story. Cheiron would never have welcomed such a pack of hellhounds into his presence. All centaurs hated dogs, and had no use for them whatsoever. Anyone could guess at this when we remember the tendency of dogs to chase after hoofed animals such as cows and horses, barking and snapping at their heels.

The name Laelaps, by the way, which appears in the list of Acteon's dogs, was also the name of the magical dog given to Procris by Minos. This hound, the fastest canine in creation, divinely fated to always catch whatever it chased, and an equally magical javelin, which never missed its mark, had been given to Minos by Artemis and he in turn gave these incalculably valuable gifts to Procris in exchange for some sex. Minos had to pay dearly for any female companionship because he was afflicted with a curse laid on him by his wife Pasiphae: Every time he had sex with a woman he would discharge, instead of seed, a swarm of ants, scorpions, spiders and centipedes. This made his love-making extremely unpleasant. Procris was aware of this and she got around it by first making him drink a potion brewed for her by the witch Circe. This cleared up Minos' little venereal problem temporarily.

Afterwards, Procris hurried happily off with her dog and javelin, and used them to win back the affections of her husband, Cephalus, who had deserted her because of her loose ways. Artemis, however, didn't like the way her valuable gifts were being swapped around for sex, and in a typical reaction – for the gods of those days – she laid a curse on Cephalus and Procris, instead of on Minos, who had started the whole thing. One day Cephalus went out at earliest dawn, while it was still dark, for a hunt with the dog and the javelin. Procris, thinking he was keeping an assignation with the goddess Eos, with whom he had had an affair in the past, sneaked after him in the dark. He heard a rustle in the brush. Thinking it was a wild animal, he flung the javelin which never missed its mark, and killed his beloved wife.

The dog Laelaps also came to an unfortunate end. A sorrowing Cephalus, trying to forget his tragedy, joined Amphitryon at Thebes where they tried to capture the Teumessian vixen, a creature inflicted on the land by Themis. The Teumessian vixen had been divinely fated never to be caught, so when it was chased by the dog divinely fated to always catch its quarry, a great commotion was stirred up in Olympus, with various of the gods each clamoring to have the divine fate of their animal upheld. Zeus finally resolved the conflict by turning both dog and vixen into stone.

* * * * * *

But, to continue with this subject of nudity in ancient and modern times, to more fully address Daphne's skepticism: Today scattered groups here and there around the world propound nudity as a way of life, arguing that it is Mother Nature's natural way. But these advocates of nudity forget that most of the world's creatures are naturally clothed in either feathers or thick hair. Except for certain repellant species, such as snakes, frogs, lizards . . . but in these naked creatures, it will be observed, their private parts do not obtrude. The procreative organs are hidden discreetly away within the body. Even so, these naked creatures are almost universally detested.

Now, in the human male, the sexual organ is of course always visible. A man cannot prudently retract his organ out of sight into his

119

body, as reptiles naturally do. So, when the processes of mutation brought the first hairless humans into the world, they were immediately faced with a problem. The first communities of hairless humans functioned in the same manner as all other animal societies, divided into more or less small groups ruled by a dominant male. What prerogatives devolve upon the dominant male in any animal societal group? Principally, it is the first choice in the right to mate with the most desirable females (which in such societies means *all* females). It was no different in the early history of *Homo desnudis*, to coin a term for the first hairless humans. The males in the lower echelons of these groups had to tread carefully to avoid friction with the dominant male, behaving always with meekness and docility. The problem was that, with the female parts glaringly visible, many normally submissive males experienced that natural male propensity when in the proximity of such a sight – that is, an erection of the virile member, a most un-submissive reaction. This would result in an immediate mauling from the dominant male, furious that any low-class male would dare get an erection in the presence of his females. Then, some clever individual in one of these early hominid societies hit upon the idea of tying a piece of stiff hide around his waist, to conceal any such manifestation, and thereby escape the dangerous attention of the dominant male. Thus, the first clothing was born. Across the centuries, the trend grew and continued, gradually taking hold upon even the dominant males, as a semblance of fairness and equality subtly spread its mask upon the façade of human relations, so that today it is largely accepted that humans, and especially human males, must never expose the procreative organ.

Besides nudity, another facet of natural behavior forbidden to civilized man is the display stratagems utilized by many of Mother Nature's creatures to attract a mate. Like the chameleon and other lizards, which flash a brilliantly colored fold of skin on their throats, Peacocks and some other birds will spread their fabulous tails, puff themselves up, and strut about, to the immense admiration of the females of their species. Fireflies find a mate by flashing their phosphorescent tail to advertise their presence and availability.

Man has no brilliant throat skin, or pretty feathers, or phosphorescent tail to flash. But still, some men occasionally feel

120

impelled to resort to "flashing," perhaps driven by the residue of some primordial instinct. These individuals will prowl the streets of a city, dressed only in an overcoat and the cut-off legs of a pair of trousers, held up just above the hemline of the overcoat with a pair of elastic bands. At what they deem appropriate moments they will suddenly, and without warning, fling open the flaps of the overcoat to flash their private parts into full view – perhaps to a bus load of school-children, or to a young lady on an escalator, or to a little old lady walking her dog. (An interesting parallel can be seen between the gecko lizard's distension of his throat skin, and the "flasher's" distension of the flaps of his overcoat.)

These tactics, however, rarely produce the desired effect of winning them a mate, if that is truly what these disturbed persons are seeking. They fail to recognize that most human females do not regard the male organ as beautiful. The flasher's unformulated reasoning seems to be that, just as a flower, which is the sexual organ of a plant, is beautiful, so must his own organ also be beautiful. But the sight of a male organ, far from awakening in a chaste woman the desire to place a bouquet of them in a vase, to gaze upon them delectably as she does with flowers, will more than likely move her to disgust. It may seem like an injustice of mother nature to the flasher, but no doubt mother nature knew what was best. Because, if sex organs had been endowed with the same aesthetic beauty as in the fragile beauty of flowers, how long could they have remained so? With all the world proudly showing off their private parts, thrusting them in each other's faces, a point of satiety would quickly have been reached. I, Jonathan Nestus, have done a lot of reflective thinking on all this.

So, behavior that aids the gecko lizard in finding a mate, results in imprisonment and humiliation for the subspecies of *Homo sapiens* we might classify as *Homo flasheriensis*. If apprehended, he is summarily hauled off to jail. And something curious can be observed thereafter – something which to my knowledge has not been previously commented upon by scholars: the measure of the punishment meted out to him by the courts bears a direct relationship to the degree to which his display was effective. For example, if the flasher's genitalia is large and prominent he will receive a harsher sentence than if it is stunted or rudimentary. The courts of law have subtle and mostly unconscious

121

ways of determining these circumstances. But in a recent case in Sandusky, Ohio, the prosecutor openly brought out before the bench the fact that the accused had a "gross erection" at the time of the offense. This unfortunate flasher received a stiff sentence. Another case in Pennsylvania, on the other hand, involved an eighty-five year old man, whose display had been rather pathetic. He drew only barely concealed smiles and probation.

Someone should make a deep study of all this. Possibly, profound implications could be derived that would contribute to a better understanding of Man and his place in the universe.

To conclude with this interesting subject, the centaur, thanks to his ambiguous nature, could freely indulge in flashing, strolling nonchalantly about stark naked, sometimes with a "gross erection," while he made bold eye contact with women.

* * * * * *

But I was telling about my plans for my ferry business. Though I had been reluctant to reveal my intentions, I eventually let the secret out – though not my reasons for wanting to do it. The news caused a bit of a stir among the centaur community at Oeta, and they even heard about it at Mount Pelion, and at Pholoe. I had to take a great deal of annoying ribbing and joking about it. Everyone began to call me Nessus The Ferryman. And everyone asked me, "Why are you going to do that?" But no one guessed at the truth. Crotus knew, of course, and Ocyrhöe had an idea, but they were good friends and they kept my secret.

122

CHAPTER TWELVE

One day, while still engaged in preparations for my move to the Avenus River, I heard that Hercules was away, gone to faraway Mount Atlas on that famous labor of the golden apples. Here was my chance, I immediately decided. I must go to Calydon and try to see Dejanira. I had been mooning and daydreaming about her long enough. It was time to do something.

It was said those apples that Hercules had gone to fetch grew on a tree which had been given to Hera as a wedding gift by Mother Earth. Hera had planted it on the slopes of Mount Atlas, entrusting its guardianship to the Hesperides, daughters of the Titan Atlas. But later on, when she discovered that those girls were snitching apples off the tree, she set the dragon Ladon as watchman.

At the time Hercules set off on this labor I shared that common belief – that the golden apples grew on a single tree, located at the ends of the earth. Later, I came to the realization that the golden apple trees actually grew on rocky headlands on not-so-distant seashores. There, gnarled and stunted across hundreds of years of their existence, nourished by the dashing foam and sea spray, they were somehow able to extract the gold which is present in all sea water, to convert it into apples with a golden crust which enclosed the edible core. But the tree was so rare, and its fruit so sought after by greedy humans, plucking the apples before they had a chance to go to seed, that it became extinct.

When we stop to think about it, there is really nothing so incredible about a tree growing golden apples. Isn't an ordinary apple tree and its fruit just as remarkable? It springs out of the barren earth, extracting, in its own mysterious way, nutrients from earth, air and water, to convert them into something totally unlike its origins. Of course, since the gold in sea water exists in such minute quantities, golden apples were somewhat small, and each tree produced only three or four. Also, a tree took hundreds of years to bear fruit. Certain

123

interested parties, anxious to guard the true secret of where the golden apple trees grew, had propagated the false information that it was one lone tree, that it grew on Mount Atlas, and that it was guarded by a sleepless dragon.

And to Mount Atlas was supposedly where Hercules had gone. But it was a lie. The cunning slob knew he didn't have to go that far. The sonofabitch had wandered over so much of the known world committing his crimes and atrocities that he probably knew where he could get some relatively nearby. He returned in less than two months, when I thought he would only be halfway to Mount Atlas, with three or four apples.

So I received an unpleasant surprise when I found him in the front yard of Dejanira's house, talking to her father Dexamenus. Two other suitors were arriving at the same time as I, and they, too, were unpleasantly surprised. They didn't stay long, quickly finding an excuse to hurry away. They knew that with Hercules present it was not only a waste of time but dangerous as well. Me, though I was somewhat taken aback, I didn't leave. Hercules hadn't spotted me as I approached, and I headed towards the back of the house. It had been a long hard trot from Mount Oeta, my quiver and bow slung across my back, and my sleek coat was glistening with sweat. So I decided to give myself a hot-walk around the back yard, to relieve my sore muscles. Unexpectedly, I found Dejanira behind the house, sitting on a stone bench under an apple tree – an ordinary apple tree, of course, not a golden one – and I faltered in my walk, trying to think of something to say to her. We had never spoken to each other before. But she knew my name, from that time at the River Avenus, and other such occasions. Each time I had contrived for our paths to cross, I had noticed what I thought were her admiring glances – cool and reserved, but admiring, nevertheless. Though, to tell the truth, I could never be sure if she wasn't just admiring me as any person will admire a fine horse. My coat was a sleek and shiny raven's-wing black, making my silvery tail all the more remarkable, a combination to evoke the admiration of the most casual of horse-lovers. On the other hand, my rippling abdominal muscles and strong arms, though certainly not as thick and powerful as those of Hercules, were nevertheless nothing to be ashamed of, and could also have been the object of her admiration.

I stopped a scant ten feet from her. For a brief moment her violet eyes met mine and then she quickly averted her gaze. "Hello, Nessus," she said, in a soft and quiet voice. "You're a long way from home, aren't you?"

This was the first time she had ever spoken to me. How sweet the sound of my name on her lips! Long afterwards, as I mused alone in my cave or in the woods, I would repeat to myself, trying to evoke a living memory of her voice, "Hello, Nessus . . ."

Before I could answer Dejanira's greeting, Hercules appeared. Massive, brutish Hercules, his stinking lion's skin draped over his tunic, his ever-present bow and arrows slung across his broad shoulders, his brass-bound olive-wood club in hand.

Hercules was about forty years old at this time. He must have been close to four spans across at the shoulders, and his biceps were as thick as an ordinary man's thighs. The bow he used was so powerful that its string was nearly as thick as the arrows themselves, and it was said that his four-foot arrows could pierce a man clear through at a furlong.

The perpetual scowl on his face deepened menacingly when he saw me, and then he sneered, "Well, well, Nessus the Centaur. Looking for some sheep to steal?" And then he turned away from me to address Dejanira.

"And how is my little peachy-weechie? Look, I've brought you a golden apple." And he took one out of the sheepskin pouch slung across his shoulders. It was small and scrawny, as I have said they were, but definitely golden.

"I only found four of them," he said to Dejanira, "but King Eurystheus will have to be satisfied with just three."

"Why, thank you, Hercules," Dejanira said, taking the wondrous apple and turning it over admiringly in her hands. A hot flush coursed through my entire human body, overflowing even into my equine parts when I saw her direct her words and her attention to Hercules.

Then the brute, remembering that I was still standing there, intruding upon his private moment, snarled at me, "What the hell do *you* want, Nessus? Why don't you run along back to your cave? And on the way, keep your hands off Dexamenus's sheep, or you'll have me to answer to."

125

And he turned towards Dejanira to add, with a little sort of half-simpering, half-adulatory smirk, grossly incongruous on his surly face, "Dexamenus is going to be my father-in-law."

Dejanira blushed slightly at this remark, but otherwise showed no signs of annoyance, or any evidence of distaste for the gratuitous insults directed at me.

"Don't worry Hercules," I answered calmly, "I'm not here to steal sheep."

And then I added, in contrived innocence, "But how can Dexamenus become your father-in-law? I thought you were already married . . . to Megara." Pretending I didn't know he had murdered her and all his children.

I saw a horrible look of rage cross over Hercules' scowling features. He seemed to turn almost purple. The look would have frightened the most resolute of beings, and I must admit that my own courage almost failed me. But with Dejanira looking on retreat would have been unthinkable.

Slowly, he took the club off his shoulder, with a certain ominous deliberation, much as a poisonous serpent will slowly raise its head to strike. He advanced a step or two towards me, the look of rage giving way to a murderous calm. "You goddamned horse's ass. I'm going to teach you to bridle your tongue."

Horse's ass! He had called me a horse's ass! Those were fighting words for a centaur, and especially in front of Dejanira. At that moment I didn't care who Hercules was. "Put down that club, you murdering sonofabitch, and let's see who the horse's ass is."

Fortunately for me, at that moment Dexamenus came walking around from the front of the house. "Gentlemen, gentlemen," he said, interposing himself between us. "Let us not engage in fisticuffs in my yard. It would be highly improper." Dejanira intervened too. She said to me, in a tense and trembling voice that revealed her alarm, "Nessus, please go. Do not cause any trouble here."

* * * * * *

So that was the way this visit of mine ended. I never said anything to Dejanira nor to her father. I was consoled by the fact that Hercules did not accomplish anything either. No father was eager to give his daughter in marriage to him. The fate of Megara was ever

126

present as a disquieting thought. Dexamenus put Hercules off for the moment, I later learned, and they had agreed to talk it over some more, after Hercules had finished another task that Eurystheus had set him – to clean the filthy stables of King Augeias in Elis.

* * * * * *

When I woke up the next morning after that dream, I was still angry. I stayed angry all day. I went that evening to Daphne's home for a visit. She lives in a duplex with her divorced mother, who always stares at me in a perturbing, penetrating way, as if puzzled as to why her daughter ever became engaged to me. She asks me many uncomfortable questions, too, about my parents, and my education and profession, and so forth. She works as a clerk at a supermarket, and perhaps Daphne has given her hopes that a rich marriage is going to lift both of them out of their doldrums. Daphne doesn't encourage me to visit at her home, and it's just as well. Her mother makes me nervous.

They were watching the Miss Universe pageant. For an hour the stream of pathetic contestants minced across the screen, in their bathing suits and high heels, to announce, in flat, mechanical and unprepossessing voices, their names and places of origin.

Daphne's mother soon got up from her seat and went to bed. I began to tell Daphne of the first beauty contest ever, reminded of it by my previous night's dream of the golden apples. At first, Daphne showed interest.

The first beauty contest, I told her, was the Judgment of Paris, when he awarded the golden apple to the fairest. There had been only three contestants – Hera, Athene, and Aphrodite. These three, at the wedding of Peleus to the mermaid Thetis, had been standing together, chatting idly, with Peleus standing nearby, when Eris, the spiteful sister of Ares, angry because someone had forgotten to invite her to the wedding, had rolled a golden apple, with the inscription, "To the fairest," at his feet.

Peleus picked it up, intending to give it to whomever it was intended, but then found himself in a quandary when he read the inscription.

The three goddesses began to squabble over the apple, each claiming it as her own. It wasn't the intrinsic value of the apple they were interested in. Golden apples were a dime a dozen to the gods back

127

in those days. They were only seeking that satisfaction that even the ugliest of women derive from being told they are beautiful. They didn't really give a fig for the apple itself.

The quarrel apparently lasted for several years, until Zeus got fed up with it and appointed Paris as judge, to settle the matter once and for all. And Paris, dazzled by Aphrodite's promise to get him Helen for a wife, never mind that she was already married, awarded her the prize. When the winner was announced, Aphrodite let out a shriek, pretending to be totally surprised. She cupped her hands over her nose and her mouth, the way all women do when they are surprised, or pretending to be, and her face took on that contorted look all women adopt when they receive good news, which seems to be a mingling of joy and anguish. At that moment she actually looked ugly. Today, all beauty contest winners still faithfully follow the tradition and react in exactly the same way.

This Judgment of Paris shows the inherent evil in beauty contests, I said to Daphne, for this one became the underlying cause of the Trojan war. And one can see how the quality of the contestants in these things has sadly deteriorated over the centuries. From the splendorous, luscious, and dazzling beauty of those Olympian goddesses, we now have these cheap floozies from Birmingham, Alabama and every other sordid corner of the world, many of whom, far from being beautiful, are actually ugly. They are hard-faced and dull-eyed; proclaiming their places of origin with peculiarly repellent voices; attracting a second look only because of their high heels and bathing suits.

"Eighty-two of the most beautiful women in the world!" the master of ceremonies was saying. What a joke.

"Look, if you don't enjoy watching this, just shut up and let me watch," Daphne said, having lost all interest in my story. "What are you so bitter about, anyway?"

I told her that in my dream the previous night Hercules had called me a horse's ass.

She gave me that look she's been bestowing on me so much lately, fraught with the implication of lost marbles and loose screws, but then she said, "Well, don't let it bother you. You'll have your revenge. You said that this Crotus guy prophesied that you were going to kill

128

Hercules."

Daphne has forgotten, if I have ever told her, the way in which I kill Hercules, which is not something to look forward to.

* * * * * *

I'm beginning to feel an increasing terror at what I know is going to happen. Every night upon going to bed I wonder if it will be the last day in the life of Nessus. There's no way of knowing, because the accounts to be found in mythology are not necessarily exact. The true event can vary in many ways. Sometimes I feel ashamed of my cowardice. Nessus himself is unafraid. He knows the great danger there is in trying to take a woman away from Hercules, but this doesn't stop him. He continues doggedly on his course.

Nessus can afford to act bravely, however. He doesn't really know what's going to happen. But me, I know what's going to happen. And my dreams are so realistic, something so entirely lifelike, that I can feel every little scratch, every little bruise that I experience in that other life. So I know that that arrow in my back is going to hurt like hell.

But maybe things can be changed. Maybe someday I can wake up in this world and find that the past is different. Maybe the past is not immutable. Maybe, knowing what that past is, I can warn Nessus. Maybe someday the knowledge I hold today can make its way into his mind in some way, and things will turn out differently.

* * * * * *

That night, before going to bed, I wrote with a ballpoint pen on the back of my hand, "Nessus, Jonathan Nestus brings you greetings from the twenty-first century. Beware the arrow of Hercules at the Avenus River." I tried to write out a fuller warning, but soon ran out of space.

CHAPTER THIRTEEN

Not long after that run-in with Hercules at Dejanira's house, I went to the Avenus river with Agrius. I wanted to scout out the exact location for my ferry business. Hercules was away again on another of his labors, bringing Eurystheus the man-eating mares of Diomedes, and I was hoping to maybe run into Dejanira again. I had been visiting her house but always Dejanira would be inside, refusing to come out, or other suitors would be present, and I had never screwed up the courage to actually declare my intentions to her father.

It was a forty mile journey to the Avenus, and Agrius and I trotted easily along, chatting upon various topics to pass the time as we ate up the miles.

"What are those strange marks on the back of your hand?" Agrius asked me at one point.

I glanced at my hand and saw that there were indeed some mysterious marks on it. I hadn't noticed them before and had no idea what they were or what had made them. I studied them for long moments. "It almost seems to be writing of some sort," I said, "but if so, it's not in Greek. The Greeks don't write like this at all.

"Maybe it's the way the Hyperboreans write," Agrius said, "those people who dwell beyond the one-eyed Arimaspians, who steal the gold of the griffins. Or maybe it's a message from some god or other. Sometimes the gods will do that. They leave their messages here on earth, writ on rocks, or carried on the wind, or in whatever way they got handy, and only the most accomplished of seers can interpret them."

I continued to pore over the marks for a long while, wondering if they could perhaps be a divine message – maybe from Aphrodite herself – telling me that Dejanira would love me forever. But Agrius soon shrugged off the problem, embarking on other tangential speculations about the Hyperboreans, the one-eyed Arimaspians, the griffins, and their fabulous hoard of gold.

"You and me ought to 'ride' north," he said, to that land beyond

131

the North Wind, and load ourselves up with some of that gold. We could buy up half the wine in Greece."

He paused for a moment to consider his own words. "But it gets awfully cold up there, they say. It snows continuously, day and night. We'd freeze our horses' asses off there. There's easier ways to get wine, I guess.

"Speaking of which, I don't understand why you want to have a steady job. I get by just fine myself without ever doing a lick of work. We get plenty of meat hunting deer and wild pigs, and borrowing a sheep now and then. The woods and meadows are full of mallow and mushrooms in the spring. Why should any centaur ever work?"

"Well," I hedged, "it *is* good to be able to have other things now and then."

"Like what?" Agrius insisted. "We don't need to build or buy a house. We don't need money for clothes, like the Greeks do . . . Oh, maybe it would be nice to be able to buy a jug of wine whenever we wanted some, but hey, man, a smart centaur can always get his hands on a skinful if he uses his noodle. Which reminds me, Hippodameia and Peirithous are getting married, and they've invited all the centaurs. The wine's going to be flowing like water there, man."

Agrius had a small skin of wine slung over his shoulder on a thong, and some bread and goat's cheese. He took the wine off his shoulder now and passed it to me. "Here, drink up. I got this wine without having to lift a finger for it. No toting Greeks across no river on *my* back. Unless it's a pretty young girl or woman, of course. But everyone to his own opinions, I always say."

We went at a leisurely trot, breathing in the fresh spring odors of the countryside, enjoying the songs of thrushes and larks that filled the air. The meadows we passed through were splashed with the dazzling colors of flowers and soft grasses, thrusting their way out of the ground, free now from the cold grip of winter.

This reminded Agrius of the legend of how the seasons had originated, and he wanted to retell the entire story – of how Demeter had laid a curse on the earth, swearing nothing would ever grow again until her daughter Core, who had been kidnapped by Hades, was returned to her. She went up and down earth, forbidding all plants to grow, until the world turned bleak and lifeless. That was the first Fall and Winter. Things stayed that way until Zeus, alarmed to see the entire earth turning into a desert, finally intervened and worked out an agreement between Hades and Demeter. It was agreed that Core, now named Persephone while in the underworld, would stay with her gloomy husband for six months of the year and then return to the upper world for the other six.

When Core returned to the upper air after the first six months, the entire world celebrated. The grass thrust its blades above the earth; the trees grew new leaves; the birds and insects sang and buzzed with rejoicing. That was how the seasons began.

Whenever it's almost time for Core to return to earth, Agrius said, she and Hades start arguing about it. He greatly resents the deal he was forced to make, and when Persephone insists that he honor it, he becomes angry. One word leads to another, and next thing Persephone knows Hades is beating the hell out of her. That's how the expression "to beat the hell out of..." originated, Agrius said. Before Persephone can return to the upper world she must have the *Hell beat out* of her. This is what causes those early spring showers, those light drizzles which occur while the sun is still shining. That rain is Demeter's tears, who wrings her hands helplessly and weeps when she hears her daughter's shrieks of fright and pain.

This was an interesting new light cast upon an old story. But at the moment my mind was on other matters. Jason and the Argonauts had returned from Colchis with the golden fleece less than four years ago, and the voyage was still a subject of keen interest everywhere. There was something related to it that I found especially intriguing, and I wanted to talk with someone about it. Agrius had only recently returned to Oeta from a trip he had made to Mount Pelion, which was not far from Pagasae, where the voyage had begun and ended, and he was up-to-date on all the latest news on the matter. Agrius was an inveterate gossip, so he didn't need much prompting to launch into the subject and its varied ramifications.

"Did you know that Atalanta is pregnant?" he asked me. "Man, that woman sure does have some gall, claiming to be a virgin. I think Meleager was screwing her cross-eyed even before the voyage. Maybe all the Argonauts were screwing her. Maybe they passed her back and forth over the oars, and each guy took his turn."

133

Jason had gone to recover the golden fleece with many of the most renowned warriors of Greece. Castor and Polydeuces had gone with Jason, and so had Idas; Euphemus; Melampus; Mopsus the seer; Palaemon, who was a son of Hephaestus; Nauplius, who was a son of Poseidon; Meleager . . . Everyone who was famous, or thereafter became famous. And even a woman, Atalanta, who was still claiming to be a virgin. Even after she had a child, some time after the voyage, she was still trying to pass herself off as a maiden. Atalanta was not one of my favorite people. The vicious bitch had killed two centaurs I knew, Rhoecus and Hylaeus, claiming they had tried to rape her.

This wasn't the topic, however, that I was itching to talk about. Hercules had accompanied the Argonauts on the first stage of their voyage, even though he had recently begun the business of his imposed labors. But somehow or other he had been left behind when the Argo made a stop in Bithynia. He blamed the twins Calais and Zeetes for this, and he later killed them both when he came upon the Argonauts on the island of Tenos.

There, he somehow became involved with Medea . . . Medea, famous as a witch and sorceress, was the daughter of King Aeetes, from whom Jason stole the golden fleece. She was a niece of that other famous witch, Circe, sister of Aeetes, who lived on an island off the coast of Tyrhennia. Medea was unsurpassed in her knowledge of all manner of herbs and poisons. She got hot pants for Jason the moment she laid eyes on him, and she helped him take the golden fleece from the serpent that guarded it, with the understanding that he would take her with him back to Greece. She was a sly and cunning woman, as can be seen in the way she tricked the daughters of King Pelias into chopping up their father and boiling him in a large cauldron, under the belief that Medea was going to rejuvenate him. Pelias was the one who had sent Jason on the quest for the golden fleece, a task that he considered impossible, and a good way to get rid of him, because Jason was the legitimate heir to the kingdom.

"Tell me," I said to Agrius, "what's the latest scoop on Jason and Medea. Is it true he's left her for another woman?"

"Oh, yeah, it's true, all right. But let me tell you something. If you're going to marry a witch, you better be sure you're going to stay with her forever. Dumping an ordinary woman is bad enough, but if you ever dump a witch for another woman . . ."

Then he told me of how Medea had taken revenge by sending Jason's new wife, Glauce, a poisoned crown and robe. When Glauce put them on she had immediately been consumed in a fierce, bone-melting heat. "She jumped into a spring," Agrius said, "trying to stop the terrible pain, but the water only made it worse. They say that she even burst into flame, and the fire even burned down Jason's palace. He was lucky to get away alive."

I had already heard the story, but I let Agrius retell it all, as the thing I really wanted to talk about festered inside me. "I've heard," I finally said, "that afterwards Medea went to Tiryns to hide out, and that she stayed with Hercules for some time. He met her when he killed Calais and Zeetes in Tenos, I've heard tell, and at that time he offered to help her if she should ever be in need."

"Yeah, that's right," Agrius said. "She was so grateful to him for letting her hide out with him that she cured him of his madness. He went stark nuts once, you know, when he killed his wife and children."

"Well, I think she did something else for him. You know that Hercules uses a poison in his arrows now. And he started using it not long after Medea stayed with him. Don't you find that to be a curious coincidence?"

This talk of Hercules and Medea was beginning to make Agrius nervous. He knew how I felt about Hercules, and he also knew that gossiping about witches and maniacs like Hercules was a dangerous business. "Oh, I don't know," he answered evasively. "He says he dipped his arrows in the blood of that creature he killed in the Lernaean swamp, the Hydra, you know."

"That's a lot of bullshit," I answered. "I know all about how that poison of his works. They say that water only makes it worse, the same as the poison that killed Glauce. That poison is so potent and virulent that only a witch could have devised it. It causes a very cruel death, and they say it's indestructible. I've heard tell that it's activated by heat – even the warmth of blood, and it contaminates the blood, so that even the blood itself becomes poisonous. Hercules should die from that poison himself, the sonofabitch."

Agrius looked uneasily around him, as if fearing that someone would hear my words. "All you say could very well be," he said, in a low voice, "but you should be careful not to go around saying those things. You know how Hercules is." And then he went on in a normal voice, "I don't know why he wants to use poison in his arrows, anyway. He's such a deadly marksman. He has to be very careful never to scratch himself with one of his own arrows. And he can't use them to hunt game, of course."

     We came out of a patch of thick forest into a flowery meadow, covered with goldenrods, daffodils, and dandelions. Agrius sniffed appreciatively at the latter. "You can make some fine wine out of that stuff. After you've picked the site for your crossing we ought to gather some to take home. No sheep around this pasture today, I see. Charaxus usually grazes them here this time of year. He must have known we were coming."

     To our left a small group of satyrs suddenly emerged from the edge of the woods, heading in the same direction we were going. Our paths converged, and Agrius called out to one or two of them by name. Shifty and beady-eyed, with long hooked noses, looking down at the ground as if embarrassed, they mumbled an answer to our greeting as they trotted along on their long splayed hooves.

     We soon left them behind, and Agrius, looking back over his shoulder at them commented, "The horny little bastards are probably going to the river crossing hoping to catch a glimpse of some women crossing the river. Funny little creatures, those satyrs. Women can't stand the sight of 'em. They can't so much as look at a woman without getting a instantaneous hard-on, you know. You can't hardly blame the Greeks for hating 'em. Did you smell 'em? Man, do they stink!"

     I felt sorry for the satyrs, for being so universally despised. Even by centaurs, who weren't exactly perfect either.

     The Avenus was still high from the spring rains. It flowed swiftly over the rocky bottom, carrying along bits of debris and patches of foam. Several other travelers were passing through that day. This crossing was on the road to Trachis, Daulis and Delphi. We met several people on the bank, traveling from Calydon to Delphi. They were wringing out their clothes, having just crossed the waters. I let them know that I would be operating a ferry business there soon.

     Then, as those people were resuming their journey, two girls came along – Chloris and Iphinoe – and they asked Agrius and me to

136

cross them over. "There you go, Nessus," Agrius said, "you can start up your business right now."

I was embarrassed at this talk of charging Chloris and Iphinoe to carry them over. I felt myself blushing. "Oh, I wouldn't charge them anything today. That will be later, after I'm officially in business." Agrius whispered to me, "What's the matter with you? You gotta start charging a fee."

But I simply couldn't do it. It just didn't seem right. It almost seemed like taking a handout, which no centaur has ever done. It caused me a bit of worry, when I realized how hard it was going to be to do this job. But it was going to have to be done. Not on this day, though. There would be time, later, to harden my resolve, I told myself.

When Agrius saw that I had no intention of beginning my business yet, he said, "Okay, you carry one across and I'll carry the other. He grinned at both the girls, who were now giggling and whispering to each other. "Nessus isn't going to charge you, but any little thing you could slip us would be appreciated. You know what I mean?" he leered at them.

Chloris swung up onto his back, holding her bundle in one hand and grasping him around the waist with the other. He waded into the cold and waist-deep waters – waist-deep for a human being, that is – while Iphinoe gathered up her little bundle and mounted sidesaddle on my back.

Having carried Iphinoe across, I returned to the other bank. I left Agrius alone with the girls, cajoling and wheedling with them as they laughed and giggled. Back on the other side I began to explore the area, looking for a spot where I could build a house or shelter of some sort. I walked slowly upstream along the bank, thoughtfully studying the surroundings. This was a beautiful place. Soon the river would be clean and clear. Behind me the meadow, covered with a profusion of flowers, extended almost from the edge of the river itself to lose itself in the woods, several bow-shots away. The far bank was rockier, and thickly wooded. There was good hunting on the other side – deer and wild boar; rabbits and partridge. I would always have plenty of game.

Dejanira and I could be happy here. I would build her a comfortable house, and we could lead an idyllic existence. Not a great many people came through – in fact it was certain there would be entire days without one customer. But there would be enough for Dejanira and I to live comfortably. I would take possession of that meadow, and either keep Charaxus away, or else have him pay me to graze his sheep on it. Maybe I would get some sheep of my own. Maybe even some cattle. If I put my mind to it, I could become a wealthy centaur, so I could keep Dejanira in comfort and style. No reason at all why a centaur couldn't do these things, just as a Greek did.

The satyrs had arrived at the river bank and they crouched and huddled beside some tall reeds, grinning, with their gaze fixed intently on the far bank. I turned my own eyes in the direction they were staring. Just visible through the trees, amidst a jumble of rocks and boulders, Agrius and the two girls could be seen. He had one of them – I think it was Iphinoe – locked in his arms as he hugged and kissed her, his wine skin and his lunch still slung over his shoulders. His horse's back was arched and he was humping away at something – at the empty air, I thought. Then, through the foliage, I discerned Chloris beneath him, half-reclining on a flat boulder, her robe hitched up to her waist and clutching at Agrius's sixteen-inch member with both hands as he thrust it at her repeatedly. The satyrs masturbated furtively.

Yes, it could be done . . . there were ways. I only needed to overcome the initial resistance and prejudice of Dejanira and her father.

* * * * * *

Later, on the way back home, I asked Agrius, "Did you actually get it inside her?"

"Naw," he said. "It's just too big for those little girls. She got me off with her hands, though. I got it all over her thighs. She'll probably use it as a charm to keep her Greek lover faithful. The Greeks got this belief, you know, that centaur blood or semen rubbed on a article of clothing will keep a husband faithful forever. That's how come we can often make out with those Greek women. They mop it up and save it."

I had heard about this curious belief before, and I pondered upon it as garrulous Agrius continued to talk. "There's some of those Greek girls that are big enough, though," he went on. "Like Hippodameia, or Dejanira. Do you know Dejanira? Man, I bet I could get eight or ten inches inside of her. She's a big girl. I guess that's why Hercules wants to marry her. He goes for those big dames, you know."

I was reassured by Agrius's words, which showed that Crotus

138

and Ocyrhöe were keeping my secret. Agrius was a good friend, who would never have spoken in the way he did if he had known I was in love with Dejanira.

"And, by the way," Agrius continued, "this Hippodameia....did you know that Eurytus is in love with her? The fool acts like he doesn't know she does it to other centaurs besides himself. Maybe he doesn't even care. If he goes to that wedding and gets drunk, there could be trouble. Are you going to be there? We've all been invited."

No, I told Agrius. I wasn't planning on going. "Mount Pelion is a hundred miles away," I said. "To me, that's a hell of a long way to go, just for some free wine."

"Well, not for me it's not," Agrius said, "I'm going to be there, to guzzle all I can while I can. And I'll take an empty skin along to fill up and take home with me. That's going to be some wedding feast."

* * * * * *

I, Jonathan Nestus, could have told Agrius that he would be well advised to stay away from the wedding of Peirithous and Hippodameia. And I could have told Nessus that he was right about the indestructibility of Medea's poison, that it is still floating around, three thousand years after her disappearance, and that it occasionally causes something called spontaneous human combustion.

139

CHAPTER FOURTEEN

With the memory of Agrius' comments on the harsh behavior of Hades with his wife Persephone fresh in my mind, I began the draft of another chapter of *A Short History of the Centaurs*. In this new chapter I wanted to more fully address the matter of how the origins of presently-existing earthly conditions can be traced to acts and actions by the gods of antiquity.

The story Agrius had told Nessus about Hades and Persephone intrigued me. I have always known that a sunny shower indicates that the devil is beating his wife. But I had never known the roots and causes of the connection before. It makes sense, when one stops to think about it. Even though it may appear almost incredible that Demeter is apparently still hanging around after these thousands of years. This would mean that some essence of the power of the ancient gods still lingers over the surface of the earth. One or two of the lesser gods and demigods are probably still around, overlooked in the general sweep made by Jehovah of the old pagan gods. Hades is gone, of course, long since supplanted by Satan, who was thrust into Hades' former domains by Jehovah without so much as a by-your-leave.

And it seems that the devil has also taken over Hades' former wife Persephone, and made her his own. Because, although the old Testament makes no mention of the devil having a wife, he certainly appears to have one today, beating the hell out of her every spring, just as Hades used to do. And today, the same as three thousand years ago, the occurrence is marked by a light shower of rain while the sun is shining brightly, the tears shed by the spirit of Demeter, who grieves to see the sad state into which her beloved daughter has fallen. Therefore, we can surmise that Persephone's altercations with Satan stem from the fact that he has high-handedly chosen to ignore the agreement she had with Hades.

The Devil treats Persephone harshly at all times, not with the consideration and respect she was accustomed to with Hades, who aside from a single thrashing once a year at the approach of Spring – a

141

thrashing that was mainly of a ceremonial nature, intended to extract all the hell out of her before she returned to the upper air – treated her mostly as an equal.

Proof that all this is so can be seen in the fact that these sunny showers usually occur in early spring, a time of year when Persephone, in olden times, would return to the surface of the earth to visit with her mother, according to the agreement worked out for her with Hades by Zeus.

I consigned all of the above into Chapter Ten, and continued as follows with,

A Short History of the Centaurs

Chapter Ten

When the sweet odors of Spring's first flowers seep down into Hell, no doubt Persephone gets restless.

"This is the time of year," she will say with a sigh, as she putters around hell's kitchen with the devil's soot-begrimed pots and pans, "when my Hades – may he rest in peace – used to let me go up above to visit with my mother."

Satan will turn a baleful eye on her and growl, "your Hades isn't around anymore, so forget it."

"Hades was so kind and considerate," Persephone will perhaps continue, as if she hadn't heard, "he didn't like to see me leave, but he knew how much it meant to me."

"Hades was an ass," Satan will reply. "He didn't know that the only way to keep a woman in line is with a good thrashing every now and then."

"One thing I can be thankful for," Persephone will continue, refusing to take the ominous hint, "is that he can't see my present situation." And thus the discussion will continue, one word leading to another, until the next thing poor Persephone knows Satan is whaling the living tar out of her and her shrieks of pain and terror, filtering out to the upper air, reach her mother's ears, who wrings her hands helplessly and showers the earth with her tears. And maybe in lands such as Louisiana, Cajuns will nod knowingly and say, "The devil, he beating his wife again."

And does this teach Persephone to keep her mouth shut and refrain from mentioning her former husband? No. The following spring she will again initiate the same discussion and it will proceed to the same conclusion. Year after year, through the centuries, it has continued. It is truly as Pausanias said,

142

referring to the Amazons, "Only with women is it true that nothing bad that happens to them takes away their appetite for trouble." *Pausanias* (I,15:2)

Of the Olympian gods, only Zeus and Hades had a spouse. All the other gods and goddesses led a single life style, although several of them were married. Hephaestus was married to Aphrodite, for example. But it appears to have been a marriage mostly for the sake of convenience, much as many persons will marry for tax purposes, or to obtain residence in a country. After her marriage, Aphrodite continued with her promiscuous ways, fornicating with gods and mortals alike. She was lucky she had such an easy-going husband, who apparently turned a blind eye on her goings-on.

Most of the gods had a very low level of tolerance towards anything they considered disrespectful behavior, and were extremely vengeful. Even Athene, reputed to be the most benign and gentle among the gods and goddesses was capable of occasional acts of savagery, as can be seen in the cruel curse she laid upon the innocent Pelasgian Marsyas, who picked up the flute she had thrown away.

Athene had recently invented the flute, and inordinately proud of the sounds she could make with it, she held a concert, attended by all the gods. But as she was playing, she noticed that Hera and Artemis were giggling, and trying to hide their laughter behind their hands. Later she got before a mirror to look at herself as she played the flute, and realized how unattractive she looked, with her bulging cheeks and eyes, and understood then what Hera and Artemis had been giggling about. So she angrily threw the flute away, and laid a gratuitous curse on whoever should pick it up.

Marsyas happened to be that unfortunate person. He went all over Phrygia playing on his newfound instrument, amazing the simple peasants there who had never heard a flute before, and who began to claim that the music Marsyas made on his flute was better than even that of Apollo and his lyre. Apollo got word of this, and challenged Marsyas to a musical contest, with Apollo playing the lyre and Marsyas the flute. The winner could do what he liked with the loser, he promised.

In the contest, Marsyas greatly impressed the judges with his music, and they were having a hard time deciding. But then Apollo turned his lyre upside down, and played and sang at the same time, and challenged Marsyas to do the same with his instrument. Marsyas gave it a good try, but found that this was impossible with a flute. So, the judges had no choice but to declare Apollo the winner. Apollo thereupon skinned Marsyas alive and nailed his hide to a

143

plane tree.

Such was the savage consequence of Athene's curse. Apollo continued to hate flute players, Plutarch says, until the seventh century B.C., when a flute player named Sakadas appeased his hatred by composing a theme for flutes commemorating Apollo's slaying of the Delphic python.

Another example of the harshness which this most generous of the goddesses was capable of can be seen in her treatment of the maiden Arachne, who had acquired great fame as the most skillful weaver of cloth and wool on earth. Ovid says that she was a girl of humble origins, the daughter of a peasant who dyed wool for a living in Maeonia. Elsewhere, we can read that she was a princess of Colophon, in Lydia. Her fame as a weaver of cloth and wool became so great that it finally turned her head, and she began to claim she was better at her craft than even Athene herself, who had invented the art. She even went so far as to say she would like to challenge the goddess to a spinning and weaving contest, to show who was the best.

Athene got word of how Arachne was running off at the mouth. She appeared before the young girl one day disguised as an old hag, supporting herself on a cane, and at first tried to counsel her with sage words of advice. "Be content," she said, "to consider yourself the best of all mortal spinners, but do not pretend to surpass any of the gods," hinting that such an attitude, besides being foolish, was dangerous. But she only succeeded in stirring up Arachne's pride all the more, and in making her utter the fatal words.

"I don't need your advise, you ugly old bag", she told the disguised goddess. "Go lecture your grandchildren! And if Athene were not afraid to compete with me, she would come here herself."

"She has come!" said the old woman, and throwing off her disguise revealed herself to the stunned girl in all her radiant glory. Arachne was too proud to back off from her hotheaded words, and the two proceeded into the famous contest. They set up their looms in opposite corners of the house, and each of them began to weave a tapestry. To tell the truth, Arachne was truly unexcelled at her craft. The tapestry she wove was so flawless that when Athene examined it she could find not the tiniest fault with it. This made her so furious that she grabbed Arachne by the hair and boxed her ears mercilessly with her loom, until the poor girl, "With a fine show of spirit," says Ovid, was driven to hang herself from one of the rafters in mortification. Then, as she hung from the rope, Athene took pity on her (or at least so Ovid claims) and lifting her up said to her, "You may go on living, you wicked girl, but you must

144

hang thus and go on spinning forever." And immediately, the girl hanging from the rope became a spider hanging from its web. Today, as the common garden spider, Arachne continues to spin as of old and still delights the world with her delicately crafted webs.

Among the legion of men and women who were the objects of a gods unjust wrath in those days, we should also mention Galanthis, changed into a weasel by Hera. Galanthis was a pretty golden-haired slave girl, the favorite handmaiden of Alcmene, mother of Hercules. When Alcmene was suffering her labor pains just before the birth of her famous son, vindictive Hera sent Eileithuia, goddess of childbirth, to Alcmene's home with instructions to delay the birth in whichever way she could. The way in which Eileithuia proposed to do this was by sitting in front of Alcmene's door with her arms, legs and fingers tightly crossed. There is great magic in crossing the fingers, as evidenced by the fact that it is still much used today. There is even greater magic in crossing the legs and arms. If Eileithuia had been able to maintain this posture long enough Alcmene would eventually have died in childbirth and Hercules would have been stillborn.

Eileithuia was sitting, red-faced with exertion, before Alcmene's door holding her arms, legs and fingers tightly crossed, while within the house Alcmene labored mightily. Just then, Galanthis, who had been passing to and fro in the performance of her chores – boiling water and whatnot – happened to spot Eileithuia and immediately guessed what she was up to. She sidled up to the goddess and said, pleasantly: "You must go in and congratulate my mistress. She has just given birth to a fine baby boy."

Eileithuia sprang to her feet in shocked surprise, uncrossing her arms and legs, and immediately Hercules was born, popping out like a cork from a champagne bottle. Galanthis then skipped away, laughing with glee at the ease with which she had tricked the goddess. But her punishment was not long in coming. Hera changed her into a weasel and also condemned her to bring forth her young through her mouth, because it was with her lying mouth that she had interfered in divine matters. Apparently, she was also condemned to copulate through her ear and in Egypt, according to Plutarch, it was believed that the weasel in that way symbolized the genesis of speech.

So, for many centuries, weasels were the only creatures in the world to give birth in this unnatural manner. Today, however, it appears that weasels have finally been relieved of this curse and bring forth their young in the same way as other animals.

In this lifting of the weasel's curse, by the way, can be seen the evidence of how the power and presence of the ancient gods has dissipated over the ages. Long ago banished from Earth and Heaven, they retain only a tenuous trace of their former power. Some of them perhaps languish somewhere in the bowels of the earth, slowly but surely advancing towards the day when they will finally breathe out their last sigh. Occasionally they stir out of their comatose state to brief moments of life and activity. Zeus, once so proud and mighty, lies feeble and helpless, deprived of his thunderbolts and the ascendancy he once enjoyed over all the other gods. But his brother Poseidon, the Earth-Shaker, will occasionally thrash about in mindless fury, causing disastrous earthquakes. Hephaestus too, will sometimes draw deep, stertorous breaths through the flues of dormant volcanoes, and with his expirations spew smoke, ashes and molten lava over the surrounding countryside.

Eventually, when all of the ancient gods have breathed their last, then, possibly, many of the decrees and injunctions imposed by them on heaven and earth will also vanish, and many stars and constellations, created by the ancient gods to honor earth's heroes, will disappear from the heavens. And if the extinction of the Centaur race was by any chance due to the divine decree of any of the Olympians, then conceivably their thundering hoofbeats might again echo over earth's meadows and Cheiron, the "divine son of Philyra," could return to Mount Pelion.

But until that day comes, it might be wise to exercise a little circumspection whenever we might feel inclined to criticize the Olympians. For some essence of their former greatness could still linger, not only over Mount Olympus, but all over broad-pathed earth.

* * * * * *

The Greek gods had inconsistent guidelines for meting out punishment and reward. Many men and women were transformed into trees and plants as a punishment while others met the same fate as a reward for their piety and virtue; such as Philemon and Baucis, who were metamorphosed into oak trees as a reward for the hospitality they had shown Zeus and Hermes when those two gods came to their home disguised as poor travelers. Dryope, on the other hand, was turned into a lotus tree as punishment for plucking blossoms from the tree which was the dwelling place of the Dryad Lotis. In Astypalaea, the women sprouted cow's horns out of their foreheads and some people said it was a mark of honor conferred upon them by Hera, because they had abused Hercules. But others said it was a punishment inflicted on them by Aphrodite,

146

because they thought themselves more beautiful than she.

Phaethon's sisters were turned into poplar trees neither as punishment nor reward, but apparently only to relieve them of their excessive grief for the death of their brother. Zeus had blasted him out of the sky with a thunderbolt, to save heaven and earth from a general conflagration, and he had gone plunging down to earth, his hair and his clothing aflame, to fall into the river Eridanus. His father, Helius, had foolishly allowed him to drive the Chariot of the Sun and the equally foolish boy had nearly brought about an irreparable disaster to all of creation.

Why was the sun god Helius so foolish as to let his young inexperienced son drive the flaming Chariot of the Sun? Actually, his foolishness consisted in making him the rash promise that he could ask for anything he desired and he would not be refused. The gods were forbidden, by their very nature, to ever go back on their word. So, when Phaethon said that the only thing he desired was to drive the golden chariot for one day, a stunned Helius had no recourse but to allow him to do so.

In Ovid's account of the affair we can see that he made a powerfully eloquent effort to dissuade him from his purpose, pleading with him to ask for anything but that. A modern-day parent who thinks he has a problem on his hands because he can no longer refuse his teen-age son the right to drive the family car would know what a real problem is if he could only have heard Helius trying to convince his hare-brained and irresponsible son that he was asking to do something that was far beyond the strength of his tender years. He told him of the many dangers that would beset his way. The Scorpion, the Crab, the Lion, the Archer – all the constellations in the heavens –, possessed of a real life and a malevolent bent, lurked in the starry byways. He told him that even Zeus himself would hesitate to climb into his flaming chariot; that the initial part of the voyage would be steep and difficult; that once at its zenith he would be terrified to see the earth and the sea so far below him; that the highly spirited horses would be very difficult for him to control on the downward part of the voyage . . . But he pleaded with him in vain. In fact, with these stories and warnings he only succeeded in exciting Phaethon's imagination and making him all the more eager to see those marvelous wonders for himself.

So Helius, resigning himself with a heavy heart to the inevitability of Fate, brought out his chariot and harnessed the four immortal, silvery steeds to it. All he could do now was give Phaethon some fervent advice on how to handle the horses, and warn him as best he could about the hazards he would encounter along the way. He cautioned him about taking the chariot too low, or too high, so as not to set the heavens on fire or scorch the earth. Phaethon scarcely listened, impatient to be off. Finally, Helius could delay no longer. He rubbed a magical ointment on his son, to keep him from being burnt to a cinder, lifted the barriers to the sky and the golden-wheeled chariot rumbled away on a pell-mell voyage over earth through the heavens.

The horses immediately sensed a strange hand on the reins, tugging inexpertly on the bits in their foaming mouths. Soon they were galloping heedlessly in whichever direction their fancy took them. They left the well marked path that Helius himself had always kept them on – he had told Phaethon he would be able to see the wheel ruts plainly marked in the sky – and dragged Phaethon on a dangerous course, just above the waters of the sea. They say the seas boiled on that day killing fish by the hundreds of thousands. Then they soared upward, scorching the heavens and throwing all the Olympian gods into great alarm. It was on this occasion that parts of the earth were burned almost to a crisp and the earth's deserts were created, when Phaethon's chariot passed a bare few hundred feet above the surface of Libya.

Panic-stricken, Phaethon struggled desperately with the reins, trying to bring the horses back on course, but he had become disoriented and could not even remember in which direction he was supposed to go.

The gods watched these goings on in a state of shock. Those of them who were away from Olympus when Phaethon first came barreling out of the east behind his runaway team, rushed back to Olympus to inquire excitedly as to what in heaven was going on. What was that insane boy doing in his father's chariot, they wanted to know. Zeus himself could not give them a satisfactory answer. At any rate, he was telling them, the danger appeared to be over, for the sun had disappeared to the west after scorching Libya dry, and by now had probably reached the end of its journey.

But he had hardly finished speaking when they all saw the flaming chariot returning once more. Phaethon had by now completely given up all efforts to control the crazed horses. He had dropped the reins and now crouched on his knees, gripping the railing on the chariot with both hands, holding his eyes tightly shut to keep out the terrifying sight of the earth, so far below. He had urinated all over himself in his fright, and as he cowered there, whimpering and whining, he was wishing with all his heart he had listened to his father.

When the amazed gods saw the ball of fire rumbling ominously towards them again, they clamored for Zeus to do something and it was only then that Zeus, with great regret, took up a thunderbolt, aimed it carefully, and blasted Phaethon and the chariot itself out of the sky.

For many days Phaethon's sisters searched for him all over the earth and finally found his moldering tombstone on the banks of the Eridanus, which is known today as the Po, in northern Italy. The nymphs of the river had collected his charred bones and buried them, placing over his grave a monument with the inscription,

> Here lies Phaethon; his father's car he tried
> And though he proved too weak, he greatly daring died.
> *Metamorphoses* – Mary M. Innes translation.

Phaethon's sisters flung themselves on the tombstone and wept and wailed ceaselessly for several months until some god or other – either because he was tired of hearing them cry, or because he felt sorry for them – turned them into poplar trees. And as poplar trees, they still continued to weep, silently shedding their amber tears into the river, to become the amber beads adorning many a young girl's neck and bosom, blithely unconcerned that they are the solidified tears of Phaethon's sisters. Plutarch, in *On the Tardiness of Divine Punishment* said that the barbarians along the River Po still dressed in mourning, in grief for Phaethon.

End of Chapter Ten of
A Short History of the Centaurs

CHAPTER FIFTEEN

There are certain days when the chasm that separates my dreamed-of existence from my present life does not seem so unbridgeable. There are mornings when, as I awaken from my deep dreams, I feel a great surprise, mingled with a keen pleasure, to find myself without my equine parts, lying in a bed like a human being. "Now I can have a chance with Dejanira!" is the thought that flashes through my half-awake mind.

And the lovelorn loneliness of Nessus sometimes persists for long moments after I'm awake. In a certain sense, it sometimes seems that my love and desire for Daphne is being supplanted by my vicarious love for Dejanira.

But I tell myself that I love Dejanira only for the sake of Nessus. I feel deeply for Nessus, and would like to see a consummation of his love. He would have a better wife than I'm going to have, to tell the truth, even if maybe he could never have normal sex with her. Dejanira, from what I've seen of her, is entirely honest and disinterested. She doesn't have her mind on money, like Daphne does. I sometimes think, what a rude shock Daphne would suffer if she finally did marry me, believing I was wealthy and had rich parents, to then discover that I'm not wealthy at all, that I'm actually poor. There would be real hell to pay, I know. But It would serve her right, for being so mercenary, for not loving me just for what I am.

Although, if Daphne were to marry me under the mistaken belief that I'm rich, she could with some justification say, if I should afterwards bitterly reprove her for not having loved me just for what I am, "I did love you for what you were – for what I thought you were – a man with plenty of money." Yet, how beautiful the love of a woman who marries a man, knowing he doesn't even have a shirt on his back, such as would be the case if Dejanira were to marry me, Nessus the Centaur.

In the case of Daphne, on the other hand, all my virtues and fine qualities are wasted. My acquaintance with philosophy, which any university graduate could admire; my extensive literary and historical knowledge; the fact that I can multiply 37 by 53.5 in my head in less than a minute – or at least I could, before I fell off that bridge –; the steadfast love I could give her . . . In fact, stripped of my fake university degree, and deprived of the wealth and the rich parents I've created for her benefit, all she would see would be a somewhat scrawny and nondescript high school dropout with, of course, no money.

But all the above considerations are purely academic. Because Daphne is showing more signs every day that she knows my true situation. On the occasions in which we get together – which are becoming ever more infrequent – the air is always thick with sly innuendos about my financial standing. A disinterested observer might say, Why don't you give up the idea of marriage and just try to have some sex with her? That would be easy to say for that disinterested observer. I would have settled for that course a long time ago, if it had ever been viable. And it is even less so now. It would take more money than I have left to get Daphne into bed. What I really need is the willpower to cut the whole business short. Because deep in my heart is the knowledge that I will never have Daphne in any way.

And I will never have Dejanira, either. I know what's going to happen. I, Jonathan Nestus, know that Nessus is going to die soon. Crotus said I would hold her in my arms, and that I would kill Hercules, but he didn't tell me the bad news. Unless something happened back in those ancient times that has never transcended to the present.

As for Daphne, what if we married and had a child . . . and what if our child turned out to be part horse? I know it could happen. As a reincarnation of Nessus, I must surely have more than the usual amount of centaur genes and chromosomes. The other day in a supermarket tabloid I saw a most astounding photograph on the front page. It was a horse with a human head. Not just the suggestion of a human head, but a head with human ears, nose, forehead, eyes and mouth. Complete human features, in short. And upon those features a rather depraved expression, such as can only be seen on a human face.

On other occasions I've noticed other news stories in some of those little publications upon more or less the same theme. Shortly after the article about the colt, there was a similar story concerning a pig. In that case, however, the accompanying photograph was not so remarkable. The pig's head – a piglet, actually, – was decidedly that of a pig, despite its marked suggestion of neotenic, human features – somewhat flatter than is normally found in pigs, true, but it had floppy pig's ears, and a pig's snout. Definitely a pig's face, not differing greatly from the face on many a piglet in a farmer's pig pen.

In the case of the horse with the human head, however . . . It was such an astounding photograph that I was compelled to furtively draw a copy of the tabloid out of its rack and thrust it onto the checkout conveyor belt with my groceries. I say "furtively," because, although I hold these publications in great esteem for the many intriguing and fascinating stories they dare to publish, yet I am aware of the scorn that many people reserve for those of us who buy and read them.

The story that the photograph illustrated, however, once I had hurried home to read it in the privacy of my apartment, was a disappointment. I had expected to read about a shocking case of intimacy between *Homo sapiens* and *Equus caballus*, transcending the normal bounds of man's love of horses; possibly even the name and photograph of the man responsible. But the article in the inside pages claimed that the little creature in the photograph was the product of a scientific tampering with genes and reimplantation, which had been carried out in, I think, Holland.

But I know better. I think it was, if not an instance of interbreeding, a case of recessive heredity – a case of centaur genes that are still floating around out there, within the gene pool of the human race. Perhaps the editors of that commendable little publication, aware of the disdain in which they are held by their peers in the publishing world, came up with the story of gene implantation in order to avoid the additional stigma of pandering to bestiality with which they might become tainted if they published the truth.

When I showed the photograph to Daphne and told her what I thought, she expressed great scorn at what she called my gullibility. "You jerk, you!" she exclaimed (she has started to talk to me that way a lot, lately), "You don't really believe what you read in that trashy little paper, do you?"

"But just look at the photograph!" I answered her. "Look at it! How can you deny what your own eyes tell you!"

She shrugged her shoulders in a gesture of dismissal. "Everybody knows you can tamper with a photograph and make it into whatever you want. You surprise me more every day. I thought you were smarter than that."

On this and other similar occasions I have felt moved to respond to Daphne at length, in order to defend my intellectual integrity. Skepticism is a healthy attitude, I tell her, but it can be overdone. I am a believer in the old adage about the relationship between smoke and fire. When we see evidence of something at every turn, there must surely be at least a grain of truth in there somewhere.

* * * * * *

Poor Agrius. His love of wine cost him his life at that social disaster that was the wedding feast of Peirithous and Hippodameia.

Peirithous was a fool. They say he had full wine jars scattered haphazardly all over the tree-shaded area where the feast took place and he neglected to take measures – some way in which to keep the centaurs from going overboard with all that free wine. He should have known that free wine and centaurs were a deadly combination, that centaurs had absolutely no restraint or will power when under the influence of wine. As Jonathan Nestus I've read in Ovid something about the fight that erupted at the feast. Who knows where Ovid got his information, but it is fairly accurate, discounting the inevitable exaggerations and occasional fabrications. It seems that people continued to talk about the terrible event for centuries after it happened, so that Ovid, more than a thousand years later, could still record the names of most of the centaurs who died there: Eurynomus, Areos, Lycidas, Lycus, Chromis, Dictys, Helops, Aphareus, Monychus . . . and Agrius, along with many others.

Ovid is wrong about Monychus, however. He escaped with his life, and he is the one I heard the story from. I didn't go to the wedding myself. I went to Calydon instead, hoping to catch a glimpse of Dejanira, and upon returning to Oeta found Monychus there, telling the story to Crotus, who also had chosen to stay away.

It seems that Eurytus, "fiercest of all the fierce centaurs," as Ovid records, was distraught and lovelorn to see Hippodameia getting married. Before the real trouble began, when he was still only half drunk, he had been trying to pick a fight with Peirithous. Then, when he was really drunk, he suddenly grabbed hold of Hippodameia as she was

154

walking past him and tried to have sex with her right then and there. Theseus tried to stop him. He said, 'Eurytus, are you out of your mind?' Which was a silly question. Of course Eurytus was out of his mind. He was bombed right out of his skull. He started swinging at Theseus, punching him in the face and chest. So Theseus picked up a heavy goblet that was on a table beside him, Monychus said, and bashed Eurytus over the head with it, killing him instantly.

For only a moment, Lapiths and centaurs stood as if stunned at this turn. Then the Lapiths swiftly took up spear and sword. The centaurs – those who were not already in a complete drunken stupor – grabbed whatever came to hand as a weapon – goblets, tables, flaming firebrands from the fireplace, boulders. Some of them uprooted small pine trees to use as clubs. Peirithous threw a spear at Petraeus and pinned him to a tree he was trying to tear up by the roots. Some of the centaurs, knowing they were greatly outnumbered and that the strength of righteousness could not be on their side, tried to retire, but they were speared and cut down from behind.

Monychus, tenderly feeling the lumps on his head, intoned sorrowfully, "Phaeocomes is dead, and so is Phlegraeus, and Hyles, and Iphinous, and Clanis, and . . . oh! so many others. Cylarrus was killed too, along with his wife Hylonome. Actually, she killed herself when she saw her husband dead."

Monychus said that all those centaurs who survived had left Pelion and were now on their way to Mount Pholoe.

The tragedy was bad news for me in more ways than one. I grieved for my friends, of course, especially Agrius. but, there were other consequences which sank in only gradually over the days. The Greek opinion of centaurs was already low enough. They said the centaurs were robbers and brigands, and drunkards, who couldn't hold their wine. They said we were sex maniacs, and inclined to molest Greek women. They said we were shiftless and lazy, and that we lived like wild beasts in our caves. A lot of this was true. Now, this latest trouble with the Lapiths would further reinforce their prejudice against us. It would be harder than ever to convince Dexamenus to give me his daughter's hand in marriage.

* * * * * *

Orpheus came by a few days later, and his presence consoled us to some measure in our sorrow over the loss of our friends. He had been on the voyage of the Argo, and now, after several years of wandering, was on his way back to Thrace. He had gone on that voyage to take his mind off the recent loss of his wife, Eurydice, and no doubt he had been of inestimable value to the Argonauts, keeping them entertained with his music through the long days and nights of sailing and rowing to their destination and back.

Orpheus was tall and skinny, with a wild and fanatical gleam in his eyes. But when he was singing and playing his lyre that crazy look would change, as if his own voice and music could soften and melt away his fanaticism. He could truly do wonderful things with that lyre, and his singing voice was something to marvel at when one considered the strange appearance of the person it came from. People said it was almost magical, and that it could move stones and trees. It was even claimed that he had out-sung the sirens when the Argo was sailing past their island.

Funny thing about Orpheus. He had really loved his wife; so much so, that it was said he had even descended into Tartarus, trying to bring her back when she died.

But the funny thing I started to say, although he had loved a woman, Eurydice, so much, yet he became a fruit after he lost her. He swore he would never touch a woman again, and he went around preaching against heterosexual love. Here's what happened to him not long after he left us that day, after the tragedy of Peirithous' wedding: He was in Ciconia, going around preaching his new gospel, and some women whose husbands had begun to neglect them, killed him, saying it was his fault. The Ciconians are a savage people, and their women are no less so. They tore him in pieces – I think they were on mushrooms, or ivy juice or something. They ripped his head right off, and threw it into the Hebrus. They say it went floating down the river to the sea, still singing.

This illustrates how dangerous a woman can become when she is unjustly deprived of sex. Orpheus, above all, should have known this truth, and have been more wary of the consequences of his teachings, because he is the one who told us the story of the Lemnian women, and the terrible thing they did when they were deprived of their husbands. The men of Lemnos had gone on a piratical raid to the shores of Thrace and when they returned home they brought a bunch of kidnapped Thracian women with them. They liked these Thracian women so much that they all dumped their legitimate wives and took to fornicating exclusively with their captives. This drove the Lemnian women insane with jealous rage. One night, after covertly plotting the hideous deed, they fell upon the men and killed every last male on the island as they slept, along with their Thracian women. Not even the baby boys were spared.

Afterwards, they had to pay the price. They were left alone for many years without a single male. The Argonauts were the first men to disembark on the island after the massacre, and they found the women there climbing the walls in unrelieved horniness.

During his visit at Mount Oeta Orpheus soothed us with many other stories and songs, and details of the voyage of the Argo. He told us of how Amycus, king of the Bebrycians had met his comeuppance. This Amycus was a vicious bully, who thought himself the best boxer in the world. He would challenge all strangers passing through his kingdom to a fist fight, confident that there was no one who could beat him. So, when the Argonauts stopped on his seashore he came to their camp, accompanied by his entire court, and without even bothering to find out who they were or where they were going, informed them that they would not be allowed to continue until the best fighter among them had put up his fists to his own. This Amycus was a son of Poseidon, Orpheus said, fathered by the god on a river nymph named Melie. He was built like a titan, and covered all over with hair like a wild beast.

Too bad for him he didn't know that the champion boxer Polydeuces was among the Argonauts. Polydeuces immediately accepted the challenge, and proceeded to beat the holy crap out of Amycus. Then, when the king's followers grabbed their weapons to avenge their defeated king, the Argonauts slaughtered them, chasing them all the way to Amycus' palace, which they sacked before turning back to their ship, loaded down with loot and several head of sheep.

Continuing on their journey, Orpheus told us, they came to the entrance into the Black Sea, where they had to negotiate the clashing rocks, a gateway composed of two gigantic rocks, moved by some mysterious force that causes them to clash together with a regular rhythm. He told us of the Mosynoechians, who fornicate out in the

157

open, like animals, but hide themselves when they eat or do other things which normal people do in the open. And he told us of the Amazons, and the iron-working Chalybes, who toil day after day without rest in an atmosphere of soot and black smoke.

Then Orpheus told of how off the Island of Thynias they had seen the god Apollo himself, flying high over the Argo, apparently on his way back from Lycia, his golden locks streaming about his head, and a silver bow in his hand. Just before coming to Colchis, they had seen the giant vulture that fed on Prometheus' liver, flying high overhead towards the Caucasus. And they had heard Prometheus screaming in agony as the bird tore at his liver, the screams ringing out over the vast sea.

And he told of how the Argo, on the return voyage from Colchis, had stopped at Circe's island, where they had seen the many weird creatures that she created with her magic potions. And of how the Argo, caught by a giant wave in a violent storm, had been stranded high and dry on the Libyan Desert, where the seer Mopsus died, just as he had foretold for himself, bitten by a viper.

CHAPTER SIXTEEN

I experienced the above fragments in the life of Nessus after the little episode with Daphne concerning the photograph of the colt with the human head. Those fragments provided me with fresh material for my *Short History of the Centaurs*, which I doggedly continue to write during every free moment. I'm a forgiving kind of guy, and even after Daphne had called me a jerk I still showed her the chapter when it was finished, still clinging, I suppose, to the hope that she would be impressed with my scholarly knowledge, and at the same time maybe convince her yet that her own views on the existence of the centaurs were mistaken.

Chapter Eleven of
A Short History of the Centaurs

The fact that Cheiron, the most famous centaur of them all, was believed to be very ancient, and even immortal, is an indication of the high regard in which he was held. His paternity was ascribed by some to the god Cronus, who ruled the universe many centuries before Zeus, and this would have made him very old indeed.

According to Apollonius Rhodius, to cite just one source, Cronus fathered Cheiron on the nymph Philyra, daughter of the Titan Oceanus. He lay with her on the island in the Black Sea which later was known by her name. But they were surprised in the very act by Cronus' wife Rhea. Panic-stricken, Cronus turned himself into a horse and galloped off, leaving Philyra alone to face the music. Philyra must have been furious at him, not only for his cowardly flight, but because he apparently did not even wait to withdraw completely from her embrace before turning himself into a horse. Proof of this is the fact that she subsequently gave birth to the weird little creature, half-horse, half-divine, who has gone down in history as the Learned Centaur Cheiron, "offspring of a lover in a questionable shape," as Apollonius Rhodius says. Other mythographers say that Philyra couldn't stand the sight of him. She loathed the idea of having to suckle him at her breast, and she begged the gods

159

to turn her into something other than what she was. This wasn't such an unreasonable request to make back in those days, and she was promptly turned into a linden tree. She could just as easily have asked that her child be made normal, but apparently the thought never occurred to her.

This story of Cheiron's parentage is entirely mythical, of course. Cheiron was born of centaur parents, the same as all other centaurs, with the exception, of course, of the original children of Centaurus.

Unlike the other races with which they coexisted, the centaurs had very small families, often only one child, sometimes none at all, compared to countless personages in the myths who had enormous broods of children. The principal reason for this was that not all centaurs were capable of reproduction, and additionally, the pregnancy of the centaur female lasted for eleven months. Their human neighbors, on the other hand, were continually in a reproductive frenzy, sometimes reproducing almost like insects, as can be seen in the examples of Danaus and King Thespius, who had fifty daughters each, and Egyptus, who had fifty sons. This low reproductive rate of the centaurs was the principal contributing factor to their eventual extinction.

Returning to the subject of Cheiron – who is too important a personage to have his history interrupted by asides, – somehow or somewhere he acquired a vast store of knowledge in all of the sciences known in those days. Though he was most famed as a healer, his broad knowledge of every conceivable subject made him a much sought-after private tutor. Despite the deep-rooted prejudice against centaurs, many parents took their children to him for instruction and learning. Besides Achilles, Actaeon, Jason and Aesculapius, he also raised Medeius (a son of Jason and Medea) and Aristaeus, a son of the god Apollo and Cyrene. This Aristaeus later became a minor deity, or miraculous hero, of Thrace and other lands and they say he invented the art of bee-keeping and was the first man to cultivate the olive. He was also revered on the island of Ceos, where he divined the cause of a plague that was decimating the population, and informed the inhabitants of the sacrifices they should make to conjure away the curse. Zeus was pleased at the actions taken and thereupon ordered the Etesian winds to blow for forty days to cool all of Greece during the hottest days of summer.

Apollonius Rhodius mentions the origin of these winds when he tells of how the Argonauts were detained at Thynia for forty days while on their way to Colchis. His story illustrates how events in remote antiquity can affect our lives today. The Etesian winds still freshen Greece during the dog days of

Summer, and modern-day Greeks can thank Cheiron the Centaur for that, because he raised Aristaeus and taught him all he knew.

No doubt, if we could but dig deeply enough into the roots of our present, we would likewise find hidden shoots connecting events in our humdrum, modern lives to many a legendary personage of antiquity, including the centaurs, and glorious Cheiron himself.

Returning to the subject of the Argonauts: Nearly every personage who accompanied Jason in his quest for the golden fleece had connections, in some way or other, with the centaurs. The names of the Argonauts crop up continually in Greek mythology, and though these connections are not always specifically mentioned, one can uncover them by delving into the more obscure aspects of each hero's life. We will not go too deeply into the matter, but one or two details should be mentioned: Jason, of course, was raised by Cheiron. Another Argonaut, Peleus, was the father of Achilles, who was also brought up in Cheiron's cave. And the fleece itself originated from certain machinations against Nephele, grandmother of the Centaur race. I will retell the story here briefly:

It will be recalled that Zeus, in order to get rid of Nephele, had given her to Athamas, to be his wife. But Nephele, true to the character of her in whose image she had been created, felt vastly superior to Athamas, and treated him disdainfully, feeling that he did not accord her the respect to which her Olympian origins entitled her. So he took another wife, Ino by name. This was the crowning insult to Nephele, and from the subsequent intrigues the two women engaged in against each other it came about that Nephele's son Phrixus (half-brother to Centaurus) was condemned to be sacrificed, supposedly in obedience to an oracle, to ensure a good crop. But at the moment of the sacrifice, a golden ram came flying down from Heaven. Phrixus and his sister Helle leaped upon its back, and the ram flew away with them towards far-off Colchis, at the easternmost confines of the Black Sea. Phrixus managed to complete the journey, but when the ram was flying over the seas his sister Helle, looking downward from the dizzying height, lost her grip and fell into the straits which have been known ever after as the Hellespont, named thus in her memory. Phrixus and Helle, therefore, were actually aunt and uncle to the first centaurs.

When Phrixus reached Colchis, he sacrificed the ram to Zeus. This seems like an ungrateful thing to do to the creature that had saved his life, but he was obeying a divine command. This, then, was the fleece that Jason went in quest of with his Argonauts a generation later. None of the ancient myths tell us why it was so important, but modern scholars speculate that it had certain religious and magical significance.

To win the fleece, Jason was put to a severe trial by its guardian, King Aeetes; a trial that he was sure Jason would be unable to pass. He must yoke two wild, fire-breathing bulls to a plow, and sow a field with dragons' teeth. From these teeth, a crop of armed men would spring out of the ground almost instantly, and Jason was required to vanquish them. But Aeetes' daughter Medea, who had fallen in love with Jason, had given him a magical ointment to protect him from the bulls' fiery breath, and she had instructed him on the way to deal with the earthborn men. Once they had begun to sprout, she told him, he must fling a large boulder into their midst. They would begin to fight over it, and then Jason must fall upon them and help them kill each other off.

Jason followed her instructions and succeeded in carrying out the task. But Aeetes, furious to see that Jason had come safely through the trial, and suspecting that his daughter had helped him, refused to honor his word and surrender the fleece. So Jason and Medea went secretly to the grove where it hung from an oak tree, guarded by a sleepless dragon. Medea put the dragon to sleep with her magic, and then Jason took down the fleece.

The city in which this drama took place, Aea, on the river Phasis, is today the modern city of Kutais on the river Rion, in the Republic of Georgia. Could we but journey to that land and that city! to perhaps see and touch an oak descended from the very same oak that grew in the sacred grove of Ares, and on which the golden fleece hung, long, long ago, guarded by King Aeetes and his sleepless dragon.

This King Aeetes, by the way, was a brother of the famed witch Circe, who lived far away on the Island of Aea off the coast of Tyrrhenia. They were both children of the Sun God Helius, and in fact, Helius stabled his horses somewhere in Aeetes' land; hence the customary reference to Colchis as the Land of The Stables of the Sun. His Colchian subjects were descended from soldiers of the Egyptian Pharaoh Sesostris, who many centuries before had passed through Colchis on his way to his war with the Gauls and the Scythians. When he returned to Egypt, some of his soldiers were left behind and they settled permanently in the area.

This pharaoh Sesostris, had an inordinate love of war and conquest, and Herodotus says that he had a curious custom: Whenever he conquered a people who fought courageously for their freedom he would erect a pillar bearing his name and an inscription of a line or two declaring how the might of his army had subjected this nation. However, if he had managed to defeat that nation easily, with little resistance, the pillar would also bear the engraving of a woman's genitals. "I have seen these pillars myself," says Herodotus, "with the picture of the genitals." But Aubrey de Selincourt, in his translation, scoffs at this. "Herodotus may have seen pillars, but the genitals are imaginary," he says in his footnotes.

I myself, however, have found no reason to doubt what Herodotus says. If he says he saw genitals, then he surely must have seen them. Why would he lie about something like that? They probably consisted of a simple V, bisected vertically, with a few curlicues denoting pubic hair. The pillars left by Sesostris, engraved in this manner, could quite possibly be the origin of the conventional symbol with which the female private parts are traditionally depicted, and which little boys – and even some adults – seem to reproduce with the ease born of instinct on public bathroom walls. So today, anyone who feels impelled to draw a representation of the female private parts on a public restroom wall should perhaps first bow his head and pay a moment of silent tribute to Sesostris the Egyptian, first practitioner of this art form.

Sesostris had a son named Pheros who inherited the throne from his father. This Pheros, says Herodotus, went blind because one day, in a fit of pique because the river Nile was in flood and its muddily roiling waters annoyed him, he threw a spear at it. The river Nile, a miraculous source of water in a land where rainfall is virtually unknown, fertilizing with its annual deposit of rich silt the farm-land along its banks, was regarded as sacred. To throw a spear at it just because it was doing its thing was the worst kind of blasphemy. An oracle told Pheros that his sight would be restored if he washed his eyes with the urine of a woman who had never made love with anyone except her husband. He hurried home and immediately washed his eyes with his wife's urine. Alas, he remained blind as a bat. He then tried the urine of a great many other women until finally he found one which restored his sight. Then he gathered together all the women whose urine had failed to cure him, including his wife, put them within the walls of a small town and burned them, town and all.

To return to the subject of Cheiron and his many famous pupils, besides training them in the sciences, the wise centaur also instructed them in the fine arts – poetry, dancing, and especially, music. For this was an age in which music and the arts held a special importance. Anyone who called himself

163

educated had, of necessity, some musical training. Even brutal, surly Hercules had once taken music lessons – until he broke the lyre over his music teacher's head because he had rapped his knuckles when he plucked the wrong strings. And, as an illustration of how intricately intertwined the lives and destinies of all the personages from Greek mythology were, Linnaeus, the music teacher whom Hercules brained with his lyre was a cousin of Orpheus.

The music of Orpheus has faded away through the centuries, and today only the glory of his name remains. It is said he was once able to move the stones and trees with the magic of his lyre. He accompanied Jason and the Argonauts on their famous voyage to Colchis, and they say that when the Argo passed by the island of the Sirens, he was able to out-charm their singing with his own music, so that they lost only one man, Butes the bee-keeper, who jumped overboard and tried to swim to the island.

Today, Orpheus is mostly remembered, when he is remembered at all, for that famous descent into hades in his desperate effort to fetch his beloved wife Eurydice back into the world of the living. She had been picking flowers in a meadow, when the demigod Aristaeus had tried to rape her. As she was fleeing from him across the meadow, she stepped on a poisonous snake and died.

Such was the overwhelming beauty of Orpheus' music that he charmed the grim guardians of the netherworld into admitting him into its lugubrious depths. The miserable old miser, Charon, child of Erebus and Night, ferried him across the river Styx without remembering to demand the customary obol. The jaws of the slavering, bronze-voiced watch-dog, Cerberus, went slack when he heard the melancholy music. Tears rolled down Persephone's cheeks, and even savage, heartless Hades himself turned from his sadistic contemplation of Theseus and Peirithous, frozen fast to their stone settee, when the sad strains began to echo in his gloomy halls. The tortured souls of the damned momentarily forgot their suffering and Sisyphus and the Danaids paused in their wearisome tasks to listen in awe to the music.

After hearing Orpheus' pleas, Hades agreed to give him back his wife on one condition. He was to lead her back up the passageway by which he had come, but he was not to look back until Eurydice was once more safely among the living.

So back went Orpheus, never ceasing to play his lyre. Up the dark, dank, and winding passageway to Aornum in Thesprotis, the pale wraith of Eurydice following after, guided by the ghostly echoes of the sweet strains.

When he emerged into daylight Orpheus impatiently looked back to see if Eurydice was still following. But she had not yet fully emerged from the passageway and he lost her again, this time forever. He only heard her faint cry of farewell as she slipped back down the passageway to the realm of the dead.

In his grief Orpheus did several queer things. He went to live among the Ciconians, a savage people in Thrace. He became somewhat of a religious nut, even becoming a priest, preaching to the Thracians and teaching them all about the god Apollo. He also foreswore women, became a homosexual, and preached about the virtues and advantages of homosexual love. His followers apparently adopted Orpheus' homosexual teachings and they began to neglect their women. This made Aphrodite angry, and she incited a pack of sex-starved, sex-crazed women to attack him one day on the banks of the River Hebrus.

Orpheus had been able to charm the guardians of hell with his music. He had made tears come to the eyes of heartless Hades and Persephone. He had been able to move trees, stones, and wild beasts with his song. But now he found that his singing and his lyre were of no avail. He learned that a woman unjustly deprived of sex was a totally implacable fiend. In a maniacal fury, they fell upon him, tearing him limb from limb and scattering the pieces along the river bank. They threw his head into the river Hebrus and it went floating off to the sea, still singing sweetly.

No musician before or since has provoked such grief upon his death as did Orpheus. Ovid says that the Naiads and Dryads of mountains and forest tore their hair and donned black garments. The trees shed their foliage and bowed their heads in mourning, and even the rocks, and the birds and beasts shed tears. The rivers and streams were swollen with tears of their own, and one of them – the river Helicorn – plunged beneath the ground when the crazy Maenads tried to cleanse themselves of Orpheus' blood in its waters. Orpheus' grieving fans would have dealt harshly with the Ciconian women but Dionysus changed them all into oak trees to save their lives.

Orpheus head drifted to the island of Lesbos where it was enshrined, and it continued to sing and utter prophecies for many years. Apollo and the saddened Muses prevailed upon Zeus to transport his lyre to heaven and it became the constellation of Lyra, which still brightens the sultry summer sky in the northern hemisphere. Though the direct perpetrators of this crime escaped punishment by having themselves transformed into oak trees, their descendants did not get away scot free. Hundreds of years later, the men of Thrace still made a custom of thrashing the tar out of their wives on certain festive occasions "to punish them for their treatment of Orpheus," as Plutarch notes in his essay, *On the Tardiness of Divine Punishment.* Plutarch, however, did not approve of the practice.

But let us return to the history of the centaurs . . .

* * * * * *

Daphne had nothing to say in praise for this chapter. That's the way she is when she figures she has extracted all she's going to get from me for the month. When the first of the month rolls around, which she has come to recognize as a time when I have a few dollars to fling around, she will begin to act more pleasant and solicitous, even asking me how my book is coming along. I'm not so dumb. I know what's what, but I just choose to pretend that I don't. Sometimes I know that *A Short History of the Centaurs* will never enjoy the light of day, to be read by the public, and that Daphne is the only fan I will ever have. So I take her as she is.

CHAPTER SEVENTEEN

After the fight at Peirithous' wedding Cheiron had abandoned Mount Pelion too, and was now living at Mount Pholoe, where the centaur Pholus had long made his home.

One day I started on the journey there, intending to pay him a visit, partly as a way to conjure away sad memories of my friend Agrius. But when I came to the Crisaean Gulf, I lost my desire for the long trip. In a little vale by the seashore I stopped to ponder on the many miles yet remaining around the Corinthian Gulf, across the isthmus, and to Pholoe.

A phantom echo sounded faintly in the distance, and this reminded me of Agrius and the story he had told me once, about the nymph Echo, and why she had been reduced to a disembodied voice. We had been traveling to Mount Pelion to visit Cheiron, and while traversing a rocky pass in the mountains Agrius had paused momentarily in his trot, saying to me, Listen to this. He cupped his hands around his mouth and let out a long halloo. And his shout rebounded from wall to wall of the mountain pass, Halloo, loo, ooo, ooo! Agrius chuckled, pleased as a child. "That's the nymph Echo," he told me. "Do you know the story?" Agrius, the same as Homadus, had had a great affinity for these tales, storing them in some special niche in his memory, and he proceeded to retell it, as we resumed our journey. The nymph Echo, Agrius said, once helped Zeus when he was dallying with some other nymphs and his jealous wife had come looking for him. Echo had stepped out into Hera's path and detained her with entertaining stories while Zeus finished what he was doing with the nymphs.

When Hera realized what Echo had done, she cursed her with the inability to speak a word unless it was to inanely repeat the words of others. Crotus told me once that hers was the first recorded case of a mental affliction known as echolalia, which as a physician he had seen once or twice.

This curse made Echo's social life rather difficult. Every time

167

she tried to take part in a conversation with her friends, all she could do was repeat the last words spoken. Then all eyes would turn to stare at her, and she was incapable of excusing herself, incapable of explaining her problem.

In her shame and embarrassment she moved away from her friends and family. She stayed only in the woods, away from all people. One day she caught sight of a young boy named Narcissus, who was out in the woods hunting with some companions, and fell instantly in love with him.

The voice and the image of Agrius as he had retold the story floated before me. "She couldn't talk to him," he had said, "on account of her problem, you know, so she used to just follow him around, and admire him from a distance. One day when Narcissus was hunting he got separated from his buddies. He stopped by a pool and started hollering out for them. 'Where are you?' he hollered out, and Echo answered him, saying, '....are you, are you!' Then Narcissus hollered out, 'I'm over here by the pool!' and Echo hollered back, '....by the pool, by the pool!' Narcissus hollered back, 'Who are you? Are you nuts, or something?' And Echo just hollered back, '....Something! Something!' 'Come here with me,' Narcissus shouted, and Echo, by this time out of her mind with desire, came running out of the woods, repeating, 'With me! With me!'

"She was real horny by this time, cause she'd been in love with him for such a long time. She went running up to him and tried to kiss him, and grab him by the member. It scared the shit out of Narcissus. He thought she must be some kind of crazy woman. He dived into the pool to get away from her, and she dived right in after him.

"But Narcissus didn't want nothing to do with her, partly because her sickness made him nervous, but mostly because he was sort of a fruit, you know, and in love with himself. He'd spend hours looking at reflections of himself in pools of water. After that, Echo started to pine away from sadness, Her body wasted away, until nothing was left of her except her voice. And that's what echoes are today, just a empty voice, repeating whatever other people say."

I shook off the memory of Agrius and moved on, deciding to go only to the edge of the sea to bathe my fetlocks in the salt water and then turn back towards Oeta. As I drew near to the seashore I began to hear the sweet sound of a woman's voice singing. Her voice, as pure as a silver bell, sounded clearly above the soft lapping of the waters on the rocky shore.

Bemused by the soothing sound, I walked slowly and quietly towards the voice. Then I caught sight of a girl, whose naked upper body was visible above the jutting boulders where she sat. I drew closer to better take in the words of her song. She was singing something I had never heard before, a strangely moving song of unrequited love,

> "Near Pagasae, in wind-hollowed caves,
> Where mermaids come ashore to sleep,
> I once heard a sister sing through the waves
> Rolling onto the sands from the deep;
> 'He loved me only for the lustrous pearls
> In the diadem that I wear,
> But hated my scales and the briny smell
> Of the sea weed in my hair . . .'"

She seemed to sense my proximity before I was fully upon her and before she had actually seen me, half-hidden as I was behind a sea-worn little crag. She stopped singing, and cast her large eyes about with a wariness of expression faintly evocative of that of a huge gentle fish, or dolphin.

I came out from behind the crag and walked up to her saying, "I'm sorry if I've disturbed you, but you shouldn't be afraid. I only wanted to hear your song." Then I saw the rest of her body, which, to tell the truth, I had wanted to see in its nakedness just as much as I had wanted to hear her voice, and I then understood why her watchful expression had made me think of a fish. She was a mermaid.

"Oh," she fluttered, "yes, you did startle me." Seeing that I was just as deformed as she was, put her at ease. She knew I couldn't too easily rape her. And besides, she could always dive into the sea to escape.

I asked her what she was doing in the Crisaean Gulf, so far from the usual haunts of her kind on the islands of Naxos and Seriphos. She was a lovely mermaid, a blonde, with huge golden scales, and a phosphorescent streak of blue running the length of her fish parts on

169

each side of her body. On the beaches of Magnesia I had seen other mermaids – brunettes, with tarpon-like scales that would flash in the sun like hammered silver coins, but those mermaids had been extremely shy, and I had never been so close to one of their kind before.

I examined this one closely now, while I had the chance. She had only the faint suggestion of buttocks, her body beginning to taper immediately after the first swelling, where buttocks would form in a human being. Thereafter it became flattened and slightly angular, just as in an ordinary fish. But her upper body was lithe and shapely, with small pink nipples on her breasts. Her eyes were very large, set high up on her forehead, so that she probably had a good field of vision forward when she was stretched out horizontally in the water. I noticed that her vagina, just above her anus (which was on the underside of her body, just as in an ordinary fish), was naturally covered by a sort of delicate little tightly-lipped bivalve conch, which was probably Nature's way for mermaids to keep water out of their vagina when they were at great depths. No doubt, when they were sexually aroused this cover would part to facilitate intercourse.

I had heard that mermaids were rather slimy, but I could see now that this wasn't so. Maybe after they sunned themselves on the beach for a while that natural sliminess would dry out, making mermaids more desirable and attractive to humans. Because I had heard many stories of human beings having intercourse with mermaids.

This mermaid, it so happened, was none other than Philomele, well known among the Greeks as a diviner. She told me that there were others of her kind in the Crisaean Gulf. She had come here recently with her parents and other family members, rounding the Malean Promontory after several days of swimming the open sea, because they had heard there were great clam and oyster beds here.

"But what are you doing so far from Pelion?" she asked me.

I told her of the trouble with the Lapiths, and that most of the centaurs had now left Pelion and were living at Oeta and Pholoe.

She examined me as we talked, her curious gaze going from my muscular human torso to my flanks and silvery tail, and then down at my hooves, as bemused at my strangeness as I was at her own. She had never seen a centaur before, she told me, which is understandable, because there were only four or five hundred of us left in the world.

170

"We are both strange beings," she said, "from the viewpoint of the Greeks. But you are less unfortunate than we sea people. I have only heard tell of woods and meadows, and I can only gaze from a distance at the mountains. You, on the other hand, can enjoy both worlds. You can always wade and swim in the sea, and you can gallop over meadows, and wander on the flanks of a mountain. I must stay always in the water or near it. I can never pick flowers, or sleep in a soft and downy bed."

"I can't ever sleep in a bed either," I said, to console her, "and I can never visit underwater grottoes, to gaze at all the sea's wondrous creatures and sunken treasures."

Then, taking pity on her at the note of sadness in her voice, I said, "Why don't you climb on my back, and I'll take you for a ride, so that you may see a little of the other world."

She hesitated a moment but then said, "I can't go too far. I must keep my tail and other fish parts wet."

She first splashed water over her lower body. then I helped her climb on my back. Her lower body felt cold and clammy on my flanks, but her breasts, pressing against my back, felt warm and pleasant. I set off at a walk away from the rocky beach, over the low hills and into the rocky crags. She clutched me tightly around the waist, trembling slightly with fear at the strange sights. We emerged upon a little meadow and I pointed out the flowers to her and told her their names – names she was familiar with but never having actually seen the flowers before. I took her to the foot of an immense oak tree, and then to an elm, and a mulberry tree, full of trilling birds and insects.

Philomele was ecstatic at the many strange sights and sounds. She exclaimed in wonder at every little new thing she saw. But finally she sighed deeply and said, "I must go back now. I am drying out too much."

So I turned around and took her back to the sea. I had been thinking, maybe Philomele could tell me something about what the future held in store for me – tell me if I had any chance of winning the love of Dejanira. I had already availed myself of Ocyrhöe's skills, and Crotus with his entrails. Philomele, I had heard, used pebbles, and sea shells.

When she had slipped off my back and into her pool at the sea shore I mentioned the matter to her. "Let me see what these pebbles will tell me," she responded. She reached down into the shallow pool of water in which she rested her tail to keep it moist. She brought up several dark pebbles in her tiny white hands, and rubbed them together thoughtfully for a while. Then she scattered them upon a flat rock beside her.

She studied them for long moments, her blond locks flowing around her shoulders and framing her fine-featured face. Finally she straightened up, and looking off across the gulf's waters in a trance-like state, spoke these words, more or less, as nearly as I can recall them,

> "Shirtless, Nessus, though you may be,
> Yet your shirt will live throughout history.
> Your destiny, Nessus, even now lurks,
> Through many fatidic twists and quirks
> Of Fate, ensconced in a leathern quiver,
> Which twice has forded a swollen river.
> Glorious Nessus! Your cunning deceit
> Shall send him to Hades in torturing heat;
> You will find in your blood the hidden way
> To make the murderous scoundrel pay."

Though I did not fully understand them, the words sent a shiver up my spine. At the same time, I fastened upon what I thought were the key words. I asked Philomele, as she appeared to come out of her trance, "What does that mean? Is the one I'll 'send to Hades in torturing heat' who I think it is? What was that part about my blood?"

Philomele only looked at me with sympathetic eyes, "I don't even know what I said. I can only give you the prophecy in that manner. You must make of it what you can."

She had to go now, she said. She had to rejoin her friends who were on another beach nearby gathering oysters. She began to pass her hands over her lower body, taking up some of the fish slime there to then rub it over her upper body. So this answered my unasked question about the sliminess of mermaids.

Then she said goodbye, slipped quietly into the clear waters, and was gone.

172

CHAPTER EIGHTEEN

Passing through the mountains on my way back home I ran into Ocyrhöe. She hailed me from a distance and when I stopped in my tracks she came galloping up, her firm breasts bouncing ever so slightly, her coppery hair streaming behind her. Ocyrhöe had moved to Mount Pholoe with her father, but she and other centaur women occasionally came to Oeta to visit relatives. Centaurs were great travelers and vagabonds, and this included the centaur women. In Aetolia, Thessalia, Locri, and Boeotia one could always run into a centaur on the roads and trails, bound for some far off place on some errand or other.

Ocyrhöe broke her gallop and came up to me at an easy canter.

"Ah, you're alone today, I see," I said maliciously.

She sensed a hidden meaning behind my words and said, blushing slightly, "What do you mean?" She stood before me, as pretty and likable as ever, brushing back her streaming hair with both hands, her bare breasts and other human parts glowing in the warm sun, her equine half shining with a light perspiration.

Ever since I had seen what Ocyrhöe did with Aeolus, my feelings of friendliness towards her had been tinged with a certain unreasonable jealousy. Even though I would reprimand myself for my attitude, saying to myself, What business is it of yours what Ocyrhöe does? You never had the intention of marrying her, and she probably knew it even before you yourself did. After all, she's a seer and prophetess.

"Last time I saw you, on the flanks of Mount Parnassus," I said, answering her question, "You were with Aeolus."

She blushed furiously now. She immediately knew that I had seen everything. "You were spying on me! But you have no right to criticize me about that. What about you, and your infatuation with that Dejanira."

"That's different," I said, "Mine isn't just a passing fancy. But you – you can't tell me that Aeolus is going to marry you."

173

"Yes, he is," she answered defiantly. "He has asked me to go live with him, just as soon as he finds the courage to tell his parents."

This was most surprising news to me, and almost immediately I saw the favorable implications it could have for me. If Aeolus would marry Ocyrhöe, maybe it would make Dexamenus' less resistant to my own matrimonial pretensions. I could point it out to him as a precedent. Ocyrhöe looked down at the ground now, and confided something else. "I'm pregnant from Aeolus. We're going to have a child."

My jealousy flared again, mixed with a certain degree of envy towards Aeolus. He had accomplished, with his puny little man's penis, what I had failed to do with my sixteen-inch member. "Hey, that's what happens when you let a man stick his organ in you," I said, "You should know that the Greeks are extremely fertile."

Then I was immediately sorry for my callousness. Ocyrhöe was looking for comfort and aid, not criticism. "Look, Ocyrhöe," I said, "if there's any way I can help you, just let me know. I'm going to start up a ferry business on the Avenus River. If you're ever in need of a place to hide out until Aeolus can marry you, you just come to me there."

I must confess that my kind offer was not entirely disinterested. lurking in the back of my mind was no doubt the thought that Ocyrhöe could help me in my suit to win the hand of Dejanira. Maybe I could send her to Calydon now and then, to act as my advocate there – to tell Dejanira how much I loved her, and convince her that I would be a much better husband to her than Hercules; to plead my case before her father, or before both of them . . .

A small tear of gratitude rolled down Ocyrhöe's cheek as she thanked me.

I was still greatly preoccupied with Philomele's prophecy. I had been turning her words over and over in my mind ever since I had left the seashore, many miles back. Maybe Ocyrhöe could provide some sort of clarification. I said to her, "I know you already told me that my love for Dejanira would bring me to a bad end. But you were only guessing, weren't you? Will you look into the future for me again, and see what it says?" We walked together to a clear pool of water formed by a little spring that trickled out of the mountain's flanks. Ocyrhöe specialized in prophecy by looking at a person's reflection in water.

We stood side by side at the edge of the little pool, looking at each other's reflection in the water. Ocyrhöe, staring for a long moment into the pool, subsided gradually into a trance-like reverie. When Ocyrhöe prophesied, she didn't talk in riddles. Everything she said was clear and straightforward. That can be bad for a seer. The gods don't like to have their mysteries revealed too clearly. Phineus was blinded and tormented by harpies for this reason. And I had heard it murmured by other seers and diviners that Ocyrhöe herself was destined to be metamorphosed completely into a mare some day for the same reason.

She lifted her eyes from the pool now, and looked into my face. "Nessus," she said, "I know you didn't believe what I told you before, but it still holds true. You are playing with fire. You must try to forget Dejanira, and you must stay far away from Hercules."

I looked away from her obsidian eyes and stared into the pool again, as if seeking there a refutation of her words.

"But Crotus said I would hold Dejanira in my arms," I muttered. "And Philomele the mermaid . . . I think she said that I would cause Hercules to perish in torturing heat . . ."

"I don't know what Crotus or Philomele said to you, but believe what I am telling you," Ocyrhöe said, "If you continue on your present course it can bring you nothing but tragedy."

She led me away from the pool's edge. Then she told me the reason she had traveled from Pholoe. Her pregnancy was causing her some worry and concern, and she had come on this long journey in search of Aeolus, to apprise him of her condition. I hoped that Aeolus was sincere in his promise of marriage to Ocyrhöe. I repeated my offer of shelter to her before we finally said goodbye, and she trotted off in the direction of Thessaly, where Aeolus lived.

I stared at her mare's body as she moved off. Her pregnancy was becoming just barely evident, noticeable only if you knew about it.

* * * * * *

I continued by the pool for long moments after Ocyrhöe had left, wondering what sort of child she would have. From other like cases I knew she could have either a completely human child or a centaur child. There was even a known case of a centauress who had given birth to a completely equine colt. Idle tongues had whispered that perhaps the father was a horse, but Wise Cheiron had reminded his people that heredity was a mystery we did not fully understand, and that given the

175

chaste and modest nature of all centaur women such speculations were unseemly.

In my obsession with Dejanira, I often mused upon the matter of interspecies marriages and their offspring. Among the most remarkable of such cases was the marriage of Peleus to Thetis, the mermaid. It hadn't worked out too well, as might be expected. Thetis only hung around long enough to get pregnant and have her child, and then one day she flung this child down on the floor of the cave where she lived with Peleus, dived into the sea, and never returned. Peleus took the child to Cheiron, who did the best he could to raise him. But Cheiron once commented to me that he believed the child had suffered serious psychological trauma and brain damage when Thetis flung him down on the rocky cave floor, and he didn't think he could ever make a decent human being out of him. For this little boy, Achilles, son of Peleus and Thetis, was sullen and petulant, with nascent sadistic tendencies.

I could never understand whatever possessed Peleus to marry a mermaid. We centaurs, great admirers of female legs and ass, could not understand how a man, for whom these appendages were certainly within his domain to enjoy, could forsake them for a woman who had only a fish's tail instead. We had nothing against mermaids. We all agreed that they were fine persons, well-shaped and proportioned insofar as their human parts was concerned. But their lack of legs and buttocks should have appeared as a most insurmountable objection to any man, we thought. Surely, for a man to mount a mermaid, with that slimy-cold scaly body, must require a considerable degree of love – or at least lust – on his part. And Thetis, I had been told by centaurs who had met her, was not a lovable person. She was aloof and supercilious, with a strangely metallic voice, and a cold, distant manner.

* * * * *

I invited myself to Daphne's home the next day, stopping by for a brief visit on my way home from work. It had been such a long time since I had seen her. She and her mother were cooking meat balls and spaghetti, and her mother invited me – not too enthusiastically, I noticed – to stay and have supper with them.

The tempting odors almost made me accept, but it would have been an uncomfortable meal. So I made an excuse. I had to get home right away and wait for a call from my investment advisor, who wanted

176

to talk to me about some stock I had bought recently. I saw the old bitch sort of perk up her ears for just the flicker of a moment, but then she subsided back into her usual dull demeanor. I think Daphne's ever-increasing suspicions about me have also taken hold on her mother's mind.

I had come to Daphne's home with the intention of refreshing within her the image of me as a man of means and resources. I wanted to drop casual references to stocks and bonds, forced mergers and acquisitions, IPO's, rising or falling interest rates, and so forth. So I sat on the sofa in the living room with her for a few minutes and talked to her of these things (carefully avoiding all mention of Nessus and the centaurs) while her mother worked in the kitchen.

Daphne, wearing a skirt and blouse, sat on the far end of the sofa, legs crossed, affording me an occasional fleeting glimpse of a small area of thigh, her attention divided between what I was saying and the TV set, sometimes briefly turning her eyes towards me with a look that was a mixture of masked skepticism and cautious credulity. One half of her knew I was lying, that the only mergers and acquisitions I was concerned with was the merger of beans and chili I would make for my supper tonight and maybe the acquisition of a package of soda crackers on my way home. But another part of her was still cautiously committed to taking me at my word. Maybe I *did* have all that money I liked to talk about, and maybe I actually did have to hurry home to catch that call from an investment advisor.

Actually, I wanted to get home so I could do something on my book while my previous night's dream was still relatively fresh in my mind. This latest fragment from the life of Nessus provided me with some most interesting information. Nessus died while Achilles, the son of Thetis and Peleus, was still a child, so he could not have known what that child grew into. But as Nessus I remember seeing that little sonofabitch around Cheiron's cave at Mount Pelion. He was just like Cheiron said he was, sullen and petulant, never laughing or smiling. No doubt it was from his fish-hearted mother that Achilles inherited his cold-hearted ways and his contempt for human life.

Achilles, which means "no lips," was named thus, it was later said, because he had as yet placed 'no lips' to his mother's breast when she abandoned him. But this is absurd. Besides, I happen to know that

177

Achilles was given that name because even in his infancy, before he grew into manhood to finally became the homicidal, maniacal butcher that can be seen on the plain of Troy, his mouth was only a lipless gash across his cruel, stony face.

No other "hero" of ancient Greece can be compared to Achilles for sheer bloodthirstiness. Even Hercules appears almost saintly beside him. On top of this he had other defects of character. Besides his complete disregard for human life, he remained childishly petulant even as a grown man, blubbering like a baby when a pretty girl named Briseis was taken away from him. He kept a fellow named Mnemon with him – the original mnemonic device – to always remind him that he should never kill any son of Apollo, because it had been foretold that if he did so, he himself was doomed to die. At the island of Tenedos Mnemon failed in this duty and allowed Achilles to kill a son of Apollo named Tenes. So Achilles, in a petulant rage, killed Mnemon. In a battle outside the walls of Troy he captured a handsome young fellow named Troilus. And killed him when Troilus refused to let him make homosexual love to him. He killed a beautiful Amazon named Penthesileia, and committed necrophily on her dead body. And this, after one Thersites had gouged out her eyes with the point of his spear as she lay dying. When Thersites taunted him for his beastly act, he killed Thersites.

When his friend Patroclus – with whom he apparently had a homosexual relationship – was killed, he went berserk with grief and slaughtered Trojans like they were going out of style. Hector, who had killed Patroclus, accepted his challenge to fight, but then apparently lost his nerve at the last moment. He turned and ran. His apologists say that he was only trying to tire Achilles out, by making him run around and around the walls of Troy. But if this was his intent, he failed to take into account that he would tire himself out as well. When he finally stopped to face Achilles, he was so pooped he could hardly stand, and Achilles made short work of him.

Then he dragged his body around the walls of Troy behind his chariot, before finally dragging him away to the Greek camp, to attend to the funeral of Patroclus. At the funeral he sacrificed twelve prisoners, along with several horses and some of Patroclus's dogs, and would have thrown Hector's body to the rest of the hounds if he had not been

178

restrained.

Even in death, his thirst for blood was unsated. As the Greeks were departing from the ravaged city of Troy, his ghost returned to demand that they sacrifice Hecabe's daughter, Polyxena, to him. All of these details can be gleaned from several obscure works cited by Robert Graves, such as Arctinus of Miletus, Tryphiodorus, Dictys Cretensis, and others.

CHAPTER NINETEEN

I decided to make that deferred trip to Pholoe before moving farther away to the Avenus. Crotus and I were hunting one day north of Mount Helicon and made up our minds on the spur of the moment to go, taking advantage of the fact that we were one fourth of the way there already. Crotus was thinking of moving to Pholoe entirely. There were better pickings at Mount Pholoe, he told me. The hunting was better, and a good living could be extracted from the travelers passing through Pholoe on their way to and from Olenus, and Elis, and Stymphalos, and the Oracle of Demeter at Patrae, and other destinations. He wanted to go to Pholoe to look things over.

We began the long journey at a steady trot, eating up the miles swiftly. We carried only our bows and a small sack with bread and cheese. That same day we rounded the Corinthian Gulf and crossed the Corinthian Isthmus. Just before nightfall we killed a deer, and we stopped at Mount Cyllene to roast it over a fire.

After we had eaten we rested and traded stories to pass the rest of the night. "Did you know that Hercules has returned from Thrace?" Crotus asked me. "He brought back those man-eating mares for Eurystheus. But he didn't get a chance to rest. Eurystheus sent him right off on another labor – to capture alive a large wild boar in Erymanthus, that no one has been able to hunt down."

I was glad to hear that Hercules had been given no rest. With any luck, maybe he would die on one of those labors that Eurystheus, who hated him almost as much as I did, was giving him. But if he was going to Erymanthus, that meant he would be coming this way, and there was a chance our paths might cross. This was bad. Hercules, as malignantly rancorous as a poisonous snake, would remember that I had challenged him, and called him a sonofabitch. If we ran into each other, I would have to fight him, a prospect which did not fill me with enthusiasm.

Hercules, brutal and sullen murderer though he was, was not completely devoid of conscience. The murder of his wife and his

181

children tormented him, and forced him to obey the oracle which had condemned him to perform those twelve labors for King Eurystheus in expiation for his horrible crime. But maybe it wasn't really a conscience, such as other people have. Perhaps it was only a superstitious fear of divine punishment, because somewhere in the back of his beastly mind the knowledge that such a monstrous crime could not go unpunished was gnawing at his spirit. I could only hope that his fear would continue unabated and that his labors would take him a long time.

* * * * * *

At Pholoe we found that we had been within an hour or two of overtaking Hercules on the trail. He had just arrived himself, and was in Pholus's cave, resting before continuing his journey to Erymanthus. Pholoe was a unique centaur community, where a great many centaurs – who did not generally tend to congregate in such large groups – had taken advantage of a network of caves ringing one side of the mountain – comfortable, high and wide caves, with rocky ledges and flat boulders all around, made to order by mother Nature herself, for the convenience of the most indolent of centaurs.

According to the terms of his servitude with Eurystheus, Hercules was supposed to perform his labors single-handed. But Hercules, besides his other defects, was a liar and a cheat. He was not alone. Lounging around the vicinity of Pholus's cave, there was a group of Thessalians, armed with bow and spear, who were accompanying him on his mission. One of them, a fellow named Ismenus, who was always fawning and sucking around Hercules, immediately spotted me when Crotus and I arrived. He came up to me to say, with a supercilious smirk, "Welcome, Nessus. Hercules will be pleased to hear that you have arrived. He was talking about you the other day."

I felt an uncomfortable feeling at the pit of my stomach. I know I'm not a coward, but at that moment I felt that to fight with Hercules was almost certain death. The time wasn't right. It wasn't the preordained moment for me to fight Hercules with any hope of coming out of it alive.

I said blandly to Ismenus, "Why, I'm glad to hear Hercules is here. We did have a slight misunderstanding once, but I'm sure he doesn't hold it against me. Tell him I apologize for my hasty words the other day, and that I wish him luck in this, his latest labor."

From inside the cave I could hear the voice of Pholus and Hercules above the hubbub of other drunken voices. Hercules was bragging about how he had outwitted Atlas when he got the golden apples. Pholus was saying, "But Hercules, how did you manage to travel to Mount Atlas and back in just over a month?" and then the menacing voice of Hercules responding, "Are you calling me a liar?" And Pholus quickly answering, "No, no, no, of course not. Who would ever doubt a word you say? I only meant . . ."

Crotus and I stood outside the cave for a moment listening. We heard Ismenus, who had immediately gone inside after speaking to me, interrupt to say something to Hercules, the exact words drowned out by the sound of one of the topers trying to sing a song, and then the snarling voice of Hercules saying, "The bastard had *better* apologize. Maybe I'll accept it, and maybe I won't. We'll see about it after I've had my wine."

I walked on with Crotus, who murmured approvingly, "You're being wise to offer an apology. Discretion is the better part of valor. Maybe Hercules wouldn't start any trouble with you, with so many centaurs around, but it's better to play it safe."

Crotus and I went to Cheiron's cave to say hello. Ocyrhöe was home with her father, and she cooked up some food for us as we conversed with Cheiron. Her pregnancy was now becoming somewhat more evident, and I thought of how annoyed with her Cheiron would be when he found out that the father of her child was a Greek. She would probably have to leave home soon. I felt sorry for Ocyrhöe, and hoped everything would turn out all right for her.

* * * * * *

Hercules and his sycophants were carousing it up in Pholus's cave. Pholus had opened a large jar of wine which was actually communal property of all the centaurs. It was said that the god Dionysus had come through Pholoe four generations earlier, and left the jar in the cave, with the admonition to the centaurs that it was not to be opened until a certain occasion, not made altogether clear. Hercules convinced Pholus that the occasion Dionysus had been referring to was his own arrival. So Pholus had opened the jar.

The centaurs in the surrounding caves and crags were angry

because of this. There was a great deal of muttering and excited commentary going on. That wine had aged undisturbed for some sixty years. It had taken a lot of willpower on their part to let it rest, anticipating the glorious occasion when they would be able to open it. Now, that maniac Hercules and his ass-kissing hangers-on were going to drain it to the last drop.

Crotus could sense trouble brewing, and said that we should cut our visit short. I resisted the suggestion, pointing out that we should stay in case our fellow centaurs needed our help. Leaving unsaid the furtive thought crossing my mind – that perhaps this might be a good opportunity to avenge the death of Homadus; eliminate this dangerous rival in my love for Dejanira; end the career of Hercules forever, taking advantage of the help I would find in more than a score of enraged centaurs. But Crotus, diviner that he was, seemed to read my unspoken thoughts, and told me that this was not a good time for anyone to oppose Hercules. He finally convinced me that it would be much wiser for us to go. We warned Cheiron that he should try to avoid trouble, that perhaps he could go talk to Hercules and convince him that he should leave. Hercules had a great friendship with Cheiron, whether real or feigned I don't know, and maybe out of respect for him he would leave the rest of the wine and continue on his way to Erymanthus.

After this last talk with Cheiron, we slung our bows across our shoulders and began the journey back to Oeta. We didn't know we would never see Cheiron again.

CHAPTER TWENTY

Daphne had agreed we would go out to dinner on Friday night. I had slipped her a few bucks some days past, to help her out with a certain difficulty – something about some funds she claimed she had borrowed from the cash box at her place of employment to face an urgent need – and she owed me. She wanted to dine at a certain expensive French restaurant she'd been to once – I forget the name of it; something like Jacques's, or Jacques LeStrappe's, or something. I wasn't too enthusiastic about the idea. I was inexorably approaching the stage at which the price of a dinner at such a place was out of my reach. But she refused to consider going to the Jack and Jill. "What's the matter," she asked, in a certain half-malicious, half-accusatory tone, can't you afford Jacques LeStrappe's?" So I had chuckled, as if amused at the question. Can't afford it? Me, with my wads of cash in several banks, and my stocks and bonds, and subordinated debentures (or whatever)? So we went to Jacques'.

Once there, I had my job cut out for me, trying to hold her attention with my conversation. Her eyes were continually wandering around the salon, following the doings of the other diners as she picked at her salad and sipped at her $80.00-a-bottle glass of Mouton Cadet.

There's very little Daphne and I can talk about. I try to appear greatly interested in her stories about the trailer homes she sells – or *doesn't* sell, actually. Because she's always complaining that she hasn't sold anything for a week, or for two weeks, or for a month. Setting me up to ask for a loan. Daphne, on her part, does not even try to pretend to be interested in the only things I can talk about. As we waited for the main course, I told her about the tragedy at Pholoe, news of which was brought to Oeta by some centaurs who came straggling in.

There had been a fight with Hercules over the jar of wine in Pholus's cave. When Crotus and I left, just two days before, they had

185

been talking of assaulting the cave to rescue what was left of the wine. They had finally worked themselves into a fury over the matter. Armed with firebrands, clubs, axes, and whatever else they could lay their hands on, they had tried to charge into the cave. Many of them had been killed, some of them by Hercules himself, and others by some of his companions.

Pholus was dead, and so were Oreus, Elatus, Hylaeus, Pylenor, Ancius, and many others. But most tragic of all, our beloved King Cheiron was also dead. He had been wounded – accidentally, Hercules claimed – by a poisoned arrow. He endured several days of great suffering, groaning in agony in his cave, attended by his daughter Ocyrhöe. Finally he expired, expressing the final wish that with his death the sentence of eternal torment upon Prometheus would be lifted. This shows how high-minded Cheiron was. Even in his agony his thoughts were upon noble and lofty themes.

Cheiron had been referring to the legend that Prometheus' punishment, which had now endured for several thousand years, could only be lifted if another immortal being should agree to relinquish his immortality and descend to Tartarus for his sake. Of course Cheiron was not affirming a belief in his own immortality. Amongst the Greeks, as I've mentioned, there was a widespread belief, fostered by the evidence of his great number of years, that Cheiron would live forever. So Cheiron's words were only a bitter mockery of what he considered a silly notion.

I don't know why I keep telling Daphne these things. Like I said, she's not interested, and more and more, every day, she's looking at me in a certain way. I won't try to describe that look, except to say it is the look a woman bestows on a man she is beginning to think is nuts, possibly dangerous, and with whom she has decided she is not going to have sex, ever.

To make her forget what I said, I began to talk of my law suit. I told her that Sam had called me the day before, and that he is becoming more confident we will be offered a deal by the city. He had mentioned half-a-million dollars. "Chicken feed, really," I said deprecatingly, "but we would get it quickly. No long wait, like five million bucks would entail."

But Daphne showed no excitement at the mention of so much

186

money. It's like she has something else on her mind.

* * * * * *

The dinner with Daphne had been on Friday night, like I said. She had other things to do over the weekend, she said. She wouldn't tell me what those other things were, and I tried to block out certain uncomfortable suspicions . . .

To cheer myself up over the long, barren weekend, I counted my prospects. Maybe something would come of my law suit soon, and I would be rich. Or maybe I would find a publisher for *A Short History of the Centaurs,* and be even richer. Then I would flash huge rolls of bills under Daphne's face. But I wouldn't give her any more money. That would teach her. Or maybe I *would* give her some, but with a strict understanding . . .

With nothing else to do, I began to work on my manuscript.

Chapter Twenty of
A Short History Of The Centaurs

Trying to make chronological sense out of the events of antiquity is a futile endeavor. Time as we know it today did not exist in those days. Time did not flow in an orderly manner until after the death of Hercules and after the Trojan war. In those days the past, the present and the future were a complete hodgepodge, with sons sometimes being born before their fathers and the lives of some of the heroes spanning many generations, although they only lived their allotted span of years. Therefore, although Cheiron was killed in the fight at Pholoe, the fact that he was still alive a generation later, raising Achilles in his cave does not constitute an anachronism.

Cheiron, by the way, was supposedly immortal, but the ancient mythographers have furnished us with an explanation of why he died. Being immortal does not mean that the person thus blessed cannot suffer great pain. The poison of Hercules' arrow made Cheiron so miserable that he now begged the gods to let him die. Prometheus, who was chained to a mountain in the Caucasus, condemned to eternally feed a giant vulture on his liver, was also immortal and he could be relieved of his torment only if another immortal was willing to relinquish his immortality and descend to Tartarus for his sake. This, Cheiron now did, seeking escape from a life which had become intolerable, and thus Prometheus' torment finally came to an end.

187

Many people forget, or have never known, why Prometheus was punished so cruelly. Many others don't even care. Prometheus was a Titan, one of the original race of giants who were born from the severed genitals of Uranus, and he was a brother of Epimetheus, and of Atlas, who holds the earth on his shoulders. He angered Zeus by tricking him into accepting the less desirable portions of an animal as his due in a sacrifice. He had been chosen as arbiter in the matter, and deceived Zeus by covering the defleshed bones over with a rich-looking layer of fat, while he hid the rib-eye, tenderloin, and filet mignon steaks under the slimy-looking tripe and tongue. Then he told Zeus to choose the portion he preferred. Zeus, apparently not as omniscient as we would expect, chose the most attractive portion, which was, of course, the bones and fat. This thereupon became the portion due the gods ever after.

Hesiod says, in his *Theogony*, that Zeus wasn't really fooled but allowed Prometheus to carry out his deception in order to punish him. At first, he punished him by withholding fire from man. "Let the buggers eat those steaks raw," he angrily muttered. This made things on earth pretty tough for a while.

But Prometheus sneaked into Olympus through a back entrance, lit a torch at the flaming Chariot of the Sun, which Helius had momentarily parked there; then, breaking off an ember, he secreted it in the pith of a hollow fennel stalk, which he carried down to earth.

So, to punish Prometheus for these crimes of deceit and theft, Zeus had Hephaestus mold a beautiful girl out of clay. He had the four winds breathe life into her and then, with the help of all the other Olympian gods, endowed her with irresistible charm and beauty. Athene helped dress her in shining robes of silver, wreaths of fair blossoms, and a crown of gold, made by Hephaestus. Aphrodite gave her sultry sex appeal and Artemis gave her litheness and grace. All of the gods and goddesses contributed their bit. But they purposely withheld from her every virtue that a man looks for in a woman. In other words, Zeus made this girl as wicked, foolish, selfish, and idle as she was beautiful, and Hesiod maintained that she is the direct ancestress of all such women on earth today, suggesting that before Pandora (for, of course, she is the one we are talking about) all women were – if not ravishing beauties – at least good-hearted, industrious, loyal and honest.

Zeus tried to give Pandora to Prometheus' brother, Epimetheus. But Prometheus had warned his brother not to accept any gift from Zeus. So Epimetheus declined the offer, probably with something like "Thanks, I had some at the office," or its ancient equivalent. This only made Zeus' anger boil over, and now, finally, he directed it upon the real culprit, Prometheus himself. He had him chained to a mountain in the Caucasus and set a giant vulture (sometimes it is called a griffon) to tear perpetually at his liver. During the night his liver would grow whole again, so that the following day the torment could begin anew. This hideous torture went on, some of the ancient sources say, for thirty thousand years. Apollonius Rhodius tells us that the Argonauts, on the last stage of their voyage to Colchis, saw the giant bird as it flew over the sea to the mountains for its daily feast. So huge was it that it made the sail on the Argo quiver as it passed high overhead. Soon after the bird had passed they heard Prometheus shriek in agony as it tore at his liver. For a long time, the vast, empty sea resounded with his screams until finally they saw the flesh-devouring fowl flying back from whence it came.

When Epimetheus saw what had happened to his brother he hastily backtracked and agreed to take Pandora as his wife.

Now, Prometheus, in his selfless love of mankind, had long before diligently searched out and imprisoned in a jar, (some say it was a box) all the Spites which afflict mankind today – hunger, pain, sickness, jealousy, dishonesty, etc., and these abstractions in turn begat children of their own. Hesiod, for one, tells us that Chaos bore black Night and Erebos, and from Night came Day and Space. She also bore,

"Deceit and Love, Sad Age, and Strong-willed Strife.
And Strife gave birth to Wretched Work,
Forgetfulness and Famine . . ."

Prometheus had entrusted the jar to Epimetheus and enjoined him to guard it carefully and never to open it. Alas, it didn't take mischievous Pandora long to come across it soon after she married Epimetheus, and she immediately opened it, probably thinking it contained jewels, or money her husband was hiding from her. Out swarmed the imprisoned Spites, like bees from an infinite bee-hive, spreading to every corner of the earth and for the first time bringing numberless afflictions upon mankind. So that all of Prometheus' efforts to shield man from these calamities were in vain. And all this was perhaps an additional source of torment to Prometheus as he paid for his love of man on the heights of the Caucasus Mountains.

Returning to Cheiron and his immortality . . . the entire concept of immortality has always been a notion that could bear some profound thought and scrutiny. In ancient times especially, with their faulty knowledge of simple

189

arithmetic, a long span of years could appear as an eternity. Hesiod, in a fragment of one of his lost works, quoted by Plutarch, says,

"Nine generations long is the life of the crow,
Nine generations of healthy men.
And the lives of four crows make the life of a stag,
Three stags the full age of a raven.
Nine lives of a raven make up the life of a phoenix;
Ten lives of a phoenix have we, fair-haired nymphs,
The daughters of Zeus."

If we assign 30 years for one generation of man, that would make the life span of the crow 270 years, the life of the stag 1080 years, the life span of the raven, 3240 years; the phoenix, 29,160 years, and the life span of the nymphs would thereby be 291,600 years, an incredible length of time for a mere nymph to live. However, it's likely that Hesiod's arithmetic was flawed, because it is commonly accepted that the phoenix lived for only five hundred years. Using this as a base, then, we can arrive at a more believable figure of more or less five thousand years as the life span of the nymphs. But even with this shortened period, it's possible that many of the nymphs of Hesiod's time are still alive today.

Immortality, whether real or simply a prolonged span of years, was something quite common back in those days. Most men and women regarded immortality as something very desirable, not having the modern vantage point that we enjoy, from where we can see that immortality wasn't always such a great thing. Many mortals of those days found this out to their sorrow.

As for instance, take the case of Tithonus, son of Ilus. Eos, otherwise known as Blushing Dawn, or Rosy-fingered Dawn, fell in love with him and asked Zeus to grant him immortality. Zeus acceded to her request, though he didn't like to do these things. But Eos had neglected to ask that he also grant him perpetual youth, so that Tithonus grew older and older, until he was a withered, emaciated and impotent old man,

"A white-haired shadow roaming like a dream
The ever-silent spaces of the east."
(*Tennyson, Tithonus*)

". . . a dried-up old fart," as modern youths will callously describe a senior citizen. While Eos, all the while beside him, remained as radiantly fair as when he first knew her, with all the glorious, sun-lit splendor and sex appeal of her youth. His voice grew very shrill and he complained constantly until finally

190

Eos, having grown tired of his incessant whining, locked him up in her bedroom where he continued to shrivel and shrink away, still whining and complaining, until he turned into a cicada. That is the reason cicadas still complain so shrilly and bitterly to this day.

Eos, by the way, had been cursed by Aphrodite so that she couldn't help falling in love with every handsome mortal she saw. She is very ashamed sometimes, because for gods and goddesses, mortal man is the lowest of the low. To consort with one is for them as scandalous as it is today for a high-born or wealthy woman to fall in love with her gardener or chauffeur. That is why Dawn blushes so much, even to this day. She was a daughter of the Titans Hyperion and Theia, and as Rosy-fingered Dawn she had the job of journeying to Olympus every morning in her silver chariot, to announce the approach of the sun, towed behind the golden chariot of her brother Helius. Then she would mount her brother's chariot and accompany him on his rounds across the heavens. Upon arriving at the stables of the sun in the east she would again journey to Olympus to announce his safe arrival. A wearisome job it must have been, day after day, through the countless centuries, riding in her brother's chariot with nothing to do but look idly down on earth and man's petty affairs. So we should forgive her if she sought solace in her pathetic love affairs.

End of Chapter Twenty of
A Short History of the Centaurs

CHAPTER TWENTY-ONE

I had been preparing my move to the Avenus river, but with the death of Cheiron and the other centaurs at Pholoe I postponed the day. Many of us went to Pholoe to attend to the funerals. A few Greeks also came to Pholoe. Some of them came only out of a morbid curiosity, but Aeolus was there too, consoling Ocyrhöe in her grief. The funeral pyres burned for several days, each dead centaur incinerated where he fell. We dragged dead branches, trees, and other inflammable material to pile over the bodies while the centaur women who had lost sons and lovers grieved and shed copious tears.

We rolled large boulders to the mouth of Pholus's cave, to blot it out forever from our sight, and many centaurs cursed his name. But none of them cursed the name of Hercules. No one, outside of myself, looked upon Hercules as someone who should be held responsible for his actions. It seems he was considered too extraordinary a being, more demigod or demon than human, to be blamed for anything.

I felt a great burden of guilt. Why had Crotus and I left when we did, knowing that trouble was brewing, and that our fellow centaurs would need our help? But Crotus assured me that we had only shown wisdom and discretion in leaving when we did. We had no obligation, Crotus said, to sacrifice our lives for the foolish errors of others. It had been sheer foolhardiness on the part of the centaurs to assault Hercules and his sycophants within the impregnable fortress of Pholus's cave. The entire blame should be placed on Pholus. He was the one who had invited Hercules into his cave and opened the jar of wine, which he had no right to do.

Later, Hercules bragged that he had vanquished the centaurs single-handed. "The fierce centaurs could not resist me," he exulted, never bothering to mention that in the fight at Mount Pholoe many companions had helped him. And if he had not used poison in his arrows, a poison given to him by evil Medea, so many centaurs would not have died. Because some of the centaurs who died had been barely scratched. In fact, the centaur Tragasus told me, Pholus and Pylenor were poisoned simply by a drop or two of blood that fell on them when they drew an arrow from a dead centaur. Some time later Tragasus told me that where Cheiron's body was incinerated a barren spot was created. Even several months later not a blade of grass had grown on it. Where the other centaurs had died, also, the same effect could be noticed. Their blood had tainted the air itself above the fire which consumed them, and while the funeral pyres had burned, birds flying overhead had fallen dead to the ground. That poison of Medea's – the so-called blood of the Lernaean Hydra – was truly the most virulent and deadly stuff the earth has ever seen.

* * * * * *

I put off my move to the Avenus for several days, and we went into a period of mourning for Cheiron and our other friends at Pholoe. During this time I heard that Hercules was back in Tiryns. He had returned from Erymanthus, carrying the live boar in a cart, pulled by a pair of oxen he had stolen somewhere. Several more labors remained for him to perform before his sentence with King Eurystheus would expire. It was later divulged that Eurystheus had ordered him to go back to Stymphalos to kill off the birds that flocked at the marsh there and caused the people of Stymphalos great annoyance, because when they flew overhead they showered feathers and excrement on their heads.

When Crotus and I had stopped to rest not far from the marsh the last time we went to Pholoe we had listened to their croaking and cackling during the night. It was claimed by some people that these were man-eating birds, that their beaks were of brass, and a lot of other bullshit. But they were just ordinary marsh birds and even before Hercules did it, I knew that a simple way to get rid of them would be to build fires, and make smoke, or maybe just clash a couple of shields around them for a while. And this last is exactly what Hercules did. It only took him a couple of days. King Eurystheus wasn't very smart or imaginative. I thought seriously of going to Tiryns, to talk to him, and give him an idea or two for some labors that would really keep Hercules occupied. I could suggest, for example, that he send him to Erytheia, at the ends of the world, to bring back some of Geryon's cattle. These cattle were a special breed unknown in Greece. It was said that they were reddish in color, wondrously sleek and fat, and very fertile. It would be a great thing to introduce the breed into Greece.

The owner of those cattle, Geryon, and his ancestry, provided endless topics of conversation around the centaur cooking fires at night. He was a child of Chrysaor, who had sprung, fully grown, from the blood of Medusa when Perseus cut off her head, and his mother was an Ocean nymph named Callirhoe. He was a monstrous being, as might be expected, being a grandson of the Gorgon Medusa. He had three heads, three bodies, and six hands. The winged horse Pegasus had also sprung fully grown from the dead body of Medusa at the same time Chrysaor was born. It hung out at the Hippocrene Fountain, and there were people who claimed to have seen it there.

As for the two-headed dog Orthrus, that guarded Geryon's cattle until Hercules killed it, it was a child of Echidne and Typhon, who were also the parents of Cerberus, the three-headed hound of hell. Echidne also bore the Hydra, and the Chimaera – a fire breathing goat with a lion's head and a serpent's body – and she was also the mother of the griffon-vulture which fed on Prometheus' liver. And to her own son, the dog Orthrus, she bore the Sphinx and the Nemean lion, in an act that has given origin to the expression, "fornicating the dog," to describe an idle and bootless occupation.

Echidne herself, was a "fair-cheeked maiden, with glancing eyes" from the waist up, but the rest of her was a huge and repulsive speckled snake. "Gloomy Echidne," as Hesiod describes her, dwelt in a vast cavern near the sounding sea and fed on raw, human flesh. Her lover Typhon was the largest living thing ever born, a child of Tartarus and Mother Earth. He too, like Echidne, was a snake from the waist down. He had snakes instead of fingers on his hands, the head of an ass, and vast, bat-like wings that could darken the sun. Small wonder that these two spawned such a frightful brood of monsters. Echidne herself, was no longer living in our time. She had been killed some time before by the hundred-eyed giant Argus.

Medusa then, was Geryon's grandmother. Perseus, after he cut off Medusa's head, found it a convenient weapon to use against anyone who annoyed him. He would take it out of its bag and flash it at those persons, to turn them instantly into stone. Perseus himself eventually met the same fate. He was having a disagreement with his father-in-law Cepheus, which escalated into a heated argument. Finally, Perseus angrily took the head out of its sack and flashed it at Cepheus, saying, "take that, you old fart!"

But Perseus was forgetting that Cepheus had recently gone blind, and Medusa's glare had no effect on him whatever. Puzzled to see that Cepheus remained unaffected, Perseus at first shook the head and slapped at it, trying to fix it. When it still didn't work, he turned it around to look into its eyes, to see what was wrong, and realized, too late, his colossal blunder.

Chrysaor and Pegasus had been fathered upon Medusa by Poseidon when he had sex with her in Athene's temple – when Medusa was still a beautiful girl – and her pregnancy had lasted for several years. That's the way it was in our times. Whenever gods, demigods, and goddesses had sex with us mortals one could never tell what sort of weird freak would be born.

Cheiron had encouraged the propagation of these stories because they served to make us, the centaurs, feel more comfortable with our own dubious descent, and to realize that there were creatures on earth much more monstrous and deformed than we. We should not feel ashamed of our descent, Cheiron would always tell us. All peoples and races have less than pure and pristine ancestors. "Whatever our true ancestry may be," he would say, "we are truly entitled to be known as 'The Cloud Born,'"

* * * * * *

When our period of mourning for the death of Cheiron and the other centaurs at Pholoe had passed, I again repacked my bag, rolled a large boulder in front of my cave entrance – to keep my ownership of it secure in case things didn't work out in my venture – and set out upon the trail to the Avenus River. I had to take a lot of ribbing from my friends as I was making my preparations. They didn't know my reason for doing this. My decision to go to work on a steady basis – to embark upon a business venture – was puzzling to them. It was unprecedented for a centaur to do this. Many centaurs didn't like to see me doing it. They thought it was demeaning, and felt embarrassed for me. But, though I felt decidedly uncomfortable about the whole thing myself, I was determined to do it.

TWENTY-TWO

On my days off from my job, my literary endeavors have afforded me many an hour of diversion. I can't see Daphne. I can't even call her. Most of the time she isn't even home, or for all I know, maybe she instructs her mother to tell me that. Sometimes, when she answers the phone herself, she acts distinctly snappish and impatient with me for calling her.

So, on weekends, I continue doggedly with my Short History of the Centaurs, which I've almost finished. Everybody will want to read it, I tell myself. Everybody has a keen interest in Greek Mythology and ancient Greek History. They just don't realize it. My book will awaken that dormant keen interest. It will sell like hot cakes. It will be a best seller. It will make me rich. Those are the things I tell myself, and then I begin to write. This is the final chapter:

Chapter Twenty-Nine
Final Chapter of A Short History of the Centaurs

The ancients cite many reasons for the cause of the Trojan war, but all agree that the stage was first set at the wedding of Peleus to the Nereid Thetis. Zeus had been in love with Thetis himself, but a prophecy revealed to him by Prometheus foretold that any child born to Thetis was destined to be greater than its father. So Zeus decided he had better pass, and foisted her off on Peleus instead.

Thetis was a daughter of the sea god Nereus. She probably wasn't too eager to marry Peleus, a common mortal, and she didn't make things easy for him. But wise Cheiron, who possessed bits and scraps of all sorts of knowledge, told him what he had to do to win her. There was a sandy little beach in Haemonia, he told him, which Thetis was known to frequent. She would emerge from the sea there to sun herself and comb the seaweed out of her hair. When the sun rose high and its rays became too harsh, she would retire to the cool shade of a nearby cave, half hidden by a growth of myrtle, and there fall

197

asleep. Here, Peleus was to accost and seize her, and hold her fast, no matter what she should transform herself into.

Peleus followed these instructions, and when Thetis transformed herself into a tree, and then a snake, and a tiger, and finally, into a squishy, slimy squid, squirting ink all over him, he clung to her desperately, though he must have been sorely tempted to let her go and call the whole thing off.

They were married in a lavish ceremony in front of Cheiron's cave on Mount Pelion. All the gods brought the usual sorts of presents they liked to dazzle mortals with – magic swords and spears; divine golden armor, stuff like that. At first the affair proceeded quite well, contrary to the usual outcome whenever the gods fraternized socially with mortals. But trouble was brewing. Someone had neglected to invite Eris, twin sister of Ares, and one of the most petty and spiteful of the goddesses. It is understandable that she was overlooked. She was such a minor goddess that in all the ancient histories she is scarcely mentioned at all. She had little importance, and of course she was not one of the Olympian twelve. As to where she habitually hung out, it is not even mentioned anywhere.

But neglecting to invite Eris was simply inviting trouble. Because, invitation or no, she showed up for the event, angry at the snub, and determined to get revenge. The way she did this was by starting a quarrel amongst the three goddesses over the famous golden apple, of course, as everyone knows.

Why was the apple so important to the goddesses? It would seem that the gods and goddesses could produce as many golden apples as they wanted out of thin air. Hephaestus, for example, could hammer out magic swords, shields, live golden dogs, and anything else imaginable, including golden apples. Hera had a whole tree-full of them far off in the West. It had been given to her as a wedding present by Mother Earth when she married Zeus, and she had planted it on the slopes of the Atlas Mountains. In those days, the Atlas Mountains were not the barren, semi-desert waste land that they are today, but rather a dreamy verdant land, inhabited by many queer creatures and plants. Springs and fountains gushed from between rocky crags, and multi-colored birds floated across azure skies. The Hesperides, lovely daughters of the Titans Atlas and Hespere, made their home here and Hera appointed them as guardians over the tree, to keep passing humans and demigods from stripping it bare. However, she later discovered that the very nymphs entrusted with its care were stealing the apples, so she set the sleepless dragon Ladon to guard it. The tree was valuable to Hera not for the intrinsic value of the fruit, but because of the rarity of the tree itself.

Equally as incomprehensible as the quarrel over the possession of a paltry golden apple was the course adopted by omniscient Zeus for its resolution: the beauty contest, with the worst choice of judge he could possibly have made, Paris, son of Priam and Hecabe. We must conclude that Zeus knew that it made no difference. The accursed golden apple was destined to be the cause of the Trojan war and he knew there was nothing he could do to avoid it.

This was the first beauty contest ever, and the three contestants were truly of unimaginable beauty. Fortunate Paris who was given the rare privilege of judging them. For the three goddesses stripped down stark naked in their desperate determination to impress him and be awarded the coveted title. Yes, Aphrodite, who had blinded blameless Erymanthus because he accidentally caught a glimpse of her as she bathed nude, and fierce Hera, who took grim pleasure in watching Ixion burn alive on a flaming wheel because he had once made love to a cloud shaped in her image . . . These two hellions, along with virginally prudish Athene, paraded one by one before a bug-eyed Paris in their birthday suits, murmuring seductive promises to him, turning around slowly and thrusting their parts in his face to make sure he would miss nothing. All this should cause us no wonderment. For today, women will still go to incredible lengths of shamelessness to be awarded the title of, let us say, Miss Prune Harvest of California. Recently, there was the much-noised case of a beauty contestant who had the gall to wear false mammaries in an attempt to impress the judges. Women go to these lengths not so much for the pecuniary rewards, be they cold cash or golden apples, as for the peculiar satisfaction that even the ugliest of women derive from being told they are beautiful.

* * * * * *

And this brings us to that tragic and melancholy period of ancient Greek history which encompasses the Trojan War. The Trojan War somehow appears to be the catalyst which brought to an end the mythic age of Greece. With the advent of the war, all those marvelous and wonderful things which had been so common throughout the world disappeared forever. The centaurs also, who had once ranged over the length and breadth of Greece, seem to have vanished, as if they had never been. It also seems that when Troy was sacked and its inhabitants massacred or carried off into slavery, a change was thereby wrought on the basic nature of time and reality. And whether this was a coincidence, or whether the war itself was the cause of this change, who can say?

Before the Trojan War, chronological time as we know it today did not exist. The change really began shortly before the war, with the death and supposed apotheosis of Hercules. Hercules existed contemporaneously with nearly all the heroes of Greek mythology whose lives span several generations. In fact, Hercules was already living during the great war of the Gods against the giants who were offspring of Mother Earth and Uranus, and this war took place not very long after the beginning of creation.

Cheiron, also, is said to have been born when Cronus was still the undisputed master of heaven and earth, since it was claimed that Cronus was his father. (When we say 'undisputed master' we are not including Rhea, who could evidently frighten him so badly that he would turn himself into a horse to escape her anger.) The Greeks, by the way, referred to Cronus as "Chronos," which is much like our Father Time, and our portrayal of the old year departing as a long-bearded old man carrying a scythe is actually Cronus departing heaven after being dethroned by the infant Zeus. The scythe he carries is actually a sickle, the very sickle he used to castrate his father Uranus, although some historians say he threw it into the sea near Cape Drepanum.

For those who take the Greek myths for just that, myths, the frequent chronological anomalies present no problem. But for those of us who know that there is an underlying truth to every one of them, an explanation of some sort is necessary. Some respected quantum physicists have in recent years suggested that the reality we perceive is only one of an infinite number of realities – as many, perhaps, as there are subatomic particles in the universe. If this is so, then this means that some realities differ from others only in the minutest of particulars, and that they exist side by side, spatially and contemporaneously. This would explain those common instances in which one person sees or hears one thing, while other persons have perceived the same thing entirely differently.

Some realities, however, are as different from each other as day and night, and their elements never, or seldom, coincide. A different kind of time exists in some of these realities – a time in which all events exist contemporaneously, and without the scrutiny of conscious beings to place them into sequential order so that first things come first and last things last. Animals are unable to arrange events in sequential order and that is one of the reasons they appear so stupid to us, when actually they are quite as intelligent as we are.

The mental constitution of bronze age humanity was something like that of cats and dogs, unable to separate events in time, and to order them sequentially. According to Julian Jaynes of the University of Princeton in his book, *The Origin of Consciousness in the Breakdown of the Bicameral Mind*, those people were actually schizophrenic, in that the two sides of their brain were not in direct communication with each other and did not function as a rational whole. The breakdown of the bicameral mind, says Jaynes, began in the Middle East sometime between 900 and 1400 B. C., partly as a result of the increasing complexity of life, which was in turn due to the increasing size of urban populations.

This last detail is significant in that one of the causes of the Trojan War was said, by some of the ancient poets and historians, to be because the gods wanted to thin out the tribes of man, which were beginning to swarm uncontrollably over the face of Mother Earth. The ancient Greek gods knew that the collapse of bicameral societies meant a grave threat to their own existence, and they tried to avert this danger to themselves by thinning out the population of the world. Ironically, the very remedy they resorted to was the single greatest contributor to the breakdown of the bicameral mind in the Greek world. And this breakdown of the bicameral mind was what ultimately led to the death of the ancient gods, since only bicameral-brained human beings could lend substance to the myth of their existence.

The chronological inconsistencies in the Greek myths are explained, therefore, by the fact that the times were not under the scrutiny of fully conscious beings. We have only to examine the behavior and customs of those times to conclude that those people were not fully conscious, which is to say, not entirely sane.

How else can we explain the actions of a people whose idea of a practical joke was to kill and cook a child and feed it to its own father? This was done by the sisters, Procne and Philomela, to Tereus, husband of Procne. They cooked up Procne's son Itys and dished him up to his father, because he had locked Procne away in a dungeon in a nearby farm and told her father that she had died, so that he could marry her sister Philomela. As a precautionary measure he cut out Procne's tongue so she could never tell on him.

But Procne wove the story of Tereus' horrendous crime on a tapestry. She sent it to her sister, who, once she had deciphered the story it told, rushed to the dungeon where Procne was imprisoned and set her free. Then, seething in rage and horror at what Tereus had done, she took Procne back to his palace and took her inside without his knowledge. That same day they butchered Procne's little son Itys and cooked him up into a sort of lamb stew, which was one of Philomela's specialties.

At suppertime, as Tereus was ravenously wolfing down his own son he asked Philomela, "Where is Itys? Why don't you bring him to the table to have some of this delicious stew? And then Procne, carrying a covered silver platter, came out from behind a curtain where she had been hiding, and Philomela cried, "Surprise! Surprise! Itys is right here, inside of you," and then she uncovered the platter and showed Tereus the hands, feet, and head of innocent little Itys, who had had nothing to do with his father's crime.

After this horrendous deed, as Tereus was pursuing the two sisters with an axe, the gods transformed them all into birds. Procne became a swallow, Philomela a nightingale, and Tereus became a hoopoe; this last a most appropriate transformation, according to Robert Graves, because it is a bird that befouls its own nest. Ancient bestiaries tell us that the hoopoe lines its nest with human excrement and that if a person smears himself with the blood of a hoopoe upon going to bed he will have nightmares of suffocating demons.

Several instances of this same practical joke (feeding a child to its father) crop up frequently in the Greek myths, and also from as far away as Persia, making us wonder if those people possessed all their marbles. Atreus, son of Pelops, did it to his own brother Thyestes, killing several of Thyestes' children and serving them up to him, showing him the heads only after Thyestes had gorged himself. And Tantalus, of course, in a slight variation of the same theme, pulled the stunt on the gods themselves, when he tried to wine and dine them on the flesh of his own son Pelops.

The Trojan holocaust then, was the single most important event that jarred the ancient world into the chronological order that we observe today. It almost seems as if the Olympian gods, shocked at the excesses and savagery of the war which they themselves had promoted, retreated within themselves in an attempt to disclaim any responsibility. They probably subsided into acrid recriminations and accusations against each other. It is evident that their presence and their power greatly waned immediately after the war – almost as if some power greater than they had stepped in to curb and punish them for their irresponsible conduct.

With the destruction of Troy and the re-ordering of time went all of the marvelous things that excite our wonder today. The serpent-tailed monsters, the Sirens, the Titans, the Nymphs and Nereids.... all retreated, either into the bowels of the earth, or into the depths of untrod forest or unsounded seas. The Dryads enveloped themselves within their oak and elm trees and were seen no

202

more. The black passageways leading down to the depths of Hell closed themselves over so that they were lost forever. Those monstrous one-eyed giants, the Cyclopes – along with Scylla and Charybdis and the Clashing Rocks – also disappeared as if they had never been. Never again did the Olympian gods walk on earth to pursue mortal maidens over verdant meadows, and no more could mortal men aspire to win the love of demigoddesses, or even of Aphrodite herself.

Along with all these marvels, which existed in a reality separate from our own, went the centaurs, the mermaids, the satyrs and many other queer creatures, who belonged to our own reality and who may have left concrete evidence of their passing, perhaps in the form of fossils, yet to be discovered some day in the future. And there could be other evidence, of a less tangible nature and which we may never recognize as such. The centaurs, for example, probably have living descendants from the original branch of their human ancestor among us today, and also living descendants from the equine branch.

Doroteo Arango, known to the world as Pancho Villa and still referred to in Mexico as "*El Centauro del Norte,*" could quite possibly have been one of those human descendants. And another intriguing possibility is that his favorite horse, *Siete Leguas,* was a direct descendant of one of the mares Centaurus mated with on that Magnesian meadow five thousand years ago, so that a complete centaur would thus have been reunited whenever Villa mounted his favorite horse. Those who dubbed Pancho Villa as *El Centauro del Norte* were perhaps obeying an impulse born of a subconscious knowledge. Alexander the Great and his horse Bucefalus could possibly have been another instance of the same kind. For there is a little known natural force, postulated by the anthropologist Hector Sabihondo, that impels the components of a vanished entity to draw together and seek each other out across many centuries of time, and this natural force is what brings about those rare but veridical instances of reincarnation and many a curious coincidence.

* * * * * *

So, where *were* the centaurs during all the years of the protracted struggle, when every other tribe, nation, and city in the Greek world toiled and fought in this sterile cause? From every corner of Greece they came with their forces: from Lyctos, Parhasios and Stymphelos; from Miletos, Lycastos and Phaistos; from Argos, Alope, Trechis and Hellas, and from every one of Crete's one hundred cities. Homer lists them all. But not one mention is there of the centaurs as being present before the walls of Troy.

Disbelievers in centaurs might point to their absence as proof of their completely mythical quality; i.e., there were no centaurs at Troy because there *were* no centaurs, and never had been. But actually, the fact that the centaurs were not present at Troy is strong additional evidence that they truly existed, and that they were half horse, just as the mythographers have maintained. Because every one of the armies besieging Troy had arrived there by ship, as Homer shows when he carefully lists which leaders were there and how many ships each had contributed to the cause, from powerful Agamemnon, who brought a hundred ships, to poor Nireus, who took a measly three. But, in the first place, the centaurs were not shipbuilders. And furthermore, even if they had had access to ships, can anyone imagine centaurs willingly climbing aboard them? Anyone who has ever tried to coax a horse into a boat will understand what I am saying. All this aside, an additional reason they were not at Troy could simply be that the centaurs sensibly refused to become involved in what they perceived as a stupid, cruel, and inhuman waste of lives.

Or, could it be they had already become extinct? No. There is strong evidence that the tribe still existed at least up to approximately 700 B.C. and possibly even well into the Christian era. However, their numbers were greatly reduced and it seems that at the end of the Trojan War there were only about fifty or sixty individuals left. Those remnants of the tribe who had been living in the ancestral caves around Mount Pelion had died out shortly after the death of Cheiron, so that now the last survivors lived in the mountainous wilds of Arcadia.

This pitiful remainder of a once proud and powerful race became extremely reclusive and withdrawn. After the social disaster of Peirithous wedding they had received no more wedding invitations, which must have hurt them keenly. Therefore, they gave up wine, which had always been their supreme joy, and also their curse. It's likely that they became very devout in their worship of their patron deity, Poseidon, since the centaurs would have shared the human tendency to seek solace in religion when fate has dealt them a few hard knocks. At the same time, recognizing the fierce prejudice which humanity held against them, they began to retreat ever deeper into the remotest corners of the Arcadian wilderness, determined to subtract themselves from all contact with the outside world.

They were successful at this because, obeying the law of natural selection, the surviving centaurs were necessarily those who had always kept their contacts with the human race to a bare minimum. Those who had run afoul of humans such as Hercules, Theseus and Peirithous were centaurs in whom the inclination to fraternize with men and attempt to rape their wives was a proclivity that was not conducive to a long life and the consequent propagation of their genes.

So effectively did these last centaurs hide themselves away, that people began to doubt they had ever really existed. Occasionally, a wandering shepherd or hunter might catch a fleeting glimpse of one, or come across a sign of their presence in the form of an abandoned cave or campfire. Then he would carry the news back to the nearby villages. Interest would flare briefly, and the entire community would be abuzz with gossip and commentary. "So-and-so claims to have seen a centaur," would be the exciting news. "Then perhaps the legend that such creatures once existed is true and some of them are still wandering around the forests of Arcadia." But then months, or even years would go by without another sighting and people would conclude that the person who claimed to have seen a centaur was mistaken, or was lying. Maybe what he had seen was only an ordinary horse and rider, they would say; or maybe he'd been squeezing the wine skin too freely.

And so, more and more, as the tragic events of the Trojan holocaust receded into the misty past, the knowledge of who and what the centaurs had been faded away beyond the memory of mankind so that finally they became only a fable. They became, in their time, what Sasquatch and the Abominable Snowman and other unverified phenomena are in ours. In the first centuries immediately following the Trojan War, having just emerged from the bicameral frame of mind, as described by Professor Jaynes, man went to lengths to deny the existence of anything which might remotely hint at a regression to that state. Man had even begun to deny the existence of the pagan gods, so that denying the existence of the centaurs was a relatively easy thing to do.

People who today have encounters with Bigfoot and flying saucers are perhaps persons who have regressed, or relapsed, into the bicameral frame of mind and thereby into a separate reality where these things truly exist. They are often reluctant to report their sightings because they know that their possession of a complete set of marbles will be put in question. This is unfortunate because these people should instead be encouraged to report their experiences and to submit to examination by psychiatrists with a view towards investigating the existence of other realities.

* * * * * *

Exactly when did the last centaur die? This is a mystery forever beyond our knowledge. Was there at some time one lone centaur who suffered the cruel fate of surviving all his friends and brothers? to look all around and find himself alone in the wilderness, surrounded by indifferent or hostile aliens? What a lonely bewildered life he must have led, perhaps sleeping in a vast empty cave resounding with the ghostly echoes of his departed friends and relatives. Sleeping uneasily, with fitful dreams of past glory; dreaming of Cheiron and Pholus, and of Nessus, who killed Hercules, while through the cave's entrance the faint light of Cheiron himself, up in the stars, shone on the cave's floor. At earliest dawn, he would stir wearily awake and, his unshod hooves resounding eerily on the cave's rocky floor, make his way to the entrance and down the mountainside to bathe his face in the clear stream flowing nearby, where formerly he had bathed in the gay company of centaur men, women and children, whose shouts and laughter were still engraved on the surrounding rocks and trees.

But it is also possible that the last surviving centaurs emigrated to other lands, perhaps traveling in the dead of night, to thwart the curiosity of idle sightseers along the way who would have thronged to see the weird spectacle of fifty or sixty men, women, and children who were half horse, half human. A well-known professor of anthropology, who wishes to remain anonymous, has suggested to me that perhaps the centaurs did indeed emigrate northward through Thrace and Scythia in an attempt to reach the lands beyond Colchis, and he himself believes there could be centaurs hiding out in the Caucasus Mountains to this day.

But the easiest thing to believe is that the centaurs have departed from earth forever, returning to the clouds from which they came. Never again will their hoofbeats echo over Magnesian meadows or around the Olympian foothills. Their caves have crumbled away and disappeared so that no one can say with certainty where any of them were. They have followed the Mermaids, Nereids and Tritons; the Nymphs and the Dryads of the oak groves; the Titans and the serpent-tailed monsters of the grottoes. They were the last of the wonderful things on earth to go and, sad to say, they were so preposterously marvelous that today no one believes they ever existed.

But up in the heavens, Cheiron the Centaur, in the form of the constellation of Sagittarius, wheels slowly across the black summer sky, straining to turn his enigmatic face downwards to where the mouth of his cave once looked out upon the southern slopes of Mount Pelion. If his now sightless eyes could see again, perhaps he would be able to make out the ghostly outlines of a little centaur girl – a red and white paint, with red-gold hair – etched into the still rocks and trees around the cave site. Then, with the image fading, he would perhaps sigh deeply, and wonder about his beloved daughter and all of his departed friends.

Meanwhile, above him towards the Pole, still intent upon his murderous errands, the constellation of Hercules at Labor forges grimly across the northern sky.

THE END
Of a Short History of the Centaurs

* * * * * *

It was a pleasant job at the Avenus River. It was midsummer, and wading into the cool waters at midday was a pleasure. When winter came, it would be a different story, but that was still some months away.

At first it was hard, as I had known it would be, to swallow my pride and do my job in the proper manner. I had put up a large piece of board and burned into it, with a red-hot arrowhead, the message:

NESSUS FERRY SERVICE
PEOPLE CARRIED ACROSS
BAGGAGE LIMIT, ONE BAG PER PASSENGER
CHILDREN UNDER AGE TEN FREE
NEGOTIABLE RATES FOR ALL OTHERS
LICENSED AND BONDED BY THE CITY OF CALYDON

But the force of habit was strong, and it wasn't easy to insist on payment for something I had always done for free. So, whenever young women, unaccompanied by husband or father, would happen to come by, I would carry them over free of charge. If the passenger was an old and feeble woman, I would also forgo payment. I mention this last to show that I wasn't a bad guy at all, as some might be drawn to conclude, given the suggestion of lechery that my dereliction of sound business practice seems to show where those young women were concerned.

Sometimes groups of my old centaur friends came by to laugh and mock good-naturedly at me. "Hey, Nessus," they would call out to me in the Pelasgian language when I would be in the middle of the river with a Greek woman on my back, "you're supposed to get paid for that, now. Don't try to get that little dish to fondle your organ or anything."

Their needling and ribbing arose partly from envy, seeing that no one else could now exercise the privilege of carrying those buxom women across, because I had a license, and they didn't. I had gone to Calydon and taken out a permit, and pledged a bond so that travelers would be protected in case of liability.

Most Greek men would swim across, but once in a while there would be one who insisted on his full rights to what was a public service. I didn't like to do it but I didn't want to lose my license, so I would have to carry the bastards over. I could have used a canoe or small barge, towing it behind me, to transport both men and women, but then I would miss that pleasure of having a woman's warm, round bottom on my back. And besides, I didn't have a barge.

The river at my crossing flowed almost due southward, and I had decided to build my house on the eastern bank, at the edge of the meadow. The western bank was rocky and wooded, more appropriate for a centaur, who always needed crags and low-hanging tree branches over which he could drape his upper body to rest. But I wanted to emancipate myself from all centaurian habits. I would build a house with special conveniences to accommodate my equine condition, and also build it in a way suitable for Dejanira.

During slack moments I doggedly carried material to my chosen site, piling up stones and scraps of lumber. I measured the site carefully, and marked out on the ground where each room and division would be. "Here will be the kitchen," I would say to myself, "and this will be the living room. Over here, will be Dejanira's bedroom, and this corner I will make into a sort of stable, with a good shelf, where I can spend the nights myself."

As I labored, I planned certain choice little spots where Dejanira and I could consort together whenever we were so inclined, and thought, sometimes, of how I would have to train myself to keep a tight control over my rectum while inside the house or stable. Dejanira probably wouldn't like it if I was always crapping and pissing on the

208

floor. And I couldn't help wondering what she would feel the first time she should see me defecating or urinating, just like a common horse. She would be bound to hear me lustily farting away, too, some day. But maybe by then she would love me too deeply to greatly care. These things did not seem to bother Aeolus, in his love of Ocyrhöe. During the funerals at Pholoe I had seen her pause in the obsequies to urinate, splattering Aeolus's feet with urine, and he had paused with her, putting his arm around her naked waist as he murmured some consoling words to her.

For the time being I spent the long – mostly sleepless – nights on the western bank, alone, with my head and torso draped over a low-hanging tree branch, dreaming away the hours. Sometimes I would stand in the open and stare at the starry sky, recalling the many stories Cheiron had told of the constellations, and the dead people they represented. Cheiron had an obscure theory on the origin of the stars, which most of us couldn't understand. The stars were thousands upon thousands of years old, Cheiron said. The various constellations did not come into existence at the time of the death of the persons they represented, but the other way around. The omniscient creators of the universe, to whom the past, the present and the future is laid out before their eyes like a painted picture, had set them in the heavens when moved by the impression of events that would occur eons later, and a seer, by looking at the stars, could sometimes foretell these events.

I would try to fathom Cheiron's meaning as I gazed upward at the Pleiades at night by the River Avenus. There had once been seven of them, and they were the daughters of the Titan Atlas. One of them, Merope, had been the wife of Sisyphus. Later, when Sisyphus was taken to hades, there condemned to forever roll a boulder up a hill, she had disappeared from the sky, never more to return. She hid herself out of shame to be the only one of the seven to have married a mortal – a mortal, moreover, condemned to Tartarus like a common criminal.

Sisyphus had drawn that punishment for revealing to the River god Asopus where he could find his daughter, Aegina, whom Zeus was fornicating in a clump of bushes. Zeus had to transform himself into a boulder to escape from her father's righteous wrath. Then, after Asopus had passed by, Zeus escaped back to Olympus, from where he blasted

Asopus with lightning bolts. He crippled him badly, and that is the reason his river flows so sluggishly to this day.

To punish Sisyphus for his blabbing, Zeus asked his brother Hades to go personally up to earth to drag him down to the Underworld. Hades went up to do so, taking a pair of magical handcuffs with him. Sisyphus, pretending to admire them, asked Hades to show him how they worked. When Hades placed them on his own wrists to demonstrate, Sisyphus snapped them shut and made him a prisoner in his house.

They say that with the god of Death thus imprisoned, nobody could die, and for a long time things were topsy-turvy on earth, with people who should normally have been dead walking around full of life. So Ares hurried down to free Hades, and Sisyphus was then hauled away to Tartarus.

He conned his way out of death's clutches one more time, by convincing Persephone to allow him three days back on earth to arrange for his own burial (he had instructed Merope not to bury him). Once back on earth he refused to honor his word, and finally had to be dragged down by force. The weight of the stone which he rolls eternally up the hill, it is said, is the exact weight of the stone that Zeus transformed himself into to escape from Asopus.

* * * * * *

After staring at the stars I would return to my tree branch, and doze fitfully, impatiently waiting for dawn. Towards the end of summer, the thought of dawn, along with the shrilling of cicadas, would bring to mind Eos – Rosy Fingered Dawn – and one of the mortals she fell in love with, Tithonus.

They say Eos falls in love with almost every man she sees, because Aphrodite laid a curse on her when she caught her in bed with Ares, who she considers her own. It makes Eos ashamed, to fall in love with those common mortals, and that's why she blushes so much, to give us the expression, Blushing Dawn. Besides Tithonus, she also went to bed with a guy named Cephalus, and with Orion, and with Cleitus, and a bunch of others. Those things don't happen any more. I guess Aphrodite's curse has finally been lifted.

Sometimes I envied those mortals who were loved by goddesses. I wished a goddess would fall in love with me, and helped

210

me get the things I wanted in life. Things like Dejanira. But then I would tell myself that I shouldn't envy those mortals who had been loved by goddesses. No good ever came of it to any of them. Tithonus turned into a cicada; Orion shot with an arrow by Artemis, who took him for a sea monster; Cephalus, killing his own wife Procris by mistake; Anchises, who screwed Aphrodite till she was cross-eyed, crippled by a lightning bolt . . .

And anyway, what chance did I have of attracting a goddess, when I couldn't even get a mortal woman to love me? How could it be, I would ponder through those long lonely nights on the river bank, that Dejanira couldn't see through my superficial defects to immediately realize that in me she would have a far better husband than in Hercules. Hercules was a slob, a drunkard, a notorious womanizer, a murderous scoundrel . . . Me, I was sensitive, kind, intelligent . . . I wasn't ugly. Many centaur women had told me I was handsome.

I sometimes felt that Dejanira really admired me in her own secret way, and that she could learn to love me. But there were other times when the sudden conviction would strike me that the strangeness of a centaur only produced in her a strong revulsion, tempered by an ambivalent fascination. That way she had of looking at me . . . As if simultaneously attracted and repelled. Was my horse's body really an insurmountable objection in her eyes? could it be that my love for her could only earn, in the final accounting, a frank loathing?

These were the questions that marched ceaselessly through my mind as I restively stamped my hooves and switched at an occasional mosquito with my tail through the long nights.

* * * * * *

Calydon was fifty miles away, and I couldn't go there every day. On the days that I did go, I had not seen Dejanira. She stayed inside her house, causing an awkward situation for me. Her father and mother must have begun to wonder why I showed up there so frequently – that is, every fifteen days or so – to reconnoiter in a semi-furtive manner around their house. I had not yet found the courage to declare myself. How could I? I didn't have a house yet, among other objections that I was sure Dexamenus would immediately raise. In fact, it was probably a mistake to be wasting my time trying to see Dejanira when I should have been busy at the river, finding ways to begin building my house.

211

* * * * * *

Business was good at the river. I didn't have passengers every day, but there were certain busy periods when I would end each day with a nice profit. I added steadily to my hoard of iron spits, which sometimes served as currency in those days, and silver coins. Sometimes a large family, with many items of baggage, would leave me an entire sheep, or a jug of wine, and bread and cheese. And of course the young women who occasionally came by without their parents, or brothers, or husbands, would reward me in richer ways than mere silver and gold, filling my need for feminine companionship until that happy day when I could make Dejanira my own. I didn't think of it as being untrue to my love for Dejanira. It was more like trials and experimentation into ways in which my marriage to her could be consummated whenever we should be married. Though it must be said that I found no true solution to that problem.

One day I began to build my house. I laid out the foundations and the doorways in a single day. Then I proceeded to methodically build up the walls with additional layers of stone, and to fill in the floors with crushed limestone, to be subsequently leveled smooth with a mixture of sand and mortar.

Centaurs and people passing through would often stop to stare curiously at what I was doing. "Who's going to live there?" was the question always asked, and I let it be known that I was planning to rent it out, for additional income. The only persons who knew the truth were Crotus and Ocyrhöe, and I was confident they would not betray my secret. It would never do for Hercules to find out. Philomele the mermaid also knew, but I felt safe in that quarter. The information was of no interest to her fellow mermaids and tritons, and she didn't have much opportunity to talk to people on land.

Crotus was an occasional visitor to the river crossing, bringing me news and gossip. One day he brought the news that Hercules had returned from his latest labor. He had gone to the land of the Amazons to fetch back the Amazon queen Hippolyte's belt. Another dumb labor. He came back after a month or so with a cheap-looking rhinestone-studded belt, which he claimed to have taken from Hippolyte. But there was no way of knowing where he actually got it. Even King Eurystheus would never dare to call Hercules a liar; but that's what he was. The

212

only force making Hercules honestly perform his labors, in fact, was the force of his conscience. And anybody who could continue to guzzle wine and murder people after having murdered his own wife and children while in the grip of a wine-induced madness couldn't have much of a conscience.

"I wonder how much time I have," I remarked worriedly to Crotus.

"He has one more labor to go," Crotus said. "He was originally sentenced to perform ten, but Eurystheus discounted a couple of those he already did because he didn't do them alone, like he was supposed to. But anyway, he has only one more."

"He hasn't done *any* of them alone," I remarked. "Somebody ought to tell Eurystheus."

"Why don't you tell him?" Crotus said. It was a rhetorical question, meant to illustrate the futility of my wish. He knew I couldn't do it, for the same reason no one else would. Word of it could get back to Hercules. "But here's some good news for you," he continued, "he has to go to Erytheia to bring back some of Geryon's cattle, for a breeding program Eurystheus is going to start. That one should take him a while."

I was glad to hear this. Apparently Eurystheus had thought it up without any help from me. But still, I didn't have too much time. I must hurry.

CHAPTER TWENTY-THREE

I labored doggedly at the construction of my house, sawing and hammering, chipping at the stones that went into the walls, shambling back and forth at a plow-horse pace with measuring string and level, hauling additional material for floors and roofing . . . Sometimes I would find someone to help me, centaur or Greek, whenever I had some way of paying them.

Winter was approaching. There was a cold bite in the air, and wading into the chilly water was becoming ever less pleasant. But I forced myself to do it. I had an excellent business here. Every traveler who came through added to my little hoard of gold and silver. Others paid me with bread, and meat, and cheese, and iron spits. And the surrounding countryside afforded me good hunting. If I persevered at my occupation I could become a wealthy centaur, rich enough to presume to the hand in marriage of any man's daughter. I could buy a few cows and sheep, and offer them to Dexamenus – not as a dowry, but as a gift – to help incline him in my favor. These thoughts, hovering constantly around the periphery of my mind, goaded me on in my house-building endeavor, and the work progressed steadily.

One day my house was finished. I stood back and admired it from a distance. I thought it looked great. Considering that a centaur had built it. We simply were not trained in these crafts. Whatever defects it might have, I thought, this fact should be taken into consideration. Afterwards I came to realize that it was a bit crude and ill-constructed. I had not plumbed the walls properly, nor squared everything to perfection. But at the moment I only felt a great satisfaction. I stood for long moments gazing at it, and trying to imagine Dejanira stepping out of the front door.

* * * * * *

That same day Ocyrhöe and Aeolus came by for a visit. They had gotten married and were living not far away. I spotted them approaching from a distance, Aeolus riding on Ocyrhöe's back. Aeolus had made a good match, I reflected. He had gained a lovely wife and a fine saddle mare, all in one swoop. Things had not been easy for them, though. Aeolus had met up with a great deal of ostracism from his fellow Greeks, and I had heard that his father and mother had nearly disowned him.

I, myself, had ambivalent feelings about the marriage of Ocyrhöe and Aeolus. On the one hand I admired him for the courage and complete lack of prejudice he had shown by marrying Ocyrhöe. I was glad for Ocyrhöe, and hoped Aeolus would be a good husband to her. The poor girl was an orphan now, since the death of Cheiron, and she had no brothers or sisters.

On the other hand, I could not help but wonder at the complete lack of squeamishness on the part of Aeolus – how he could ever bring himself to actually have intercourse with a woman who, when you got right down to it, was really mostly a mare. As I think I have already mentioned, even for a centaur the carnal act with a centaur female provoked a vague feeling of unease, the faint sense that we were committing an unnatural act, because of the aesthetic leanings of our human psyche.

True, I was fantasizing and planning to make a woman, Dejanira, commit a similar act by marrying me, with my horse's organ and everything, but I rationalized to myself that it was not the same thing. A horse's organ should rightly be something to attract a woman's admiration, but a mare's genitalia should not be an object of eroticism to a man. This would be sheer bestiality.

In this regard, then, we centaurs were not entirely free of prejudice either, as I have already hinted. Furthermore, the love of Aeolus for Ocyrhöe transcended the sexual, and he loved her in spite of, not because of, her mares parts.

When they drew near I was further surprised to see that Ocyrhöe was wearing some sort of top, to hold and encase her breasts. To centaurs, a woman's breasts were not the same object of erotic fascination as they were to the Greeks. We did appreciate the aesthetic beauty of a woman's breasts, but we admired them quietly and

216

reverently, not with the eyes-agog lust of the typical Greek. The sight of a pair of breasts did not necessarily excite us, unless they came in conjunction with a pretty face and other body parts. It looked like Aeolus, living as he did in close contact with the Greeks, had prevailed upon Ocyrhöe to cover her breasts, to deprive those men of any opportunity to leer at them and make comments upon their size, and their succulence, and so forth.

After exchanging greetings I waved a hand proudly at my new house. "What do you think of it?" I asked them.

"It looks . . . nice," Aeolus said, after he had stared at it a while. "Who's going to live in it?"

"Oh, I think I'll rent it out," I answered. And I wondered if I could still depend on Ocyrhöe to keep quiet about what she knew.

I invited them to step inside, and Aeolus sat at the table I had installed in the dining room, drinking wine and eating a roast leg of mutton as we conversed. Neither Ocyrhöe or I could sit with him, of course, but we stood – she at his side and I across from them – at the table in convivial company. She was now well advanced in her pregnancy, and they did not seem to be worried about what their child would be, whether horse, or human, or both. Perhaps Ocyrhöe, being a seer, already knew that it would be an entirely human little girl. It can be read in the literature of later centuries that this little girl was named Arne. Although Aeolus, perhaps in a defiant gesture towards the bigots around him had tried to name her Melanippe, which means black filly.

When Arne grew into womanhood she had children of her own, and she named one of them after its grandfather. This second Aeolus is the one who was entrusted with the guardianship of the winds, and who on his island hosted the wandering Odysseus when he was returning home from the Trojan war.

* * * * * *

One of the legends of our time was of a place called the house of Rumor. In a place where earth, sea and sky meet, in the center of the world, is a many-windowed, many-doored house made of echoing bronze. There, an old woman named Rumor lives, and every secret in the world, of things that are happening, things that are to happen, and things that have already happened, is whispered to her in that house by the four winds and their children. To this house one day, came the rumor that Hercules had captured the cattle of Geryon, and was expected back in Greece any day. He had killed Geryon and his dog, and was now driving some of those cattle across rivers and plains towards Greece. And the rumor went winging its way over earth, sea and sky, to reach my ears at the Avenus River.

The news was electrifying, jarring me into a complete sense of reality. The time had come for me to act. I must go to Calydon and ask Dexamenus for the hand of his daughter Dejanira in marriage. I had been putting it off for one reason or another for many days. Actually, it was probably for the single reason that I had not worked up the courage. It would have been best if I had been totally deprived of all outlets for sexual gratification. Then, driven on by the goad of nature, I would probably have spoken to Dexamenus long ago. But in my occupation of ferryman many opportunities had come my way, which it was not in the nature of a centaur to reject, and I occasionally accepted the gesture of girls and women, traveling alone, who insisted on showing their gratitude for being carried across free. Of course it was as Agrius had said: A normal sexual congress was virtually impossible.

Now, with the news of the imminent arrival of Hercules, the time had come to take unequivocal action, to take the most important step in my life. I needed to select the most propitious day possible to make my bid. We centaurs were not welcome at Delphi, Dodona, or any of the other famed oracles of our day, where I could have obtained advice. They were too far away anyway, and I had no time to waste. Luckily, on the next day after I heard the news, Crotus came by for a visit. I asked him to divine for me, as he knew how, the best possible time for me to make my move.

I brought out a sheep I had gotten as payment for the crossing of a large family, and after we had butchered it he studied the entrails. After long moments of poking at the smelly mess with a stick, he finally spoke up.

"Nessus," he said, "all I can see for you, if you go to Dejanira's house now, is complete failure. The best time for you would be twenty days from today, at the next full moon. But I know the problem this would present for you, because by that time Hercules will be back, and with him around I wouldn't recommend that you go there at all. So, it's

218

up to you. Don't blame me, however, if you go there now, and things don't go well for you."

This was a dilemma. On the one hand, talking to Dejanira's father at this time implied a strong probability of total rejection. But if, to improve my chances, I waited for twenty days, it would surely be too late. I finally decided upon a compromise – to put it off for only ten days.

As it turned out, this was just long enough to make my visit to Calydon coincide with the arrival of Hercules himself, finally finished with his labors, and determined, in his brutish, pig-headed way, to take Dejanira away with him that same day.

* * * * * *

Dejanira's house stood somewhat isolated in a field on the outskirts of Calydon, so I became aware that Hercules was present while I was still some distance away. He was sitting on one of several stone benches in the front yard under an old fig tree which was now barren and leafless in the early days of fall. Dexamenus sat before him on another bench, the two engaged in earnest conversation. Hercules was waving one ham-like hand in the air to punctuate his words; he rested his other hand on his olive wood club, planted in the ground between his legs. His bow and quiver of arrows was slung across his massive shoulders, as usual.

Another suitor was there also, a fellow named Achelous. Not the river god, of course, but just a tough Thessalian of the same name. He was apparently the only man courageous enough, or desperate enough in his desire to make Dejanira his own, to pit himself against Hercules. He awaited his turn now, sitting on another of the benches under the barren fig tree, as Hercules spoke his piece.

Achelous and I shared something in common: we both labored under the handicap of an abnormality that set us apart from the generality of mankind, although his was not as pronounced as mine. In his case it consisted in the fact that he had a pair of horns growing out of his head, just like a bull. Aside from this deformity, though, he was a handsome man, powerfully built. Achelous, to explain his horns, let it be known that his father was his namesake, the river god. I had often

219

reflected that much was to be learned from the example set by Achelous, who far from considering his deformity a handicap had turned it, rather, into a mark of distinction, attributing it to a divine paternity.

But then, Achelous could make that claim because he was not the member of a racial group with that distinctive feature in common, as was the case with the centaurs. Everyone knew, moreover, that the earth was full of many men and women with various other abnormalities, sired by gods, demigods, Titans, winds, tree spirits, Tritons, and even animals, but they also knew that the centaurs sprang from the bestial actions of Centaurus, who was himself the offspring of a criminal act.

Anyway, whatever the cause, Achelous had a pair of horns growing out of his head.

I endeavored to approach the house cautiously, remaining unseen, and made my way to the east side, from where I hoped to overhear the words of Hercules and Dexamenus. I found a slave who was peering around the corner of the house, stricken with awe to see the fabled Hercules in the flesh. Several head of Geryon's cattle, about forty of them, showing the effects of the tremendous journey from Spain and across Europe, were grazing dispiritedly around the house. They were strikingly handsome beasts, even after the wear and fatigue of the long drive. The slave told me that Hercules was planning on taking Dejanira with him that day, and that he was going to embark the cattle at Chalcis, to cross the gulf, and then on to Tiryns.

Hercules was too engrossed in his business to notice my arrival, so I wandered in my disconsolation towards the back of the house, hoping to find Dejanira there again. I wandered to the apple tree where I had last seen Dejanira some months before. Two or three forlorn apples still clung to the barren branches and I plucked one of them, to examine it listlessly, looking from it to the back door, longing to see Dejanira step through it.

There is something about the act of longing for something in an intense manner when certain other emotional conditions are present. Magical effects are sometimes produced. Maybe when we direct our will toward the attainment of a desire even when we have given up hope, we thereby circumvent the opposition of the gods, who think we have stopped trying to force things. Because now, after I had given up

220

all hope, though still continuing to stare at the back door, wishing to see Dejanira step through it, my wish came true and Dejanira stepped out. She didn't see me until after she had closed the door behind her.

She was aglow with a soft inner light which seemed to have descended upon her at this moment in which her fate was being decided with her father. A soft pink suffused her cheeks, and her ash-blonde hair shimmered like the webs of a thousand golden spiders, shining in the sun of a clear autumn day. Never before had she appeared so lovely.

I dropped the apple to the ground untasted, and advanced towards her. Her eyes and her hands fluttered again in nervousness as they had that other time I had seen her here. And again, as that other time, I found myself speechless. I approached to within three feet of her, still vainly trying to think of something to say.

She spoke first. "Hello, Nessus," she said, "Aren't you cold without a shirt?"

"Dejanira," I finally stammered, "I've come to take you with me. I've built a – built a fine house at my river crossing, and I want you to come live with me. I – I got plenty of food, and I have a good income from my ferry business. I make a good living there, and we'll always have plenty to eat and drink. I can't offer you no golden apples, like Hercules, but I'm a better person. There would never be no other woman for me, but just you."

Having begun to speak, the words now flowed with increasing ease. I told her I loved her, that I wanted her for my wife, and that I would make her happy. "Forget that brute Hercules," I ended, "and that guy Achelous. Hercules is a filthy, repulsive slob. He murdered his last wife, you know, and he's had a bunch of others. He'll drop you too, just as soon as he gets tired of you. Me, I would love you forever. No one else can ever love you the way I do. I have loved you from the first day I saw you."

Dejanira had been looking at me with an expression I can't describe or define. Was it shock, amazement, tender love, or what? Sometimes we see only what we want to see. At that moment I decided that her expression was one of overpowering love – love and regret. "Nessus," she finally answered, "you know I can't go with you!"

From the front of the house the voices of the three persons discussing Dejanira's future came easily to us on the tiny breeze wafting

221

the words from that direction. Hercules was saying, "Look here, Dexamenus, let's just cut the bullshit. You already gave me your word that I could have your daughter as soon as I finished my labors, and I don't think you would dream of going back on your word. Besides the fact that you couldn't possibly marry off your daughter no better. I'm a son of Zeus himself. I'm famous all over the world. People have heard of me from one end of the world to the other – from Erytheia, beyond the Hesperides, from where I've just returned with Geryon's cattle, to the land of the Amazons, where I fought the Amazons and captured that bitch Queen Hippolyte's girdle. I wiped out the Stymphalian birds; I killed the Lernaean Hydra; I captured the Erymanthian boar alive; I defeated the so-called indomitable centaurs single-handed – killed about fifty of the sonsabitches –; I've been down to hell itself. I don't know why I'm telling you all this. Of course you already know that you couldn't ever do no better than to have me for your daughter's husband. Especially since her only other suitor is a freak."

Achelous spoke up. "Whoa, there, whoa, there Hercules. Let's not get personal here. These horns I have are living proof that I'm a son of the river god Achelous, for whom my mother named me. As for you, we would just have to take your word for it that you're a son of Zeus. And all those labors you brag about, why did you have to do them? Everybody knows the reason, so I won't mention it."

Achelous seemed to be wavering between audacious courage and sensible caution. He did not have the nerve to mention, outright, Hercules' murder of his wife and children. He knew how furious this made Hercules.

But then, having held back from the brink, he retorted to some inaudible comment Hercules made. It must have been something very insulting, because he said hotly, "Well, if you're a son of Zeus, then your mother's husband, Amphitryon, is a cuckold, and your mother Alcmene is a whore!"

These were deadly words. Dejanira and I, standing face to face, momentarily silent as we listened to the exchange, heard Hercules say, with a murderous calm, "I've already listened to you for too long. I'm going to rip those cow's horns of yours off and stick them up your ass."

"Gentlemen, gentlemen," we heard Dexamenus say, "this will never do...."

222

Then we heard a great scuffling and thumping, as of two powerful bulls fighting over a cow. On Dejanira's face was a look of alarm and distaste as she heard the sounds of the contest going on in front of the house.

"Dejanira," I said, making one last effort to win her, "climb on my back and let me take you away from this ugliness."

"Nessus," she answered again, "you know very well I could never go with you. Why, how can you even think of it? You – you . . . we're different!" She appeared to grope for the appropriate words. "How can I say it . . .? you're not human! You are more of a horse than anything else!"

Her words would have been too cruelly devastating if I had accepted them at face value. But in her words and in her voice I read another meaning, whether because that other meaning was really there, or whether because the kindness of Providence sometimes protects our sensibilities in that manner, I cannot say today. At that moment, however, I was almost sure that what she really meant to say was, "Nessus, how I wish I could go away with you! I, too, have loved you since the first day we met. But to go away with you would be your sentence of death." She could not speak these words, I told myself, because she felt that in order to save me she must be cruel.

The fight in front of the house had ended almost as quickly as it had begun and we could hear Achelous groaning. Then Hercules came around to the back of the house holding one of Achelous's horns, which he had broken off, in one hand. His face was still purple with rage and exertion, and it turned even darker when he saw me. "You again!" he exclaimed, advancing towards me with a menacing air, "what the hell are you doing here?"

But Dejanira restrained him with her soothing voice. "Hercules, please don't fight anymore!"

Hercules flung down the horn and took Dejanira by both of her hands. "All right, my little darling," he said, and his voice had never sounded more loathsome to my ears. "I'll do as you wish for now. But I have won you today as my wife. So go inside and pack your clothes and shit. You're coming with me today. My bed, a hero's bed, is waiting for you in Tiryns."

223

Dexamenus now came around to the back of the house and grasped Hercules by the arm with his usual bland remonstrances to keep him away from me. Dejanira bowed her head, as if in submissive modesty or in dejection, I couldn't say which, and went into her father's house to pack her bag.

* * * * * *

I returned to the river, with my heart as heavy as lead. I cursed myself for a coward. Why had I done nothing? Why didn't I challenge Hercules, as Achelous, certainly not my superior in strength, had done? Why had I valued my life so much at that critical moment, when now my life was not worth living? Then I rationalized my pusillanimity, saying to myself, "But Dejanira wouldn't come with me. She told me. If she had given me the smallest indication that it would have done me any good at all, I would have fought Hercules."

And so it went. From dawn to dusk, and on through the sleepless nights, I alternated between cursing myself for my lack of resolution, to excuses for my behavior. And the image of Dejanira's face, every word she said to me, every gesture and expression, in those minutes before she vanished from my sight into her house, passed and re-passed before my mind.

The full grip of winter was upon the land now, and I often passed the nights in my house, in the special stable, and sleeping upon the special shelf I had built. The large and empty rooms were depressing. Dejanira dwelt like a phantom in the kitchen and living room, and at every turn. She floated before me when I left the house, and when I returned to it her shadow would be there waiting for me.

* * * * * *

But gradually, as the cold winter slowly gave way to warmer days, Dejanira, as an ideal, began to dissipate and her place was taken by another Dejanira, a highly physical Dejanira, with whom I could fantasize having physical love. This was more bearable, and my life became less of a torment.

Sometimes I would dream of Dejanira – dream that I held her in my arms, and that my organ, in some miraculous manner, with either myself or Dejanira accommodating my dichotomous nature, would penetrate into her vagina. Sometimes, if I happened to be sleeping under the soughing trees, I would wake up in the middle of one of these

224

dreams to find myself hugging a tree trunk and humping away at the empty air with my erect organ.

* * * * * *

And this makes me wonder sometimes if perhaps I, Nessus the Centaur, did not contribute in those days to that phenomenon I have spoken of earlier – I mean the interbreeding of flora and fauna. I, Jonathan Nestus, am not a botanist or other kind of scientist, so I don't know how long that plant known as centaurea has been around in the world, or that other one called Centaureum umbellatum. How did those plants get their name? Could they possibly have originated as a consequence of one of those dreams?

CHAPTER TWENTY-FOUR

Some days ago Sam dropped by to talk. He set his brief case on the dining room/kitchen table and sat on one of my rickety chairs to deliver some bad news. The city, previously willing – almost eager, it might be said – to settle out of court, had now, for some mysterious reason, suddenly decided to contest the matter in a trial. Sam couldn't understand what had happened. He had suspicions though. He questioned me closely in regard to what he called my 'mental problem.' Was I telling him the truth? Was I really having those delusions, and did they really begin after the incident with the police?

And then he asked another question, a more uncomfortable one: Could there be any other cause that the city attorneys might adduce as the reason for my mental condition?

The questions made me uneasy, not because he was referring to my other-life experiences as "delusions" and as a "mental condition," but because I knew I had not been entirely open with him. So, after hemming and hawing for a moment, I told him about the fall from the bridge.

As I told him the story, each word seemed to affect Sam's already discouraged demeanor even more, like air visibly leaking out of an already half deflated balloon. He was silent for a moment, and then asked, "And have you told anyone about this fall?"

"Oh, no. Absolutely no one."

And, as he continued to stare at me, as if waiting for me to finish my answer, I finally added, "Except for my fiancée, of course." Even as I pronounced the word "fiancée," I knew how ridiculous it must sound to Sam's ears. Sam had met Daphne once, and he probably knew that any idea of marriage between Daphne and me was sheer fantasy.

Sam's expression became even more downcast. "I want you to ask her who she's repeated the story to. But I think it's plain now why we've just lost our case – a chance for a good settlement, maybe even half-a-mil." His expression now became one of weary resignation, such as can be seen in the faces of all inveterate losers. "I shouldna been counting on this case so much. With my lousy goddamn luck, I shoulda known something like this would happen."

He picked up his briefcase to leave, with what seemed to me an air of finality. He spoke a few somewhat bitter words as he paused at the door, in his bitterness now abandoning completely all traces of gentility in his accent. "Let me give you some advice. Don't never tell a woman nuttin. Don't even tell her what you had for breakfast. Don't tell her what time you took a shit . . ."

* * * * * *

Before Sam's visit I had been calling Daphne for several days. Her mother would answer the phone, and tell me that Daphne was away, without expanding her information. She was sorry, she would whine, but she was doing her laundry, or cooking, or washing the dishes, and didn't have the time to talk to me.

After Sam left me I immediately called again. Once more her mother answered, sounding faintly impatient, as usual. But this time she told me: Daphne was on a vacation – gone on a fun-ship cruise, or something.

I wondered how she could afford it. She was always complaining about the lack of money. And I felt hurt that she had not even told me she was going. Three or four days later I called Sam and told him I had been unable to talk to Daphne; she was away on vacation.

"Oh, yeah," he said, "she's got plenty of money to go on vacations now. She sold you out. I've got my sources inside city hall. Someone slipped her a couple thousand – I think the police have a special fund for things like that. I don't know if we want to go to trial. With her testimony, I don't think we have much of a chance . . ."

* * * * * *

It's a safe guess that Daphne is gone for good. What sense would it make for her to sell me out for a measly two-thousand dollars, when she had such an excellent chance of sharing in several hundred thousand with me? The answer seems to be that Daphne didn't want to share anything with me. For her, two thousand in the hand was the far better bargain.

Yet I continue to hope that I'm wrong, that Daphne will return from her fun-ship cruise and call me, to tell me it has all been a misunderstanding. But logic and common sense tell me that Daphne is gone, that I have lost her forever. Well, not exactly *lost*. You can't lose what you've never had. But I *have* lost many thousands of dollars . . . in my ruined law suit, and in those expensive dates, and in a five-thousand dollar engagement ring. Although, placed alongside the loss of half-a-million dollars, the loss of a five-thousand dollar engagement ring is small potatoes.

* * * * * *

Three thousand years away, Nessus had problems of his own. Nessus is lucky, in a way. He only has to bear the heartache of having lost Dejanira. Me, I have not only his sorrows on my mind, but my own. I grieve with Nessus for his loss of Dejanira, and now I also have the sorrow of having lost my Daphne.

* * * * * *

With Dejanira lost to Hercules, why did I continue to cross and recross the chilly waters of the Avenus River?

I think it was because I continued to cling to hope. Maybe Dejanira was not lost forever. I had recently heard rumors that Hercules had taken part in an archery contest held by King Eurytus of Oechalia, in which the prize was Eurytus's daughter Iole. It was just as I had told Dejanira. Hercules was already chasing after other women. Dexamenus might just as well have given his daughter to a pig. It would have been no worse a match. To hanker for another woman while having such a priceless jewel as Dejanira for a wife showed the utter swinishness of Hercules' nature.

He won the contest, of course. The sonofabitch's marksmanship with the bow was absolutely uncanny, whether he was shooting at a stationary target or a moving one. No one could recall a single instance in which he had ever missed his mark. It was said that when he killed the twins Calais and Zeetes they were a furlong away, zigzagging as they ran, trying to frustrate his aim. King Eurytus, however, had refused to hand over his daughter to Hercules, claiming that he had been

229

ineligible to participate in the contest, because he was already married to Dejanira. I wondered what Dejanira thought about all this. Maybe she would remember I had warned her this would happen. Maybe she would get angry and leave Hercules, and then maybe I would have another chance. Although it would be galling to have her in this way, a leftover, one of Hercules' used-up rejects. The only way I could ever be comfortable with Dejanira now was if Hercules were dead.

* * * * * *

So I stayed on at my crossing, sustaining my body on the proceeds of my business by day and feeding my soul with impossible dreams at night. Sometimes I slept in the gloomily empty house, and sometimes I would stay on the far bank of the river, among the trees, passing the cold nights under a large sheepskin cloak, which I draped over my human and equine parts like a caparison.

Crotus would come to visit occasionally. "How long are you going to live this way?" he would ask me. "Why don't you come back to Oeta, and forget this foolishness of working for a living, like a Greek."

I hedged. "This isn't so bad. And now I've gotten used to having a steady income. I get everything I need here . . . don't have to steal sheep anymore, and my supply of wine is assured. Besides, I have a lot of fun carrying those girls over. Some of them are very grateful. You should hang around here with me, and see for yourself."

But Crotus, grown more reflective and wiser from the recent events that had caused such an impact on the centaur race, seemingly having aged a quarter of a century in the short span of two years, was no longer greatly interested in girls. "I don't think it's healthy," he said, "to get mixed up with those girls. I agree more and more every day with Cheiron, may he rest in peace. He always preached that we centaurs should stick to our own kind."

Ocyrhöe and Aeolus would sometimes drop by for a visit too. Although it was hard for Ocyrhöe because, after an eleven-month pregnancy, her child had been born. And since her little child was entirely human, she had to carry her in her arms, just as an ordinary woman would. With centaurlings, the centaur mother never had to do this. A centaur child could run on its own legs almost immediately after birth. Ocyrhöe's child was a pretty little girl with jet-black hair.

* * * * * *

230

Spring was drawing near. Down below in Hades' dominions Persephone's quarrels with Hades were beginning again as the time to return for her six-month's stay with her mother approached. Hades becomes sullen and angry at this time, resentful that he has to relinquish his wife for six months, all to please Demeter and his brother Zeus. Persephone, like most women, has never learned to tread cautiously at this time. Instead of conducting herself in such a way as to avoid irritating her husband, she provokes him until the next thing she knows, Hades is whaling the tar out of her again.

So Demeter was again wringing her hands helplessly, as she does every year, and shedding heartfelt tears – which were falling upon the earth as light showers, even though the sun was shining – upon hearing her daughter's shrieks of pain and terror.

Then the day came when Persephone packed her bag and returned to her mother's side for her annual stay. Spring was wafted over the world, and the goldenrods and daffodils, the poppies and the marigolds, splashed their colors over the meadow at the Avenus River.

Whenever Crotus or Ocyrhöe came by I longed to ask them for news of Dejanira. I wondered if she really loved Hercules. I wondered if she was pregnant already. Hercules, the sonofabitch, was extremely fertile. Every woman he touched became almost instantly pregnant. I wondered if Dejanira ever thought of me. Maybe she was sorry she hadn't climbed on my back that last day I saw her, to let me carry her away, to live with me forever.

Although the unasked questions burned within me, I always held my tongue. I couldn't bear to mention the names of Dejanira and Hercules to Crotus or to Ocyrhöe. Especially with my ill-constructed house looming there on the bank, since Crotus and Ocyrhöe both knew the reason I had built it. And both of them sedulously avoided all mention of anything which they knew might cause me pain and embarrassment.

One day, however, Crotus himself began to talk about the doings of Hercules. I listened with a keen ear, while pretending that the gossip was of little interest to me. Hercules was threatening King Eurytus over that business of the archery contest. He was insisting that Eurytus had to give him his daughter, whether he liked it or not. The fact that he already had a wife, he had let Eurytus know, was irrelevant.

231

He had won Iole fair and square and he was going to have her.

Then Crotus revealed some other news about Hercules and Dejanira, which he let drop in a studiedly casual manner. They had been living in Tiryns, but they were going away from there now. Hercules had gotten into some trouble. He had killed a little boy there at a banquet, for spilling water on his feet. Hercules claimed it was an accident. He had just meant to give the boy a little tap on the head. But the resentment against him for this latest outrage had grown too strong, so he had decided to move to Trachis. He and Dejanira had just started on their journey five days ago, Crotus said.

Even as a centaur, for whom these things were more or less commonplace, I often marveled at the facility with which news was disseminated in those days throughout the Greek world. We ourselves, the centaurs, were one of the principal means through which such news and gossip was spread. To us, a forty mile jaunt was as a short stroll on a lazy day. Given a good reason, we could cover fifty, sixty, or more miles in the same time. So this fresh news that Crotus brought me from faraway Tiryns was not surprising.

Crotus further revealed the fact that Hercules and Dejanira were first going to pay her father Dexamenus a visit in Calydon. So they would be coming this way. "They'll probably be here tomorrow," he said.

I felt something like a hot and cold fever surge through me. My equine heart continued to beat at the normal rate, but the heart in my human breast began to pound. I tried to hide my emotion from Crotus. I tried to speak in a normal voice as I said, "Oh, well, I'm not really interested in Hercules' doings. But if they need help getting across the river, I'll take any business that comes my way."

My casual air did not deceive Crotus. "Nessus," he said, "you must do your best to avoid any trouble with Hercules. Don't even look at his wife, and don't let him goad you into anger. A soft answer turneth away wrath, you know, even with Hercules. It's not a good time for you to make trouble.

"Maybe it might be a good idea for you to go away until they've gone to Calydon and back. Your cave at Oeta is still vacant. Come on back with me, and we'll have a great time – I have a large jug of wine, and we'll get us something to barbecue tomorrow night.

"Hey, don't worry about me," I said, "my trouble with Hercules is water under the bridge. As for Dejanira, I never even think of her anymore."

But the very mention of her name had been like a flaming firebrand thrust into my chest. I wasn't going to lose this opportunity to see her again.

CHAPTER TWENTY-FIVE

A beautiful morning shortly after the spring equinox. The returning sun warms the earth and the energy which during the winter is spent in keeping the body warm now seeks other outlets. The smell of fresh grass and flowers, the buzzing of bees, and the trill of mocking birds and meadow larks floats lazily around the warm air.

From the distant woods, a partridge was calling. I wondered if it was Perdix herself, the sister of Daedalus, mourning for her lost son Talos who was killed by his uncle, jealous to see that he had invented the saw by casting in iron a copy of a serpent's jawbone he had found.

The river was quite high. Far upriver, heavy spring showers were falling, and the current carried bits of debris and the river's characteristic patches of dirty foam. All morning I had looked for ways to stay occupied – sweeping the floor of my house with a long-handled sedge broom, carrying water in a large jar into the house, cleaning out the ashes from the hearth . . . For no special purpose. Only to dispel the restlessness which nagged me. Whenever I was outside the house my eyes were constantly turning – obsessively and involuntarily – towards the direction from which Dejanira and Hercules would be approaching from the southeast.

It was past noon when I saw them coming. They emerged from the woods, far across the meadow, on the road which came from Boeotia and distant Tiryns. As they approached I saw that Hercules had a pack on his back – no doubt the bare essentials of their personal belongings. Dejanira carried a small bundle slung over one shoulder – perhaps her clothing and other small articles. I wondered why the sonofabitch had not gotten her a horse, or a cart or something. He himself, of course, could never have ridden a horse. No horse could have lasted for long carrying his four hundred pounds. But If Dejanira had been my wife, she would never have had to walk. I could have carried her to the ends of the earth, her thighs warming my back, her smooth arms and soft hands around my waist.

Hercules, for once without his usual retinue of ass-kissing hangers on, showed evidence of being in a foul mood. He flung the pack off his back with a curse as he came to the river's edge, and turned his baleful and bloodshot eyes, first upon me and then on the sign I had posted.

His lips curled in a sneer. "Well, well, if it isn't our friend, Nessus the Centaur! Become a porter now, have you? I guess you don't get no wedding invitations anymore and have to work for your wine now, huh?"

This was a cruel allusion, of course, to the tragedy of Peirithous's wedding, where so many fine and noble centaurs had died.

I let Hercules' goading words roll off my back with a slight quiver of flanks and shoulders, and as he turned his attention away from me to examine the swollen stream, I turned my eyes towards Dejanira, now more alluringly beautiful than ever. Her ash-blonde hair was still combed in her usual style, coiled and piled on her head, and her soft violet eyes, under their arching brows, still retained a faint trace of maidenly modesty. But now her once nubile body had bloomed into the full flower of womanhood. Her firm high breasts were larger, more turgidly swelling with lactatious promise. Her hips were wider, her legs and thighs fuller, and her abdomen, though showing no evidence of pregnancy, swelled exuberantly beneath her thin white robe. The soft breeze pressed her garment to her thighs and I could faintly discern the bulge of her pudenda, and imagine the curly, ash-blonde hair with which it was probably adorned. Marriage had done great things for her body.

Dejanira blushed faintly at my examination. At the same time I thought I saw in her violet eyes, as she looked at me in that sidewise way she had, a faint hint of repressed longing. At that moment I was sure that Dejanira was in love with me. I felt the certainty that she, the same as I, grieved and sorrowed that a relationship between us could never be.

And then again, maybe I was mistaken. Maybe she was only thinking what a shame it was that such a magnificent horse was ruined by having an upper human body melded onto it. Maybe I read

236

something in her expression that was not really there. Because I longed so desperately to believe that she felt towards me the same way I felt towards her. I will never know. Now, across the abyss of three thousand years since those moments, I still feel a great sadness when I think of it.

Hercules, occupied in checking out the swollen stream, did not notice my devouring examination of Dejanira. He cursed to himself. "What kind of a goddamn operation are you running here," he said to me. "Don't you have a barge or a boat? I'm going to complain to the authorities in Calydon about this. I don't see how they could have given a horse's ass like you a license to operate a public service."

I remembered the advice of Crotus and, with an effort, reined in the almost overpowering urge to respond in a different manner to Hercules.

"I'm getting a barge soon," I told him instead. "Don't worry about that. For now, as a special favor to you, I'll carry Dejanira across at no fee whatsoever. I'll carry your pack across, too."

"Don't call her Dejanira, horse's ass. That's my wife you're talking about."

Again, my rage almost overwhelmed my good sense. This despicable, wife-murdering sonofabitch telling me I couldn't speak the name of Dejanira. But from his repeated use of the epithet "hipporchus" I knew he was deliberately trying to goad me into anger.

So I only replied, in a mild voice, "Of course, I meant Mrs. Hercules."

"What do you think, sweetheart," the slob said to her. Will you be all right?"

Dejanira turned her head aside and murmured something to Hercules in a low voice.

He replied, in a normal tone, "Don't worry about that, sweetheart. I'll be right here beside you."

He took his bow and quiver off his shoulders, talking to me the while. "There's a little matter pending between you and me, Mr. horse's ass Nessus. You called me a name once, some time ago. No one has ever called me that and lived for as long as you have. But we'll wait until a later time. I have other things to think of today."

Then he took off his lion skin and his shirt and wrapped both around his bow and quiver of arrows. He whirled this bundle around his

237

head once or twice and gave it a heave, throwing it to the far side of the river. Then he threw the brass-bound club that he was never without after it. He stood a moment looking after it, no doubt relishing the opportunity to display his massive, naked musculature to Dejanira, with testes and organ hanging hugely.

"You go first," he said to her. "I'll be right behind you." And to me he said, "Just keep your horse's ass hands off her, you hear?"

Dejanira left her little bundle with Hercules' pack and approached , half hesitantly, to mount on my back. A tiny quiver began to course uncontrollably over my entire horse's body in anticipation of her touch.

So that what followed may be better understood, I must try once more to fully explain the nature of a centaur's mental processes. I have already explained that, though we had a human head and brain, sometimes the unbridled passions of a virile stallion would surge through us, wiping out every vestige of restraint and reason. I don't know at what moment, if ever, I decided to do what I did. It wasn't when I had mildly answered Hercules' insults by offering to carry Dejanira across the stream at no charge. Nor was it when he threw his club and his deadly bow and arrows across the stream as he prepared to swim across himself. For even without his club and his bow Hercules was still not someone to be trifled with.

As a matter of fact, the idea was never actually formulated in my mind. But when I felt Dejanira's soft hands on my quivering withers as she prepared to mount on my back, the fatidic resolution was half formed. Then, when I felt the weight of her warm ass and rounded thighs on my back, I ceased to be in control of my faculties.

Hercules had waded knee-deep into the swirling water and was looking back to see if I was following. The next thing I knew, I had reached behind me to sweep Dejanira off my back and into my arms. Holding her by the waist and thighs over my shoulder, I wheeled swiftly on my hind quarters and galloped off with her.

I really don't know exactly what I intended to do with her. There was no idea clearly formulated in my human mind. An uncontrollable equine passion had taken over my will. But I guess I had decided that I was going to try to have sex with her.

I heard Hercules bellow behind me, "Nessus, you son-of-a-bitch! What the hell do you think you're doing? Come back here!"

"Go fuck yourself!" I flung back at him over my shoulder and galloped heedlessly away, trampling the frightened flowers beneath my thudding hooves.

"Nessus, Nessus, what are you doing!" Dejanira gasped, "Hercules will kill you!"

"Dejanira," I panted in mid-gallop, "come away with me. I will take you far away, where Hercules can never find us. He can never love you as I do. I will be good to you, Dejanira!"

But she only answered, "Nessus, stop and put me down this instant!"

I was holding her fast with my arms around her waist and thighs, and she was beating against my back with her hands as she demanded to be put down. Her obdurate attitude, the sensation of her soft body on my shoulders, her hands pounding on my back – all combined to snap the last remaining thread holding my reason together. I freed one hand and began trying to rip off her thin robe as I ran.

I finally stopped about a quarter-of-a-mile away, panting and gasping for breath from the exertion and the emotion. Now I put her down, but without letting her go. Grasping her around her supple waist I lifted her off the ground again, crushing her to my chest and kissing her lips, her face, her eyes, with fierce passion. I fancied that I could feel her melting in my arms like a huge blob of warm wax at the mouth of a raging furnace. Savagely, I ripped away at her tattered garments to expose her glowing mammaries, her smoothly gleaming thighs and rounded abdomen. I even caught a fleeting glimpse of her pudenda, covered, just as I had imagined, with fleecy, tightly-curled ash-blond hairs. It was a maddening sight, and I began to thrust ineffectually in its general direction with my horse's organ.

But for a centaur engaged in an enterprise of this sort (I must be honest and call it what it was, rape), a great degree of cooperation is necessary on the part of the rapee. Dejanira's body would have had to be five feet longer, or my organ five feet longer, to have had any chance of success. And Dejanira was not cooperative. She knew, of course, as I surely must have known somewhere in the back of my mind that to see his wife raped before his very eyes was something Hercules wouldn't like very much.

Here, surely, with the high drama and intense, traumatic emotion involved, must have been an instance to give birth to some strange creature such as those which were known in those times to occur from spilled seed and other like accidents, as has been recorded by many mythographers. Maybe here, and not beneath the trees on the banks of the river, is where Centaureum umbellatum originated.

So engrossed was I in my fruitless efforts to effect a congress with Dejanira that I failed to realize Hercules had recovered his bow and arrows, recrossed the river, and was now within bow shot of us. Some of the ancient mythographers say he shot me with his poisoned arrow from half-a-mile away. This is obviously an exaggeration. But he *was* quite a distance off when he loosed his arrow. So far, in fact, that after it thudded into my back to emerge at my chest, I had a good while to think of several things. I thought, as I sank down on the asphodel, that Ocyrhöe - not Crotus and Philomele – had been right. I thought of how lucky I was that death would take me before the poison could take effect; because to die from the effects of the poison would be a much more excruciating death.

I looked down at the arrow protruding from my chest. The fierce courage of the centaurs was a byword in those times. Without hesitation I grasped the protruding shaft with both hands and pulled it all the way through. I glanced at it briefly before I let it drop from my fingers. Beneath the thin film of my blood with which it was covered I could see the dark stain of the poison, and tiny bubbles beginning to stir over it.

The blood poured out of the cruel wound and flowed down upon the shocked but uncomplaining asphodel. Dejanira stood beside me, clutching the tattered remnants of her robe to her body, looking down at me with an indefinable expression on her beautiful face. What was it – shock? pity? love and regret? Or was it simply relief? The unanswered question torments me even today.

Hercules had taken the time after letting his arrow fly to return three or four hundred feet to the river bank to retrieve his clothing, and now, through a little window on the ground formed by three or four little crocus-like flowers, I could see him sauntering casually up to watch me die. How I wished I could stand up once more for just an instant, and have revenge before I died. But my sight was becoming blurred. My ears were filled with a vast roaring. The end was so near that the terrible pain had ended. I hoped the sonofabitch would touch my blood. It was surely poisonous by now. Then I thought of something. It was not the words of Philomele that prompted the thought, but rather the other way around. It was only after the thought occurred to me that I remembered her words, and finally understood them. *"You will find in your blood the hidden way . . ."* I remembered, too, the words of Agrius about the Greek belief in the magical powers of centaur seed and blood. At that moment I accepted what must surely be the truth. Dejanira did not love me, and never had. She was in love with her husband, Hercules, and aware, no doubt, of his propensity to change wives just as frequently as he changed his underwear, if he ever wore any.

I reached out for a shred of Dejanira's tattered robe, picked up the bloody arrow lying by my hand and wiped it clean with the cloth. Before Hercules could reach us, I gasped out my final words to her. "Dejanira, let me do something for you before I die. Hercules is going to leave you soon – a girl in Oechalia named Iole. Take this blood. Don't let it touch your fingers, and don't expose it to sunlight. Rub some of it on one of your husband's shirts next time you think he's going to see her. It will be a love charm that will keep him faithful to you forever."

Poor dumb Dejanira. Maybe tricking her into killing her own husband was not an honorable thing to do. But in the fierceness of my hatred for Hercules there was no room for decency or conscience. And anyway, I was sure I was doing her a favor.

CHAPTER TWENTY-SIX

The death of Nessus was a traumatic experience for me. I was unable to go to work, and called in sick. I passed the rest of the day in my pajamas, drinking coffee, pacing restlessly around my confined spaces, trying to shake free from the memory. It had been so vivid and real, as I have said all these experiences were. Dejanira's face continued to float before my eyes, and there was a nagging pain in my back and chest.

Gradually, as the day wore on, it eased and I was able to breathe freely again. But .those last-dreamed events passed over and over through my mind. One thought predominated. Nessus was dead. I would never relive his life again. I would never see Dejanira again.

Then, over the days, other thoughts filtered in from the edges of my mind. I thought of my own loss – Daphne. She, also, was irretrievably gone. But I was surprised to discover that I could say, Fuck Daphne, good riddance. Daphne couldn't have held a candle to Dejanira. And she had committed a most vile act of treachery, ruining my chances of a rich settlement with the city . . . and this, after making me spend all my inheritance money on her.

Instead of mourning the loss of Daphne, I found my melancholy yearnings, more and more, turning to Dejanira. I began to ask myself, did I really deceive her? Could it be that Dejanira understood me far better than I suspected? Surely she couldn't have been so dumb. Surely, she must have *known*. Surely Hercules would have warned her about the great danger from anything his arrows touched. And as my own eyes had filmed over just before dying, I seem to remember that her eyes had been filmy too, as if with tears, and her lips formed words I could no longer hear, as she wrapped the cloth I gave her in another piece of her tattered robe and secreted it in the remaining shreds of her garment.

Maybe Dejanira did love me. Maybe she hated Hercules as

much as I did. Maybe it was she who first called the poisoned tunic which killed Hercules "the shirt of Nessus," as a tribute to my memory, and hanged herself after Hercules died, not out of grief for him, but only because with his death she had accomplished the only purpose left to her in life. Maybe those last words I could no longer hear were, "Nessus, I love you. I will avenge your death." I long to believe these things. But I can never know with any certainty.

And, does knowing how Hercules died – ranting, raving, and cursing heaven and earth as his flesh and his bones melted in the fierce heat of his own poison – give me any satisfaction in this life? Sometimes it does. I read Ovid's description of Hercules' death over and over. I have to take Ovid's word for it. But I wish I could go back again and talk to Crotus and Ocyrhöe, and my other centaur friends. For all I know, maybe Dejanira left some sort of message that has not survived the times, explaining why she hung herself, explaining that she had known perfectly well what she was doing when she poisoned Hercules.

But other times, I know that it doesn't matter. All of that was so long ago.

* * * * * *

Sam says we will go ahead with a law suit in court, but those things take years and years. And there is a good chance we will never see a dime. So I must continue to slave at Crompton's. Day after day I must get up, shave, dress, go to work, come home, eat my beans and chili, stare at the TV screen . . . And somewhere in time I know Nessus lives. He gallops free as the wind with his friends Homadus and Agrius and Crotus. They drink wine together in their caves in the evening; they barbecue savory mutton over their fires, and exchange gossip on the doings of the neighboring Greeks and Lapiths

* * * * * *

It is dawn again, and I must get up. It is nearly time to go to work. But I continue in bed, putting off the hateful moment for as long as I can. I have been wondering whatever became of that house I built on the banks of the Avenus River. Did someone ever live in it? Could there perhaps still be some faint sign of it left, that I would recognize if I saw it today? If anything ever comes of my law suit, maybe I'll make a trip there, take a long vacation, and look for it. Maybe I can stand again on the exact same spots where Nessus the Centaur stood three thousand years ago, find the spot where I died, still marked out on the ground with a barren patch where no grass will grow – on the self-same spot where I last looked into Dejanira's eyes. Maybe I could even reclaim the site of my old house and build a new one, and set myself back in business at the river crossing, with a barge or a boat . . .

But now I must get up. I sigh deeply as I leave my bed and begin to dress. I wish I was still Nessus the Centaur. I wish I was back at the Avenus River, making my living by crossing the clear waters every day. A certain dream has been haunting me lately. A sweet-sad dream, in which Dejanira walks alone through a field of goldenrods and daffodils towards the river crossing, her white robe shimmering in the golden sunlight of a warm spring day. And I stand there, with the cool water flowing around my fetlocks, waiting for her.

THE END

Other Alondra Press Books

Island Journeys, by Patti M. Marxsen
Take a lyrical journey with this author across time and across seven islands with a common thread of French history.

The Other face of Murder, by Gil Porat
An outstanding first novel by a doctor-writer, dealing with a mysterious murder among friends. Dr. Gil Porat joins the ranks of other medical professionals who have made of writing their second love after medicine.

The Canyon Chronicles, by K. Gray Jones
A historical novel of Utah and the conflicts between Mormons and Gentiles during the epoch from the mid 1850's to the early part of the 20th century. A novel that is "sure to please some and infuriate many others."

Rio San Pedro, by Henry Hollenbaugh
The author's memoirs of his life as a crocodile hunter in Central America in the 1950s. Jonathan Galassi of Farrar, Straus & Giroux says, "There is a wonderful sense of presence in this novel."

The Origins of Fortune and Misfortune, by Armando Benitez
A quasi-serious metaphysical treatise purporting to explain why some people are fortunate and lucky, while others are not. It is comparable to *The Soul's Code* and *Fooled by Randomness*, but more readable and entertaining.

Rhyme of the Fall of Berlin, by Henry Hollenbaugh
A powerful mock-epic poem of World War II, encompassing the birth of Adolph Hitler, the invasion of Russia, Stalingrad, the fall of Berlin, and the death of Hitler and Eva Braun. Written in eight-line rhyming stanzas, sometimes as a parody of poets from Homer and Dante to Milton, Shakespeare, Keats, Byron, and others.

Visit us at our website www.alondrapress.com